Love

Led By

the Spirit

D0840753

by

PAT SIMMONS

ISBN- 13:978-1533332592
ISBN-10:1533332592
Editor: Chandra Sparks Splond
Proofreader: Judy at Judicious Revisions
Beta reader: Darlene Simmons
Cover design: Nat/Bookaholic Fiverr.com
Author photo: Angie Knost Photography

Readers' Praise for Pat Simmons

5 Stars. "Oh my goodness. I so enjoyed Jet's story, even though it left me heartbroken for her, and her struggles. Jet's story added "filing" and depth her and to "Crowning Glory", and is the perfect lead in to "Love Led by the Spirit". The excerpt has me excitedly waiting the book to come out. I am so pulling for Jet and Rossi!" — Reader Jewel on *JET The Back Story*

5 Stars. "I enjoyed the insight into Jet's mind. I understand her character. She is interesting. Whenever an author creates a character that develop strong feelings in readers, that is an excellent author. Well done Pat Simmons." –Amazon Customer on *JET The Back Story*

5 Stars. "This book is for EVERYONE whom feel there no second chances in life, Mrs. Simmons is the BEST CHRISTIAN AUTHOR the Lord as best the world to know through her books, I always want to be a better person after reading her books, a better Christian, a better everything. This is truly a must read books.— Theresa Cartwright Lands on *Crowning Glory*

5 Stars. "Truthfully, there was absolutely nothing about this story to dislike. This was an awesome Christian fiction read. Miss Simmons pulled us into this story to the point of making you feel as though you were friends of the families involved. Well done Ms. Simmons; well done. I'm beginning JET right now; I will be anxiously awaiting *Love Led By The Spirit.*—Vanessa Hunter on *Crowning Glory*

5 Stars. "Pat has done it again! There is nothing like a praying, caring man...and that's exactly what the main male character is like. Where is my Tyson???? I like the friendships that the main character, Monica, had with her friends. We all need a ride or die friend or three in our lives. Great job, Pat!" –LeeLee, reader on *Every Woman Needs a Praying Man*

Can't wait to read Love Led by the Spirit.

"Even with all the deadlines, meet and greets, conferences, retreats, you still pour yourself into your books giving fully of yourself ALWAYS leaving us with a treat that's uplifting, encouraging, enlightening, spiritual, moving, exciting, wonderful and amazing. I say with a heart of gratitude. You still are my favorite author.
Don't grow weary while doing good."

Thank you so much, Nicole. This story is for you!

Dedication

To all the ministers God has called and chosen to do His will. God bless you and give you strength to every the torch until the end.

Acknowledgements

Special thanks to Becky Rosner, Marketing Associate, and Paul Woody, Special Counsel, American Poolplayers Association for answering my questions.

Editor extraordinaire Chandra Sparks Splond for bringing my characters to life and loving this story.

To family and friends, Kerry, Simi, and Jay, thanks for your support, and so many others who have blessed me with their prayers and purchases, so that I can continue to write Christian inspired stories. Thank you!

Chapter 1

Minister Rossi Tolliver didn't have enough fingers to count the number of women inside and out of the church who would say yes if he proposed. God knew he wasn't boasting. It was a fact that these sisters wanted a man of God for a husband. In turn, he wanted a woman of God for a wife. He only dated practicing Christian women baptized with water and fire, yet something was always amiss.

He sighed and rubbed his eyes. It was a Saturday morning in early June, and Rossi was supposed to be studying a passage in his Bible, but his mind kept drifting. When he looked out the window from his downtown St. Louis loft, his imagination came alive. He could see himself bike riding alongside a companion on the riverfront or sharing a bag of peanuts at a Cardinals game at the nearby stadium.

At thirty-five, Rossi was the oldest of four sons and the sole minister in a mostly practicing Christian family. If a Tolliver had a crisis, he was the one they turned to. In essence, their problems became his to petition before the Lord. Not that he was keeping tabs, but he had an ever-growing list.

It was well known that Rossi took God's anointing over his life seriously, so it seemed like everybody had an opinion about what type of woman would make him a perfect wife. He recalled a conversation at a recent family get-together.

"She has to be pretty—I'm thinking about my grandbabies," his mother, Laura Tolliver, stated, *"if any of my sons care to give me any." "She has to love the Lord, not be prone to anger, have a gentle spirit, be kind to others, and be a faithful churchgoer,"* Aunt Sharon, his uncle's wife, added to round off the ingredients for his ideal wife.

His father, Rossi III, or Ross as the family called him, gave the so called benediction to end the discussion. *"The most important factor to consider is your wife's willingness to work with you in the ministry. That, son, is a true helpmate. Why do you think I fell in love with your mother? Laura is a peacemaker."*

Talk about pressure. They gave him a checklist when all he wanted was a woman who loved God and him—period.

Their unsolicited advice reminded him of the stern talk they gave him about his responsibilities and their expectations before he took his date to his junior prom. He closed his Bible. There was too much distraction in his head to reread Mark, chapter two for a third time. *"They that are whole have no need of the physician, but they that are sick: I came not to call the righteous, but sinners to repentance."* Instead of meditating on verse seventeen for the upcoming community outreach program, his heart seemed to scold him: *You need a wife.*

"I got that," he said aloud, flustered. He stood and wandered through his spacious bachelor pad. Would his wife want to redecorate? Would she want to live there?

His family meant well, but... "All those are good qualities, but you've all forgotten about the most important criteria: She has to have my heart," he explained to the bird that landed on the window's ledge.

It pecked on the pane as if it was trying to get his attention. Frowning, he noted it was a sparrow. Hmm. The rarity of seeing that type of bird made him reach for his Bible again and flip through Matthew until he stopped at chapter ten. He scanned the verses, then reread twenty-nine through thirty-one: *Are not two sparrows sold for a farthing? And one of them shall not fall on the ground without your Father. But the very hairs of your head are all numbered. Fear not therefore, you are of more value than many sparrows.*

After praying for years for "the one" to cross his path, was God sending him a Word? The Lord had heard his every prayer that were as numerous as the hairs on his head. Maybe this was confirmation that only one woman could complement him. "Who has my heart, Lord?"

An alluring face flashed before his eyes: Jesetta "Jet" Hutchens.

Rossi smirked. The beautiful Jesetta *couldn't claim three out of five of those qualities.* He gritted his teeth, doubting she would ever possess two of those attributes. *Or will she?*

To his cousins' displeasure, Jesetta was due back in town in a couple of days. After almost a year's absence, Rossi wondered whether he had planted enough spiritual seeds in her life and God had caused them to grow during her time away from home. If so, how would everybody handle the news that Jesetta would be his wife?

Keep praying, the Lord whispered.

***

St. Peter's Cemetery in Normandy, Missouri, right outside the St. Louis city limits was Jet's first stop when she arrived back in town from Nashville. The cemetery on Lucas and Hunt Road was one of a few historic cemeteries in the area that didn't have a separate burial area for blacks.

While most natives would go for the White Castles burgers, Ted Drewes Frozen Custard, or Imo's pizza, not Jet. Her connection was buried six feet under in Section 25, Block D, Lot 4 and Plot 6. She didn't need a landmark to find her baby sister, Diane. Jet hadn't lasted nine months in Nashville living with her former college roommate, Layla Keyes, even though she enjoyed working as a manager at her friend's franchised boutique hotel, a position for which she was way overqualified. But it was something to keep her busy.

The drastic move had come years after a botched robbery claimed the life of her only sibling, and Jet struggled with getting on with her life. Personally, Jet thought she was progressing fairly well—until her friend put her out, literally. Layla was sticking to her story that it was for Jet's own good. That was debatable. As far as Jet was concerned, Layla was removing the training wheels off her tricycle on the road to recovery. She hadn't seen it coming as the two of them ate dinner.

"Part of me says stay here. You're at peace here, and I like the company," Layla had said.

"Not to mention, you have me as cheap labor," Jet reminded her, although it wasn't about the money.

Layla grinned. "Besides that, I know how close you were with Diane and how much you love her little girl. If you can't make a decision, then I will. Jesetta Hutchens, I'm putting you out."

She had shrugged. "No problem. I can get my own place like I wanted to do in the beginning."

"And I'm firing you, too, so you have nothing here. Go home."

Jet blinked. "Don't you want me to give you my two weeks' notice?"

"Nope. Because I'm giving you one week to go home. Enjoy the summer with your niece. Don't let Dori grow up without you. You're her only connection to Diane, so don't come back." She grinned as if to soften the blow.

So here she was again, mentally starting over for a third time after her sister's death. She parked her car and took a deep breath as her eyes watered. Maybe her best friend had been right. Jet should have never abandoned Dori. She should have stayed and fought for her right to stay in her niece's life.

Grabbing the bouquet of flowers, Jet stepped out of her car in her dress boots, not bothering to change into her flats like she often used when she came to the cemetery. She had walked the path so many times for almost seven years that her footprints had created a path for others.

Her deceased parents were buried not far away, so she stopped by their gravesite first. Next, she veered left and counted the paces to Diane's brown glazed headstone.

She dared herself not to blink as she whispered the inscription, "Diane Lovanne Hutchens Tolliver. Loving wife, mother, and sister." After a series of breaths, Jet blinked to rid the moisture that blurred her vision. *And dead at twenty-three.*

Two months shy of her twenty-fourth birthday. "Murdered," she choked out. A robbery gone badly had claimed the lives of sixteen innocent people. Her sister, who had run to the store for a few items, had walked into a death trap. Was there really such a thing as wrong place, wrong time?

Jet sniffed as she squatted to place the flowers on Diane's grave. "Sis, I'm back. Since you've been gone, I haven't been the best role model for Dori, and I'm so sorry, I've been so, so mad at God for taking you away." She paused and fumbled through her purse for a tissue.

Usually when she visited Diane's grave, she carried a washcloth because her tears were so heavy. Maybe the short time spent in Nashville did help heal wounds.

Tears washed My feet, the wind whispered in her ear, but she didn't understand what that meant.

She blew her nose and sniffed. Her demeanor instantly changed when she thought about her brother-in-law. "Girl, if you could, you would roll over in your grave at Levi's choice of a woman to replace you and be the mother of your child."

It wasn't the first time Jet had vented about the former Karyn Wallace to her sister's headstone. A young mother of a month-old daughter, Diane's life was cut short. As if that weren't heart-wrenching enough, the ultimate betrayal came when Levi married an ex-felon, a convicted murderer. That had been a slap in the face.

No one seemed to share her concern about Karyn being unfit to a mother her niece. Jet's suspicions that something was amiss about the woman came to light at a grief counseling session.

Rossi had tagged along for support, as did her brother-in-law, Levi, and his then-girlfriend, Karyn. The heart-wrenching personal stories of loss evidently had been too much for Karyn to handle because she freaked out and confessed she didn't mean to kill someone. The knee-jerk reaction and temporary insanity that followed caused Jet to lash out on behalf of all victims and slap Karyn silly. Of course, Jet regretted her actions days later—well, it was longer than that, but she did eventually feel bad about it.

Jet blinked, not wanting to revisit her own irrational behavior. She had been a peacemaker growing up, so that was definitely not her character. Only for her niece's sake did she plan to be cordial to the new Mrs. Tolliver, but she was going to watch her like a hawk in case Karyn got any ideas about harming Dori.

Funny, she missed St. Louis when she was in Nashville. Now, she missed Nashville because she had started to heal emotionally and spiritually. She chuckled. A Bible had been in her possession all the time, and she had never bothered to study what it said until she moved away. Of course, she would follow along whenever she attended a service with the other Tollivers to support one of Rossi's speaking engagements, but her anger never allowed her to see past the words.

Layla had forced her hand to get help, which led to Jet actually reading her Bible regularly. Since she was back in Dori's life to stay, she was open to some spiritual counseling from Rossi. That was if his girlfriend, Nalani—Karyn's sister—would let him out of her sight. Another twist of fate. The only thing she had in common with Nalani was they both were loyal to their only sibling, a sister. Nalani was a petite size four, fair skinned, and sported a short hairstyle. Jet was five-ten and a size fourteen with long black hair and rich brown skin. They both had curves. Men seemed to prefer smaller women, calling her full-figured. Since when were hips considered full-figured?

She glanced up into the clear ocean-blue sky to draw her mind back to the present. This was the hand God had dealt her, so Jet was going to play it like a poker champion—and she had never gambled a day in her life.

The clouds floating above her seemed to empty her mind. In a trance, she squinted at what appeared to be figurines shaped like men on horses, angels with trumpets, and a body on a cross. Were her eyes playing tricks on her?

You have the victory, God whispered. *Read Proverbs 21:31.*

Bewildered and frustrated, Jet frowned. She saw no victory in her current situation, and the few times God did speak to her through the scriptures, she wasn't quite sure what He was saying.

Maybe Rossi would guide her. He seemed to be eager in the past, but that was before Nalani turned his head and dug in her claws. Honestly, she was surprised the two hadn't tied the knot yet since Rossi appeared to be enthralled by her beauty.

Before she knew it, Jet had been at the cemetery for more than an hour. This had been her place of peace before the storm. She took a deep breath and worked a smile on her face.

"It's time for me to go, Diane. Whatever is broken inside of me will get fixed, I promise, and I won't abandon Dori again—ever." She swallowed, then her voice trembled. "Also, I…" She paused. She had to say it, "I won't be back. The next time we meet I guess will be on the other side." *Whew,* she exhaled. Jet was finally closing the door on the past so she could move forward. "Lord, You said You would help me if I asked. I need some type of spiritual overhaul," she whispered, bowing her head and closing her eyes.

Her lids fluttered open as she squatted again. Bringing two fingers to her lips, she kissed them, then touched the headstone. "I love you."

Standing, she rubbed her hands on her pants. Despite her willingness to leave, her feet wouldn't budge. It had nothing to do with her designer boots sinking into the soft ground. "Come on, I can do this." She gave herself a pep talk as she spun around, then froze. An imposing man stood next to her car, watching her. Dressed in black from head to toe, his buff figure was intimidating. Her weapon of choice while screaming would be to take off one of her shoes. The stacked heels on her boots were weapon ready.

His face came into focus as he began his calculated steps toward her, then Jet recognized Rossi's signature swagger. Fear left her, and the sense of peace she had returned.

As if he wasn't handsome enough with his silky black goatee and deep dimples, the groomed beard enhanced what God had already made perfect—if that made sense. The determination on his face kept her staring. When he invaded her physical space and his cologne crept into her nostrils, she shivered. "What are you doing here?"

"Waiting for you, Jesetta."

Chapter 2

"Excuse me?" Jet blinked. Her long lashes teased Rossi. "You stalking me?"

While she waited for his answer, Rossi took his time admiring her beauty. Her hair was brushed up into a ball—only a few strands had escaped the bondage. With flawless skin, her features were profound. She didn't need makeup, yet he noticed a hint on her cheeks and lips.

The black-and-white short trench coat seemed to be a part of her black pants. The boots gave her more height so he could gaze into her brown eyes, which had carried a hint of sadness since Diane's death. "This was my third drive-by since Levi said you would be in town today. I came this morning, at lunch, and this afternoon. I'd have returned this evening if I had to."

"A phone call would have saved you gas." She twisted her pouty lips.

Woman, I missed you. She was back, and her sass was in full force. He smirked. After Karyn married Levi, he and Jet had drifted apart. According to Jet, he'd started dating her nemesis' sister, Nalani.

What could he say in his defense? Karyn's sister was pretty and surrendered to Christ—something Jet had refused to do. In his opinion, he had done all that was humanly possible to lead Jet to Christ. He was tired of fighting her. All the prayers in the world couldn't keep the peace between the Wallace sisters and Jet.

That was in the past. Things had changed. Although he considered himself a patient man, he had waited forty weeks to be this close to Jet again, and lately his heart had become impatient when it came to Jesetta Hutchens.

Love is patient, longsuffering. God whispered a portion of 1 Corinthians 13:4.

"Welcome home." He opened his arms for a hug, but she didn't budge. Already, they had entered into a standoff.

"Uh-uh. I'm not hugging another woman's man." She shifted her stance and planted a fist on her hip.

He cleared his throat and slipped his hands in his pants pocket. "Nalani and I haven't been together in months." He frowned at her chuckle. "You act like you're not surprised."

"I'm not." She strolled past him toward her car. He spun around and fell in step beside her.

Should he be surprised that she wasn't surprised? "Why not?"

She shrugged but kept walking without missing a beat, weaving around headstones as if she was on skates while he had to steady himself on the unleveled ground. "You dated her longer than any other woman of yours I met. For a moment, I thought Nalani had you. Imagine two sisters married to two cousins. Yep, I thought she was the one." She lifted her hand and deactivated her car alarm.

At first, Rossi did too. "She wasn't. I got blindsided."

At her car, she turned and gave him a blank expression. "I guess that happens to the best of us."

"Yeah." At one time he could read her expressions and anticipate her moods, but it was as if her emotions were encased in lead.

"I'm sure Dori is waiting on me."

That little girl made Jet's world. If only he could convince her that God had more for her than misery. He grinned. "She is."

Jet's face glowed. "Then I'd better go."

"Wait." Rossi placed his hand on the handle, stopping her from opening the door. She squinted. "Where's my hug?" He didn't care if he sounded pathetic.

"You're serious?" Throwing her head back, she laughed, showing her perfect set of white teeth. When she wrapped her arms around his waist, Rossi trapped her in an embrace and began to pray. "Lord, Your will is perfect. Thank You for bringing Jesetta home for Your purpose. In Jesus' name. Amen."

She mumbled Amen and stepped back, chuckling. "Some things never change with you, Tolliver."

He wiggled his brow. "You'll be surprised that some things are changing." Rossi opened her door and she slid behind the wheel of her Lexus, a car he had recommended she purchase.

When she glanced at him, a sunbeam cast the perfect light on her face. Maybe he gave up on her too easily. "Thank you. I wish you had prayed for peace, strength…"

"God's will is perfect. Everything we need is in His will." He patted the hood of her car. "Buckle up. I'm following you."

"I would argue that I don't need your services, but your cousin might be trippin', so again, some things never change."

"God never changes." He thought about the numerous scriptures that said as much from Numbers 23:19 in the Old Testament to James 1:17 in the New, but he doubted Jet would welcome the encouraging Bible verses. Without another word, he trekked to his SUV, which was hidden by a monument of a headstone.

Honestly, Rossi didn't know what kind of reception she would receive at Levi's. Dori would be ecstatic because he could tell she had been missing Jet. Karyn would be guarded. His cousin Levi was unpredictable. Since he was very protective of his wives—past and current—Levi would be suspicious.

Besides being first cousins, they had founded Tollivers Real Estate and Development Company. They were tapped as minority contractors for many projects that involved renovating, restoring, or new construction. Their company was flourishing.

When Levi got word that Jet was moving back to St. Louis, he was in a miserable mood. It had been doom and dread for days in the office.

"That woman is pure evil," he told *Rossi with a sneer before they started their morning meeting.*

"No, that woman is a wounded soul who needs Jesus," Rossi countered.

"I hope the Lord helps her before she gets here because I will not put up with her foolishness."

Well, they had less than an hour's drive from the cemetery to 15672 Fair Park Lucie Court in Fairview Heights, Illinois. That would be twenty-three miles of prayer time.

Chapter 3

"You have no say in who your brother-in-law marries." Layla's pep talk replayed in Jet's head as she gripped the wheel tighter. "Your focus needs to be about your niece's well-being. Be there for her."

Jet nodded. "I can do this." She could act fake for Dori's sake, but pretending took way too much energy. She should know because she had been acting like everything was back to normal for years. When in reality, Jet was walking around with an opened wound.

Something had to give. Judging from Levi's clipped tone a week ago when she informed him she was moving back, she'd better brace for hints of drama.

Forgoing the radio, she used the quiet time to prepare for a mental battle. She didn't know what she was walking into. In the almost nine-plus months since she had been gone, had Levi and Karyn turned her niece against her? Her heart dropped at that possibility.

Glancing in her rearview mirror, Rossi's vehicle was in sight as she crossed over the Mississippi River from downtown St. Louis to the Metro East in Illinois. Was he going to referee or babysit? She lifted her eyebrow. What really happened between him and his love connection with Nalani?

Soon, Jet turned into the familiar subdivision and parked in front of the Tollivers' two-story house. She took a deep breath and prayed, *Lord, help me to hold my tongue.* Getting out, she didn't pause for Rossi as she followed the path to the porch and pushed the bell.

The door opened seconds later, and she came face-to-face with Levi. He didn't mask his suspicious frown, and she refused to care. Suddenly, Dori screamed and raced to the door. She jumped in place, grinning ear to ear, while waiting for her father to invite Jet in.

When he finally did, Rossi was behind her. "Hey, cuz." Levi nodded at Rossi. "Jet."

"Auntie, Auntie," Dori said and hugged her tight. Jet could tell she had grown a couple of inches, but she would be seven soon. Her hair was wild in two loose ponytails. Otherwise, she seemed happy.

Dropping to her knees, Jet closed her eyes and held on to her niece for dear life. "I love you."

"I love you too," Dori replied, giddy with excitement in her voice. It was such a contrast to the still atmosphere around her.

Shutting out the world, Jet wished this moment would never end. She was glad Dori didn't wiggle out of her embrace. When Jet opened her eyes, she realized she had an audience: Levi, Karyn, Rossi, and the new baby—toddler—Levi Jr.

"See my baby brother." Dori hurried to the boy, then struggled to pick him up with Karyn's assistance.

"Umm-hmm." Jet nodded, but made no effort to take the child. She glanced at his mother. "Hello, Karyn." See, she could be civil.

"Welcome to our home." Karyn's smile seemed genuine enough. She wasn't as petite as her sister had been, but it was evident she had added pounds.

"C'mon." Dori tugged on Jet's hand. "I want to show you my room."

Be respectful. Jet looked to Karyn for permission. Karyn granted it with a nod, and Jet was glad to escape their scrutiny.

Since her last visit more than a year ago, Dori's bedroom had been repainted in lilac and updated to include two bookshelves—one packed with books and the other with the porcelain dolls Jet had started to collect for her. Jet smiled. Dori was a voracious reader, and her love for books was what brought her father and Karyn together.

"See my clothes?" Dori opened the door to reveal everything neatly hung and arranged by color. She pulled out one outfit after another to show her favorite outfits. "I use to like pink, but that's for babies. I like purple now because…"

Jet listened attentively until a long shelf on the wall that displayed family photos caught her eye. Although she responded to Dori's chatter at the right moments, she crossed the room and picked up the four-by-six frame and swallowed, staring at the photo. Jet thought it was of her as a little girl, but it was actually Diane's grade-school picture.

She hadn't seen this picture in years. She turned around. "Where did you get this?"

"Mommy," Dori stated, then began to show her the latest electronic games and books.

Not wanting to confuse her niece by asking for clarification of who was the mother, she asked instead, "You do know who this is, don't you?"

"Yeah." Dori bobbed her head and pointed. "She's my first mommy, Diane. Mommy says I look like her."

"You do." Cradling the frame in her hands, Jet sat on the twin bed and stared. Kudos to Karyn. At least the woman wasn't trying to wipe her sister's memory from Dori's life.

"Mommy also said—"

Jet squeezed her lips together as she struggled with hearing Dori call Karyn mommy, but that was her problem. She would have to work through it.

"I also look a lot like you." She grinned. "You're pretty, Auntie, so I guess I'm pretty too."

"Yes, you are." Jet's heart warmed, and she brushed back the wild hair from her niece's ponytails using her hand. They talked—or rather, her niece chatted away while Jet listened and watched her. She could stay holed up in the room for days, but evidently Little Levi wasn't having it as he banged on the door.

"Doree! Doree!" he yelled, followed by more banging.

Dori opened it without hesitation, and her baby brother wormed his way inside and made a beeline for his sister's toy chest. Amused, Jet watched the sibling interaction. She was glad Dori had someone.

Her niece fussed at Little Levi about touching her things the same way Jet used to yell at Diane for playing with her toys. Those were the good days where their parents sheltered them from bad people. *Lord, please protect them.*

The boy was handsome and favored Karyn more than Levi. Evidently, the Tollivers didn't have strong genes. She chuckled to herself, but her giggle caught the child's attention because with Dori's stuffed animal tucked under his arm, he wobbled over to her. He shoved it in her face and laughed.

Seconds later, Levi appeared in the doorway. "Jet, can we talk?"

Might as well get it over with. "Sure." She stood.

"But we haven't finished playing, Auntie." Dori looked disappointed.

"I'll take you to the park," she promised and followed Levi to the kitchen.

Once they were seated at the table, Jet folded her hands. If her brother-in-law was expecting her to throw the first verbal assault, then he might as well take a nap. Her focus was her relationship with her niece, not him or Karyn. As they eyed each other, Jet silently corrected her earlier assessment. Dori's brother did favor his father.

Why was the house so quiet? Eerie with children—and where were Rossi and Karyn? Finally, Levi pushed his glasses higher on his nose and cleared his throat.

"Unless you've changed, nothing has changed between us."

Her? "Excuse me?" Why was it she who had to change? No, she refused to take his bait. He was right. Wasn't that what she told Diane? She was prepared to make changes in her life. However, he could be a little more sympathetic.

"I protect what and who is mine, and that is my wife—Karyn—and my children. I never kept you from Dori, but that was before you became disrespectful, belligerent, conniving..."

Any woman would be suspicious of another woman trying to take the place of her sister. The stakes became higher when she read about Karyn's past. Despite knowing what Karyn had done, Levi married her anyway without any concern for his daughter's well-being. Now who was the crazy one?

As Levi continued to mount his threats, Jet had to tune him out. Otherwise, she would give him a piece of her mind.

Only when a vein twitched in his forehead did he settle down. She knew he loved fiercely. She had witnessed it firsthand with Diane, so his theatrics weren't a surprise. Besides being older than him by three years and taller too, she had to remind him of his place. She leaned forward. "I suggest you check yourself. I am your late first wife's sister. Disrespect me and you're disrespecting her. Furthermore, you might not have a problem with Karyn killing her own child, but if I were you, I would keep an eye on her. And as for Dori, if she puts a mark on my niece, I will have social services here so fast to launch an investigation—"

"Are you threating me?" Levi stood and sneered.

Jet got to her feet too. "Call my bluff." Why was she letting this man provoke her?

"Sweetie, can I talk to you for a moment?" His wife appeared from nowhere and interrupted the showdown.

"Yeah, we need to talk." Rossi stood behind Karyn.

Her opponent took his eyes off her long enough to glance their way, and so did she. Both were shooting Levi daggers. *Good.*

Watching Rossi shove his cousin out the back door, Jet exhaled, then dropped to her seat. She bowed her head, closed her eyes and massaged her temples. How was she going to make a civil relationship work? When she heard the chair scrape the floor, she looked up. Karyn had taken her husband's seat. Did she have any energy for a round two? She didn't think so. She would use the intermission to leave. Some homecoming.

***

"Please don't go," Karyn asked softly. "I'm sorry for the things my husband said to you and the manner in which he said them." *Lord, help me win her over to You,* she silently prayed, then she took a deep breath. Studying Jet, she saw Dori, the daughter she'd legally adopted not long after she'd gotten married.

Jet tapped her long nails on Karyn's glass table. "Levi doesn't mince words. He meant what he said, and so do I. Only for Dori am I willing to be nice, but I'm watching you. I lost one loved one, and I'll do whatever necessary to keep from losing another one."

Her implication was understood, which was why the truth hurt. As long as Karyn lived, until the day she died, she would reap the condemnation from others because of her actions. God had forgiven her and given her grace to bear the shame. The key to her mental stability was to forgive herself and live each day, which was never promised. "I understand your pain."

"How?" Confusion draped Jet's face. "I don't think you do." Sitting back, her guest gave her a mock laugh. "You have a sister and I don't."

She nodded. "True. I have a sister who I love dearly, but I have a son who I miss daily." She swallowed, replaying the day she was studying for college exams, stressed at being a new mother, depressed about losing her mother and being abandoned by her boyfriend—the father of her baby.

How did she know that squeezing her infant son too tight to quiet him would kill him? She was later diagnosed with postpartum depression. "Before I was even sentenced to prison, I was paying for my sins. God forgave me, but it took a long time for me to forgive myself. If you never forgive me for what I did, which had nothing to do with you, I'm okay with that." She swallowed to keep the tears at bay.

Though your sins be as scarlet, I have washed them white as snow, God whispered Isaiah 1:18. *Keep trying with Jet.*

Shifting in her seat, she regrouped. "Please get to know me as Karyn Tolliver, not the woman I once was."

"You're asking a lot. When I see you, I see what the newspaper said you did."

"Yes." She sighed. "And when God sees me—and you— He sees us as prized possessions after He cleans us up after our self-destruction," she said as Dori ran into the kitchen.

"Mommy, can I change Little Levi's diaper?" The expectancy on her face tugged at Jet.

"As long as it's not number two. Be careful, and I'll check."

"Okay! Auntie, come see me change my brother's diaper. I know how."

Jet glowed around Dori. Her smile actually reached her eyes. "Sure, sweetie." She stood, and Karyn eyed her heels. She wondered whose height Dori would take. Maybe she would consider enrolling her into some child modeling just in case her daughter started to inch past her.

Karyn peeked outside the sliding door at the Tolliver cousins camped out on her deck. Thank God Rossi was there to calm her husband down. She loved that man and thanked God every day for him, but she didn't need him to fight her battles, especially with Jet. Jesus was doing that.

Before her incident, Karyn never had to work hard at being someone's friend. She and her younger sister, Nalani, were Miss Personalities—outgoing, charitable, and the social butterflies as children of an Illinois senator.

Prison changed her. She was guarded and chose her friends carefully. Her best friends were also former felons, but all three had surrendered to Christ while in prison. Once they were released, they gave back to the community by opening Crowning Glory, a full-service salon and barbershop that helped people get back on their feet.

Jet became not only a thorn in Karyn's side, but the sides of Buttercup and Halo who had tied the knot once their probation period had expired. Now, the two of them were hoping to start a family soon. At the time, Jet worked as the finance manager at the bank that was reviewing their business proposal. She initially turned down their loan. That's when Nalani came on the scene and forced Jet's hand to reverse the decision.

To say there was bad blood among Jet, Halo, and Buttercup was an understatement. Levi barely tolerated her. Karyn was determined to be her friend. At least Rossi, the man of God that he was, was long suffering when it came to Jet. No one was better than him at winning souls for Christ.

Karyn joined them in the bedroom and watched from afar as Dori meticulously wiped her brother and sprinkled a little baby powder on his bottom. Once she was finished, Little Levi scrambled off the bed and made a beeline to Karyn. She smiled at his toothy grin.

Jet praised Dori with accolades about how caring she was and the good job she'd done. Dori beamed.

"Well, sweetie, I'd better go so I can get settled." Jet turned and looked at Karyn. "Unless you have any objections, I would like to take my niece to the park tomorrow."

"For a picnic?" Dori's eyes widened in excitement. "Yeah."

"Yes."

"Can Little Levi come? Dori pleaded.

Almost in union, they both said no, then glanced at each other. Karyn wondered about Jet's reason. Did she not want to be around her son? A stab stuck in her heart. Since they already had a family gathering, she had a perfect excuse to avoid a direct answer. "Do you mind a rain check? The Tollivers are celebrating Uncle Ross' retirement."

Of course it was rude not to invite Levi's sister-in-law who had been part of the family before her, but she didn't want to make that call.

"I cash in rain checks," Jet said in a no-nonsense tone before kneeling to give Dori a goodbye hug. When Little Levi waited for a hug, Karyn scooped him up. She didn't want to give Jet a chance to reject her son. They both had trust issues to overcome if they were to have a shot at a genuine friendship.

After waving goodbye at the door, the children returned to their toys while Karyn prayed. *Lord, help us to love one another.*

Minutes later, she stepped out on the deck, and informed Levi and Rossi that Jet had left. Rossi looked disappointed; her husband, relieved.

"Well, I guess I'd better head out," Rossi said, then turned to Levi. "I know humility isn't in any of our DNA, but it's a must have to walk with Christ. Jet's not your enemy, cuz. The devil is."

Levi acted like he didn't hear him.

Once Rossi left, she lit into her husband. "You should be ashamed of yourself. You didn't have to be so mean spirited to Jet—your daughter's aunt."

Levi squinted. "You do remember this is the same woman who attacked you, almost got you fired, sabotaged your business…shall I go on?"

"No, you shouldn't." She planted a fist on each of her hips and lifted her chin. She wasn't backing down. "I want to mend fences, win a soul for Christ—"

"I was defending your honor. Setting down the house rules," he added smugly and folded his arms.

"Sweetie," Karyn purred. She knew how to get his attention, and his stance relaxed. Her handsome husband was a gentle giant, but he hadn't been in her shoes where she desperately wanted someone's—anyone's—forgiveness.

Lord, please help us to love one another and mend this family, no matter what it takes, she prayed.

Chapter 4

While eavesdropping on Levi and Jet's conversation, Rossi debated with Karyn which one should step into the ring. "I'm going in."

"Me too." Karyn stepped into the kitchen before him.

"Hey, I wasn't finished," Levi fumed when Karyn stopped him mid-sentence.

"Trust me. You are," Rossi said and physically shoved him out the door to the deck. Levi might be shorter than him, but his cousin was solid, so he wasn't going willingly.

Once outside, Rossi folded his arms like a bouncer and blocked Levi's path from re-entering the house. "Have a seat."

"Are you crazy? She may try to hurt my wife." His nostrils flared like an irritated bull.

Rossi needed to calm himself down too. As boys, they would horse around and throw punches. As men and practicing Christians, they settled their disagreements through prayer, but his cousin was making it rough. "I mean it, Brother Levi. Grab a chair."

Calling him Brother gave Levi pause. Whenever Rossi went church mode on a family member, they knew there was no compromise. Levi complied, but it wasn't without some grumbling. "You owe Jet an apology."

"For what?" He leaped from his chair. "She came into my house…"

"And did nothing." Rossi continued to block Levi's view as he walked to the table and took a seat in front of him. "Jet came in peace. I've never seen her hold her peace, but she did—until you went too far. She's right, man. I know how much you loved Diane. She wouldn't want you treating her sister like this."

"I loved Diane, and I love Karyn."

"And as a brother in Christ, what about Jesetta? Doesn't she deserve and need your love?" He paraphrased a couple of verses from 1 Corinthians 13. "Love suffers long and hard. Love is kind and doesn't behave badly, and most of all, love is not easily provoked." Tilting his head toward the door, Rossi shook his head. "From where your wife and I were standing, you failed, bro. There was no love on your part."

The conviction must have pricked Levi's heart because he bowed his head and groaned. Putting his hands on the glass-top table, he glanced up. Weariness was in his eyes. "What am I supposed to do, huh?"

"Pray for Jesetta. God took her sister away. Dori's getting older. Your daughter doesn't need to feel or see this friction between two people she loves. You've recovered. Now pray that Jet does too." He paused and chose his words carefully. "And a word to the wise, don't ever talk to her like that again."

Levi squinted. "Are you threatening me now? Over Jet?"

Rossi wasn't about to confirm or deny his cousin's accuracy. As protective as Levi was of Karyn, Rossi's heart was coming to Jet's rescue, but he couldn't compromise allegiance to God's work. He repented. *Lord, I know according to Romans 2:11 that you show no partiality to us. Help me, Jesus, to judge situations fairly. Help me, Lord. Help me to bring peace to Levi and Jet.*

"Are you?" Levi frowned.

"No, cuz." Rossi shook his head. Until God resolved the tension, it was going to be a balancing act when Jet and Levi were in the same room. "If you need to fast and pray to overcome this tension, then I suggest you do that. God hates hypocrisy. As saints, we are not to be guilty of it." He needed to tend to Jet's wounds—if she had any after the tit-for-tat with Levi. "I'm heading out. Do you want prayer before I leave?"

"Nah, I'm good." Levi stood.

Since when did a saint turn down prayer? Rossi got to his feet too. "Well, we're going to pray anyhow." He bowed his head. "Lord, in the mighty name of Jesus, You are not the Author of confusion, so we come before You naked with our sins and ask that You forgive us and give us more grace to overcome this trial. In Jesus' matchless name."

They both said "Amen" together.

When Karyn informed them that Jet had left, Rossi's heart dropped. They had a lot of catching up to do, and he had hoped to spend some time with her today.

"Was she okay?"

"Are you okay?" Levi asked his wife.

"We'll both be okay, eventually." Karyn eyed her husband.

Rossi took her "you're in trouble now" look as his cue to leave. He said his goodbyes. As he walked out the door and to his SUV, he debated if he should call Jet since he had no idea where she was staying.

Common courtesy overruled his desire to see her. He decided to give her space and head home, but Jet stayed on his mind during the drive to his loft. Less than twenty minutes later, he strolled through his front door, frustrated. Jet was not to blame for the turmoil. Calling it as he saw it, he put the blame on Satan who was the master of confusion. Rossi began to pray and rebuke the demons that caused mischief whenever Jet and his cousin were in the same room.

Once peace had recaptured his soul, he ended his petition to the Lord. His stomach growled, but he craved seeing Jet to satisfy the hunger reigning in his heart. First, he wanted to know where her heart was with him and God.

Hours passed before he called her. "Did I wake you?" Checking the time, it wasn't nine o'clock yet.

She yawned. "Just taking a nap."

"You're getting old on me already, huh?" They chuckled together.

"No. Tired. I drove from Nashville earlier, remember? Then I had to deal with your cousins. The Tollivers are draining."

"Hey," he said, feigning insult. "I'm a Tolliver."

"Umm-hmm. I know. You're included when you get on my bad side." She paused, then added, "But you're okay."

"You mean I'm not your favorite?" he teased her.

"Nope. Get in line behind Dori."

"Fair enough. So…" He crossed his living room and flopped in an oversized chair. "If you're not doing anything tomorrow, the families are getting together to celebrate pops' retirement. I'm sure everyone would love to see you."

Silence, then finally, "I don't think that's a good idea. I don't have energy for back-to-back drama."

Rossi sighed. Maybe he was pushing too hard too fast. He had no comeback. Once Levi decided to marry Karyn, it didn't take long for her to win over the family. Everyone was glad when Jet stop coming to the get-togethers because of the tension she brought. Of course, no one would go on record confessing to that. "I want the best for you, Jesetta," he said softly.

"Thanks," she replied in a softer voice. "I believe you."

"So what are you doing tomorrow?"

"Probably house hunting."

"Want some company?"

"I don't think I'll win brownie points taking away the favorite son from his father's party. I'm a big girl and a home girl. I know my way around."

Jet didn't know he was willing to show up late so that he could put the wheels in motion to woo her not only to God, but himself. "You have no idea how much we love you, especially me." That part was true… Well, it might take pulling teeth for Levi to admit to that. "What about Sunday? I'm the speaker/preacher for our annual family and friends' day."

"Although you do hold my attention, I think I need to keep my contact with Levi and Karyn to a minimum—for now. I'll look for another church to attend."

She was looking? Rossi perked up. He liked the sound of that. "For the record, Levi changed membership after they got married. Since Crowns for Christ was instrumental in Karyn's salvation and they work with the prison ministry, he felt they should be unified in helping others..."

"Who were in prison," she finished. "To this day, I still don't understand how a woman can kill her baby. Then again, I don't understand how anyone can take another person's life." She released a mock chuckle. "It's a twist of fate that they can move on and I seem to be stuck. How can they just move on?" Her frustration was apparent.

"It's never okay to sin—never. God does forgive, Jesetta, and to be a Christian, we have to ask God to help us to forgive one another. Let me give you two scriptures to consider, and I hope you will come Sunday and support me."

"You don't need my support."

"Trust me, I do."

They were about to disconnect when Jet yelled, "What about the scriptures?"

Rossi blinked. She was actually reminding him? Good sign. *Thank You, Lord.* "Read Genesis chapter four and verse fifteen. No—make that the entire chapter in the Old Testament and Matthew chapter five in the New Testament. You'll learn about the magnitude of God's forgiveness."

"Okay. See you Sunday." *Click.*

He roared at her antics. Jesetta was back, and Rossi was going to enjoy getting to know Jet as a woman after his own heart.

Chapter 5

Jet thought about reconsidering Rossi's offer seconds after they disconnected. The Tolliver family get-togethers were legendary—food, fun, and fine brothers. She first met Rossi at one of their parties. If anyone wanted to host a male auction, the contestants were on deck. The Tolliver clan was made up of good-looking men, including Levi and his younger twin brothers. Rossi was the oldest of four siblings and three years older than Daniel, five years older than Titus, and seven wiser than Chaz.

Amazingly, their resemblance was unmatched as if they were quadruplets. Some were practicing Christians, a term she'd heard Rossi say, a few were trudging in lukewarm water—another Rossi Tolliver term—yet Jet understood neither.

Besides Levi and his younger brother, Seth, who happened to be a twin to Solomon, most were unattached. She thought about the former Tia Rogers who had married Seth. The woman had a magnetic personality that easily drew people into her circle of friends. Jet was one of them.

When Diane was alive, Jet's presence was expected at the parties. No invitation was needed, and she rarely missed a gathering, but things changed after Karyn's past was revealed. The Tollivers seemed so accepting and forgiving. Was it part of their Christian duty? It didn't matter as Jet's appearances became less frequent until she stopped going altogether.

"Yep, I made the right decision to decline Rossi's offer," she said to herself. Jet's sanity depended on keeping minimum interaction with the Tollivers.

She stood and strolled across the thick carpet to her sliding patio door. Stepping outside, she observed the buzz of the crowd below her hotel room—workers, shoppers, and tourists having places to go. Leaning on the railing, her mind wandered again.

Levi had so irritated her by the way he had approached her, then Karyn's chatter confused her. What was God thinking when He snatched Diane, a loving mother, away from Dori, and allowed Karyn to take her sister's place? Where was the justice in that? Then the woman blamed her actions on postpartum depression. That nonsense just plain annoyed Jet.

Obsessing over the Tollivers took way too much brainpower. Jet took one final glance around downtown St. Louis and stepped back inside her suite. After working at Layla's luxury hotel, she couldn't see herself staying anywhere that didn't rate four stars. And the Magnolia Hotel was amazing. She gave herself a month or so to decide where she wanted to live.

As far as income, Layla insisted on keeping her on the payroll as a consultant until Jet found work. With a finance degree and banking background, Jet hoped to have a job within a week, but there was no rush. She knew how to manage money, and over the years she had invested and saved well.

Still, there was no place like home, and before moving to Nashville, Jet had built a lavish house in Illinois not far from Levi to help with Dori. Since her services were no longer needed, Jet decided to stay in St. Louis again. *Levi.* She huffed. She was so proud of herself that she held back. Diane would be proud too.

Reconcile with your brother before coming to My altar, God whispered. *Read Matthew 5:24.*

Jet paused. Rossi had suggested that same chapter. Was that a yea or nay from the Lord? Frowning, Jet's jubilation was instantly deflated. Since she began reading her Bible more while in Nashville, she liked it when the Lord spoke to her every now and then, but it always seemed to be in a riddle, and she was clueless how to decipher it.

As she reached for her Bible, her phone chimed. Seeing that it was Layla, she answered it, flopped on the sofa, then crossed her ankles. "Hey, girlfriend."

"Hey nothing! I've waited all day to hear from you to see how everything went," she fussed. "You're calm, so that means your homecoming was well received, right? I'm crossing my fingers."

Her cheerleader. She and Layla had hit it off instantly when they met at Vanderbilt University in Nashville. They were both tall at five-feet-ten. Layla had rich dark skin and had been wearing her hair in stylish cornrows. Whenever they used to walk into a party, they grabbed attention. Who would have thought thirteen years after graduation neither of them would have found their soul mates or have at least one child?

Maybe men were intimidated by their independent nature and professional status. Whatever the reason, they both were thirty-five, and their clocks were ticking. Yes, they were professional women. They were inseparable in college, but over the years, life had gotten in the way, and they'd lost touch. They reconnected after Diane's death. When Jet had confided that she needed a clean start, Layla had opened her door. They promised to stay better connected this time around, and already Jet had forgotten to touch base with her friend. "Well, uncross them."

Layla groaned. "Uh-oh. Do you need any reinforcement?"

"Nope. No 'man down' here, but—"

"But what?" Layla pressed. "Do I have to leave my business here to come down there and get in your business? What's going on?"

Closing her eyes, Jet sighed before explaining. "I felt like my brother-in-law picked up where we left off." She shook her head. "Granted, it was strained, but I was willing to be fake for Dori."

"You can't let that man get to you."

"Right, says my best friend who kicked me out to the wolves."

"I did not!" Layla argued, then chuckled. "You've been running from your pain, and left untreated, it will kill you. I just want to see you move on and share memories about Diane without breaking down."

"Hey, I have gotten better." Jet refused to let the pain and hurt consume her anymore. "I only cried—two times."

"Three," Layla corrected. "I was keeping track. Remember, keep reading your Bible."

Bible? Jet thought about the scripture God pointed her to before Layla called.

"Have you seen Rossi?" Layla asked, interrupting her thoughts.

Why was she grinning before she answered? "Yep. He actually came to the cemetery."

"Huh?" Layla repeated. "I didn't know you planned to stop there. How did he know? Did you tell him?" She rattled off questions as Jet replayed the scene in her head.

"I don't know how he knew. He just showed up." Her voice drifted as she strained to recall his very words. "Actually, he said he had been watching out for me."

"Hmmm." Layla chuckled.

"What?"

"Oh, nothing... So how was Dori?"

Jet smiled. "Cuter than ever and getting taller, and she's starting to look more like me." Proud, she beamed at the assessment.

"So are you glad to be home?"

"Time will tell, despite being homeless because my friend kicked me out, and unemployed because my friend fired me..." She couldn't finish as Layla burst out laughing, and Jet joined her.

"You know you're welcome to come any time to visit, but I felt you needed to be there and fight until the end."

"You were right. I'm not about to let Levi or Karyn intimidate me."

"Good. I'm a phone call away if you need me, but it seems Rossi is even closer. Are you sure he doesn't like you?"

"Of course he likes me—as a domineering older brother who thinks he can boss me around." Her stomach growled. "Listen, all this recap is making me hungry."

After they disconnected, Jet reached for the menu and ordered room service. While waiting, she grabbed her Bible, but her mind was still on what Layla said. Rossi liking her as more than a charity case?

Nah, she doubted it. He had too many options out there to focus on her.

***

Saturday afternoon, Rossi's mind was elsewhere as he mingled with family and friends at his father's retirement party. One person was missing, and he wondered what she was doing.

"Rossi, please tell me that crazy woman's not back in town," Nalani Wallace, Karyn's younger sister, said as she strolled to his side.

He schooled his expression before glancing at the woman everyone thought was the perfect match for him. Nalani was fiercely loyal to Karyn, a people person, polished, classy, and would call on politicians if she needed favors—like making sure Jet's bank reversed the decision not to approve the loan for Crowning Glory salon.

Yes, the petite diva was a force to be reckoned with. And like any full-blooded man, Rossi had been blindsided by her beauty and charm too. Once she surrendered to Christ, he pursued her as a wife candidate. The two had dated heavily for months, causing Rossi to wonder if his attraction was lust building within him or true love. It wasn't until he was on his knees crying out to God for direction about whether Nalani was the right one for him that the Lord spoke.

Rossi, your heart knows. God whispered nothing more.

He'd searched his heart and concluded Nalani was missing something. He just couldn't put his finger on what it was. If he had to hold out until he was fifty years old, Rossi was determined to find the woman who would love him because of what was in his heart, not his title or bank account.

He and Nalani's courtship slowed, and eventually, they decided to be friends or in-laws. Now he looked at her. Where Jet was tall at five-ten and curvy, Nalani was five-four or five easily without the six-inch heels she teetered on at the moment with an appealing shape too.

Both women were beautiful and classy. Nalani had the features to pull off the short haircut that accented her face. To sum Nalani up in one word: stunning. Jet wore her hair long with curls that bounced with her every move. It was her flawless brown skin that was eye catching. He had seen her with and without makeup. Jesetta Hutchens had a gift from God. She was naturally beautiful. One thing both ladies had in common was their love for their sisters.

"She's anything but crazy. She suffered a great loss as you had when Karyn was incarcerated. Only you have Karyn back. Jet has nothing," Rossi explained gently. "She has every right to be here. Dori is her niece."

Not only did he want to be Jet's protector, but he wanted to defend her too. She was a good woman. "Her story is not yours and yours isn't hers. Pray for her, Nalani."

*Hmph*ed. She folded her arms and jutted her delicate chin. "I'm going to be praying alright that she tiptoe around my sister or…"

Rossi could feel his nostrils flare. "Or else what, Sister Nalani? Don't step out of the will of God to enact revenge. Jet's not saved—yet. Show her the love of Christ."

Nalani lifted her eyebrow and looked away, waving at a few family members. "I'll pray more for me that the woman doesn't test me."

"Noted." He shook his head, then slipped his hands inside his pockets.

He saw his cousin in the distance. Levi walked up to him. "I thought Jet might have tried to invite herself. *Whew*. So glad she didn't." He grinned and took a sip from his bottled water.

"My sentiments exactly," Nalani added.

"Cut her some slack, Tolliver. She might surprise you. Jet may turn out to be a better Christian than most believers, including us." With that final statement, Rossi excused himself so he could speak with his parents.

"Congratulations again, Pops." He shook the elder Rossi's hand. "You've been a good role model." He kissed his mother's cheek.

"Thanks, son." He looked over Rossi's shoulder. "I heard Jet was back in town. I thought she would be here."

"She is. Maybe she felt she wouldn't be welcomed," he said to both of them.

"We've all had devils to fight. I can't imagine the loss that young woman suffered. I hope she got some counseling and with prayer, God can make her whole," his father said sincerely, genuinely liking Jet.

"Amen," his mother said. "She just needs a double dose of love."

Rossi wanted to pat his chest and confess that he had that taken care of, but he held his tongue. His family was too vocal about the right woman for a minister. If he had the Lord Jesus' stamp of approval, that was all that mattered.

Chapter 6

Sunday morning, Jet stretched as she snuggled under the comforter. The day before had been a good one as she explored old hangouts across the area. For the first time in months, she looked forward to Sunday service where she'd hear a Word from God that would touch her soul. With Rossi preaching, she hoped God would speak to her. All other sermons paled compared to his.

So today was family and friends day at Living for Jesus Church. She no longer felt like family, and she doubted anybody missed her at the retirement party. Suddenly, she missed Layla. At least when she visited churches in Nashville, she wasn't alone.

Getting up, she tapped the Pandora app on her phone and gathered her items for the bathroom. She had set up her selection for female gospel artists, and those singing sisters were her companions all day Saturday.

Already she had some favorite songs, and one of them played while she was in the shower: "Free" by Kierra Sheard. She didn't know if the song was new or old, but the words seemed to seep into her pores. Jet desperately wanted to be free once and for all of the pain of losing Diane. Some days, Diane's death hit her hard.

When the singer said to lift her arms, Jet did that just that. Tears streamed down her cheeks. She followed the prompting by the artist to be free from burdens, the mind games, the past, and more. By the time she stepped out of the shower, Pandora had played two or three more songs, but that one stuck with her.

Jet realized as long as she stayed mad at the world, she could never be free. She made a promise to Diane and herself that she would move on.

As she dressed, Jet prayed, *Lord, I know You speak to Rossi, but speak to me today. I don't know how many people will be there, but I need a message.*

After applying her makeup, she brushed her long mane up into a ball on her head. She liked the youthful look it gave her. Next, Jet put on a royal-blue sleeveless dress and chiffon duster to cocoon her from the slight chill in the sanctuary, then slipped on her shoes.

She swiped up her Bible and purse, then headed to the lobby for breakfast. Jet nodded at the patrons.

Working in the hotel business for nine months gave her an eye to discern if guests were enjoying their experience. She couldn't help but assess the same thing that morning.

Jet acknowledged a few appreciative stares from men with a smile, but she didn't linger. She planned to do things differently when she dated again. She didn't want or need Rossi's or any of the Tollivers' approval. If a man could make her happy, put up with her occasional moods— hormonal or otherwise—and make her laugh, then he would be a keeper. But first things first, she needed to connect with God as Diane had done.

At the buffet table, Jet filled her plate with fruit, then requested a made-to-order omelet. Half an hour later, her belly was full, and she was behind the wheel of her car. She was about to pull out the garage when she received a text.

Remember today is a new day. Don't let yesterday's stuff ruin it. Call me after church.

She smiled at Layla's message before replying. Rossi's preaching, so I know I'll hear some good stuff. She tapped Send and drove off.

The Tollivers' church was centrally located off I-270. It was a magnificent white stone structure with acres of parking. The thousand-plus membership wasn't a mega church, but it definitely was too large a crowd to make her feel at home. She would find a church with a more intimate setting where she could grow little by little.

Jet was relieved that Levi had changed his membership to Karyn's church. After parking her Lexus, Jet crossed the lot to the entrance that had a bold sign overhead: *Enter expectantly, depart triumphantly.* She smiled. Jet hadn't noticed that before the few times she'd visited. She hoped that would be the case today.

Although she had read the entire chapter four of Genesis as Rossi suggested, she didn't understand God's logic behind protecting the first murderer with a mark on his forehead to keep him from succumbing to the same fate. Cain had murdered his flesh and blood as Karyn had done with her son. Whether God had sealed Karyn with a mark or not, whenever Jet saw her, she saw a murderer.

"Enough," she mumbled, then smiled at the ushers as she stepped into the lobby. Knowing in which section the Tollivers sat, Jet veered in the opposite direction, then she bumped into Rossi's mother, Laura.

"Jesetta!" The woman, who was inches shorter than Jet and fashionably dressed, held onto her hat with one hand as she encircled her arm around her with the other. "I've missed you." Her eyes sparkled. "My son told me you were back in town, and I had thought you would be at the party."

Why did she suddenly feel guilty? "To be honest, I didn't want to be a party crasher."

"Nonsense. Party crashers are overrated." Laura Tolliver *tsk*ed then looped her arm through Jet's and steered her in the direction she didn't want to go. "We're sitting over here." She pointed.

"I know. I thought I would sneak in and out." She was hoping Laura would take the hint.

"Nope." She proceeded to march down the aisle where the other family members were sitting. They waved and smiled, easing some of the tension. She got sandwiched between Tolliver sisters-in law. That meant there was no escaping Laura and Levi's mother, Sharon, who she once was very close to, any time before the service ended.

"Our lost sheep has come home," Laura whispered to Sharon.

She hugged Sharon, but Jet was cautious. After all, Karyn was a Tolliver now, so by default, Jet distanced herself from family.

"I've missed you." Sharon's eyes watered.

Jet nodded and blinked as she looked away. She didn't want to start bawling. Then as if sensing eyes on her, she glanced toward the pulpit and met Rossi's stare. He gave her a mock salute. She giggled. Some things never changed. From the hugs and Rossi's gesture, Jet dropped her defenses.

The praise team finished a string of melodies, the church secretary read the announcements, and then Pastor Bryon Brown walked to the podium. "Praise the Lord, everyone! Our speaker today is no stranger or guest. He and his brothers were baptized here, and he's worked with our youth tirelessly in kingdom building. Please stand as Brother, Minister, and Preacher Tolliver gives us what the Lord has given him."

Rossi stood and Jet noted his swagger to the podium under thunderous applause. Jet and the two pews of Tollivers screamed the loudest.

The only time she'd seen him bashful was when others gave him accolades as a minister. "Thank you." He motioned for everyone to be seated. Jet grabbed her Bible, anxious for God to speak to her.

"Before I give you my text..." Standing tall and confident, Rossi commanded the audience with his deep voice, "I want us all to consider our guilt today. Have you ever been angry at God for something someone else did, but you blamed God for their behavior? If you are blaming God for the bad stuff, who gets credit for your blessings?" He paused for them to consider his question. "There is one God, and His name is above every name—Jesus, and our guilt doesn't separate us from Him."

Jet considered herself a smart, educated woman, yet Rossi had dumbfounded her.

"If someone sinned or committed a crime, we want the maximum punishment as justice."

"Amens" circulated around Jet, so she added her own. Rossi smirked and nodded. "What if it were you? Wouldn't you want the grace of God to get off the hook? The blood that Jesus shed keeps you from getting caught and tried in the devil's court. Repentance keeps God from punishing you for every wrongdoing conceived in your mind, then committed with your body."

She gnawed on her lips, scanning the crazy things she had done and said in her lifetime that could have gotten her in trouble, but like he said, Jet hadn't got caught. She thought about when she slapped Karyn after hearing her admit she had killed someone. The woman could have pressed charges for assault—and she would have deserved it—but Karyn didn't. Had that been God's grace?

"Now—" Rossi patted the podium—"you may open your Bible to Genesis four."

So he had given her a preview of his sermon by telling her to read Genesis chapter four. She smiled, thinking she was privy to something others had no advance knowledge of.

"In verse seven, God tells Cain how to stay in God's graces, simply by giving Him the best sacrifice. We all know that didn't happen because he became angry with God for rejecting his sacrifice. He took his anger out and killed his baby brother. Wow." Rossi stepped back, folded his arms, then shook his head.

He was quiet for a moment, then said, "Lord, help us not to get so angry that we sin. When you get a chance, study Ephesians 4:26."

She made note of that scripture in her phone to read later. Up until this point, she didn't realize how bad the fallout could get from her anger, especially at Karyn. Jet had to admit bodily harm wasn't out of the question when she saw the woman.

"This is a mind-boggling chapter because God didn't give Cain the punishment we think he deserved. Despite his disobedience, God protected him from the same fate with a seal or mark of protection..." His manner of preaching was so convincing and compelling, people didn't stir. Soon, he closed his Bible. "Nothing good can come out of being angry with God—or others. This is the altar call. Please stand. If you came angry today, leave it here. Repent before you do something crazy. Cry out to the Lord Jesus, and He'll answer. Come today and let God put His seal of the Holy Ghost on you. Come..."

Jet took a deep breath, then exhaled. How many times had she heard Rossi's plea, only to ignore it? Her heart pounded as she contemplated her next move. She rested her Bible on the seat next to her, and Laura touched her hand but didn't say a word. Swallowing back the uncertainty of what she was committing to, Jet stood and climbed over the Tollivers as they clapped and shouted, "Thank you, Jesus."

Stepping into the aisle, she bowed her head. This wasn't a catwalk to the altar. She didn't care who was watching or if she was the sole one. Anger would no longer rule her life. Instead of being directed to one of the ministers, Rossi came down the steps and waved her toward him.

"What do you want from the Lord today, sister?" he asked as if he didn't know her.

"I want God's forgiveness and His seal," she mumbled through her tears as Rossi's strong hands gently squeezed hers.

"If you repent, He will forgive you instantly, then complete His salvation plan for you with the water baptism to be buried with Him, and Jesus will give you the Holy Ghost, so you can be resurrected when He returns." He paused.

"This is between you and God, Jesetta. Talk to Him," he softly urged her. "Not me."

Hearing her name on his lips calmed her spirit. "Lord, please forgive me," she whispered until two women, dressed in all white, came to her side and led her out of the sanctuary into a small room. She wasn't the only one changing her church clothes for white pants and gowns, mumbling to God. Soon, Jet joined other candidates at the pool's ledge. Surprisingly, Rossi was in the water, standing between two other ministers. She couldn't recall a time when she heard him preach, then watched him baptize folks in the same service. Her mind was jumbled with too many thoughts to reason why.

When she was the next to step down, instead of going to the last minister as she had seen others do, she was directed to stop in front of Rossi. When their eyes met, she relaxed at his smile.

"Cross your arms over your chest, Jesetta." She did as he instructed. "Once you repented, God planted the seed for your salvation walk to grow. This anointed water will not only wash away your eternal sins, but sins that were waiting in the wings. Finally, God promises you the Holy Ghost, and it will increase your faith in Jesus."

She nodded, believing every word he said in a low voice as if it was just them in the pool instead of four others.

"Whatever your struggles are from here on out, trust God to help you, no matter what."

"I will." Jet nodded as her heart pounded with a mixture of excitement and fear of the unknown as Rossi gripped the back of the white garment she was wearing.

Lifting his arm, he said in a loud voice, "My dear sister, upon the confession of your faith and the confidence we have in the blessed Word of God, we now indeed baptize you in the name that is above every name by which we must be saved and that is the Lord Jesus Christ for the remission of your sins. Acts two tells us you shall receive the Holy Ghost."

Closing her eyes, Jet trembled as Rossi pulled her back, submerging her under water. She became lightheaded. As soon as it seemed like she was drowning, Rossi guided her to the surface with measured strength. Whatever heaviness she took into the water seemed released. Either the angels were singing or she could hear Kierra Sheard's "Free" in her ear.

Opening her eyes, she heard Rossi shouting, "Hallelujah," but she was too mesmerized by the vision of a ball of fire coming at her.

As she opened her mouth to scream, it slammed into her, and the next thing she knew, she heard a different language coming out of her mouth.

Her body felt slack as arms began to wade in the water. She couldn't control her movements or her tongue, yet she knew Rossi had not let go of her.

The roar of excitement in the auditorium sounded like a stampede of thousands of horses running endlessly.

"Today, you're sealed as a bride," Rossi said.

In a daze, she glanced at him. His eyes sparkled, his smile gleamed, and the expression on his face was pure relief. "Welcome to the Body of Christ, Sister Jesetta Hutchens."

She grinned widely, but she wasn't in control of her tongue, so she lifted her arms in praise. In her mind she screamed, "God, tell Diane I got it."

Chapter 7

W *hew.* Rossi had baptized hundreds during his ministry and never before had God shown him a vision and spoke so fast that it caused him to wonder if he'd heard right. *I present your bride.* He repeated what God had said at the same time he blinked and saw Jet no longer in her white baptismal gown, but a wedding dress that would rival royalty.

He exhaled again as he quickly dried off to redress and get out to the sanctuary and Jet. "Let the wooing begin," he said with a grin as he buttoned his shirt.

Had God whispered something in her ear? He hoped so. He was tired of the on-and-off casual dating scene. He wanted a wife and children.

While on his knees, God gave him the morning sermon. Rossi had been speechless that it was the same text he had given Jet the day before. That wasn't a coincidence. As the youth minister at Living for Jesus Church, this had only been the second time Rossi had been asked to speak during morning worship. That wasn't by chance either. "Thank You, Lord, for bringing her home."

When he entered the sanctuary, he spotted his family huddling around Jet. As Rossi approached, his path was intercepted several times with hugs from the mothers in church.

"You preached well, young man. All you need is a wife," one said.

"I couldn't agree more." He beamed while keeping his eyes on the subject of his affections.

The men gave him hearty handshakes and pats on the back, then there was the flow of single sisters. "Minister Tolliver, you were magnificent." Sandi Coffman smiled. The sister was pretty enough and sweetly saved, but there was no attraction on his part. Plus, Rossi tried to steer clear of the dating pool from his church. If things turned sour, he would have to deal with rebellious spirits every time he came to God's house.

He thanked her, nodded to other happy faces, and gently pushed aside family members to get to Jet. "Excuse me. Excuse me, family."

Spinning around, Jet greeted him with a glow on her face and tears in her eyes, and the curve of her lips signaled pure joy.

"I got it, Rossi. Jesus gave me His gift." She looked as if she was about to burst with excitement.

He chuckled, stuffing his hands in his pockets when he really wanted to gather her in his arms and bury his nose into her hair. His senses heightened when she walked in with his mother. Her blue dress captured his attention. It definitely was her color, and her hair, which was originally trapped into a ball hours earlier was now spread across her shoulders.

She flew into his arms and hugged his chest, thanking him. In response, he trapped her again, forgoing the proper church protocol on singles interaction. The Lord did say she would be his wife, so he shared her hug. Finally, he stepped back. "Let's celebrate." His eyes sparkled at the idea of them finally together for him to spill his heart.

"That sounds like an excellent idea," his mother stated. "We can throw an impromptu get-together—"

Shaking his head, he stopped Laura before she got carried away. "I'm thinking simple, Mom—dinner."

"Oh." She frowned, looking from him to Jet. "Well, okay, but you know salvation is the reason to celebrate."

"Thank you, Mrs. Tolliver. Maybe another time." Jet's face continued to glow. Her expressive eyes were wide with wonder.

Not pressuring her, his family members accepted her answer, and one by one, gave her hugs and congratulations.

Once they were alone, Rossi casually asked,

"So do you have plans for dinner?"

After picking up her purse and Bible, she seemed to float toward the exit. "Not really. I'll grab room service at my hotel."

"Not even a small celebration, Jesetta?" He used his thumb and finger as a demonstration. "Don't you know the angels are rejoicing over one soul that repents?"

"Wow." Jet's eyes sparkled. "Over me," she said breathless, then squinted. "Where is that in the Bible?"

Her eagerness was not only endearing, but sexy. Rossi winked. "Luke 15:7–10." Her eyes closed as if she was making a mental note. "So where are you staying anyway?"

"Magnolia." She kept strutting to her car.

He reached out and touched her wrist. She spun around. "You mean the Magnolia that is within walking distance from my loft?"

"That's the one. Four stars."

"There are unoccupied lofts in my building. I can put you in one of those free of rent," he fussed. Four stars came with a luxury price tag.

Her lips curved into a smile. "Thank you, but I didn't come back to be a burden on the Tollivers. I plan to—"

"You can tell me all about your plans over dinner—my treat. Soul food or classy?" He wasn't going to take no for an answer.

"Surprise me." She shivered, and Rossi was about to give her his suit coat, even though it was a perfect June afternoon with a slight breeze. "I can't believe it. I saw something while I was in the pool I'll never forget."

Yep, they were finally on the same page. Hallelujah. Rossi smirked. "Me either."

***

Jet was giddy with excitement. She never thought she could have so much peace, but she did. It was as if nothing mattered. Nothing—food, clothing, nothing. All she wanted to do was see Jesus and talk to Him again.

She couldn't wait to grow stronger in the Lord. She smiled as she spied Rossi trailing her to the hotel to drop off her car. She lifted her hand in the air, and he waved back. She giggled. She was actually praising God.

More than anything, she wished Diane was alive. She was having one of those moments where only a sister would understand. But she had Layla. Unfortunately, her friend was probably still at church. She sighed, and she could feel a rumbling coming up from her stomach. She blinked, and her mouth moved as the Holy Ghost began to speak through her tongue. She loved this experience.

Not only was God in control of her tongue, but the wheel. She had no problem exiting off the highway to Washington Avenue.

"I love you, Lord!" she screamed when she stopped at a red light. Luckily, no one was next to her to give her strange looks.

After driving to the hotel entrance, a valet opened her door. Rossi parked behind her, stepped out, and tipped the valet in advance.

"Give me a minute to change."

He shook his head. "There's no need. You'll still be beautiful."

She had actually blushed at his compliment as he reached for her hand and guided her to the passenger side of his SUV. Once she was strapped into her seatbelt, Jet closed her eyes. When she opened them, he was staring at her with an expression of awe.

"Is this what Diane experienced?" She didn't care about the answer, but he whispered, yes. Why did she fight God's blessing so hard and for so long? Taking a deep breath, she closed her eyes again to relive those moments with God. "You know I want to go to that cemetery and tell Diane all about it. Silly, huh?"

Rossi touched her hand. "There is nothing silly about what you're feeling. I'm here. I used to be your confidant. You can tell me anything, Jesetta. That will never change."

Bowing her head, Jet couldn't lie if she wanted to. "I didn't want to come between you and Nalani."

"I respect that then, but this is now, and there is no Nalani and me." She nodded. "Now, if you're in the mood for French or Italian cuisine, I would love to take you to The Crossing in Clayton."

Her eyes popped opened. She worked in Clayton for years before moving to the Metro East and then Nashville. Nothing in Clayton was cheap. She turned to him. "Isn't that kind of pricey? The Crossing is the place to impress your date."

Rossi's husky laugh made her smile. "Says the woman who is staying at a four-star luxury hotel."

She shrugged. "Layla negotiated a deal." He intertwined his fingers through hers and squeezed. She shivered at his touch and stared into his eyes. He was so handsome.

"Back to The Crossing, I am trying to impress you. This day is cause for a celebration."

"Oh, okay, but if you don't have enough money, I have my debit card," she teased.

"You got jokes, huh?" He winked, and she blushed. Jet could count on one hand since she'd known him how often he'd winked at her. That was twice within the span of an hour. "I have you covered, Miss Hutchens."

She didn't have a doubt. As CFO of his own real estate and construction company, Rossi and Levi, the CEO, were doing very well. They'd developed an area of East St. Louis with shops, eateries, and residential spaces and named it Tolliver Town.

She had avoided the place after she rounded up some friends to protest the grand opening of Crowning Glory, the salon Karyn owned with two other ex-felons, which catered to ex-felons to help them get back into the work force.

Closing her eyes, Jet prayed. *Lord, forgive me for being mean-spirited.*

Forgiven. His whisper tickled her ear until she bit her lip, smiling.

Once they parked on Forsyth, Rossi helped her out of the car, then took her hand. He squeezed it as they entered the restaurant.

"I guess you're really excited I surrendered to God," she said once the hostess had seated them.

"Ecstatic." He smiled, and this time, his twin dimples winked at her.

Her heart fluttered at the sight. She reached across the table and took his hands. "Thank you so much for always being my friend and big brother."

After giving her an odd expression, he became quiet. At the same time, their server introduced herself.

"You know what I like, so order for me."

He nodded and plucked at the hairs on his goatee as he scanned the menu. "Let's start off with the mixed greens salad, and we'll take the day's special."

Once the pretty server disappeared, Jet shook her head. "I still can't believe what I experienced."

Rossi leaned back and anchored his chin in the curve of his fingers and watched her. He wore an amused smirk as he listened to her.

"I know we've had an undefined relationship over the years, but I need you to be something different," she said.

He perked up and sat straight. "Yes, name it."

"Since you're a minister, can you counsel me? I don't want to be like Cain ever again."

He was slow in answering. Maybe she had asked for too much. "You mentioned seeing some type of vision. What was it?"

"Like a ball of fire," she rambled on. "I can't believe you didn't see it."

He shook his head. "Evidently, Jesus had me programmed to a different channel."

"Rossi," she pressed, "am I asking too much for you give me one-on-one attention?"

He leaned across the table and met her halfway. "You can never ask too much of me. I'm invested in your spiritual growth too. Trust me."

Their server returned with their drinks, and someone else behind her brought their salads. After thanking them, Jet closed her eyes and bowed her head. When Rossi didn't say anything, she looked up. "What are you waiting on? Come on. I'm hungry."

He grunted then curled his lips. "You are so cute, church girl."

She stuck out her tongue as his large hands engulfed hers.

"Lord, this is a day You have made, and we rejoice in it. Thank You for Jesetta's salvation and the salvation of the others today. Please sanctify our meal by removing all impurities, and help us to help those who are hungry. In Jesus' name. Amen."

She didn't open her eyes right away and allowed the prayer to echo in her head.

"Hey, are you okay?" He squeezed her hand.

Fluttering her lids, she looked at him and nodded. "For the first time in my life I feel like someone loves me. Strange, huh?"

"It's not. God's love is unmatched, and love from a godly man is irreplaceable."

When their meals arrived, they continued to chat between bites, but mainly Rossi listened as she tried to find words to describe her baptismal experience and answered her Bible questions. Soon, she paused when she noticed his stare and empty plate. "Your eyes are laughing at me," she accused him.

"Nope. My eyes are appreciating God's beauty made whole."

She smiled. If this salvation thing made her this attractive, then maybe the man who was to be her husband would come calling soon.

When he yawned, Jet checked her watch. They had been there for two hours. "Come on. I guess I'd better let you get home and get ready for work."

He didn't argue as he stood, then helped her out of her chair. When he pulled in front of the Magnolia Hotel, she turned to him. "Thank you for counseling me. I plan to be the best Christian ever."

"Amen." He parked the car and walked around to assist her. Before going inside, she hugged him. "Good night."

Once she was in her hotel room, she kicked off her shoes and began to undress. Next, she tapped Layla's number and put the phone on speaker.

"Hello?"

"I got the Holy Ghost," Jet screamed and danced in place.

"The what?"

"I'm finally drama free. I repented, and Rossi baptized me today." She told Layla about the ball of fire, then added, "And before I came out of that pool, I was speaking in a language I've never heard spoken."

"What did you say?" Layla asked.

Jet shrugged and thought about it for a moment. "Honestly, I don't know, but it was a high that I didn't have to pay for. When Rossi took me to dinner—"

"Hold up. Rossi happened to baptize you, then he happened to take you to dinner? What else did Minister Rossi do today?"

"Preached. He agreed to counsel me, so I asked him about the evidence of the Holy Ghost—the speaking in tongues."

"And?"

"Evidently, the Bible talks about unknown tongues, which are heavenly. The other tongues could be any of the sixty-five hundred languages spoken in the world today. That's what Rossi said."

"Girl, I do good to speak proper English and a little Spanish."

They chuckled. "He gave me scriptures to read that explain the differences." Jet found her notes and told her friend where to find the passages. "Acts 2:4-7: *And they were all filled with the Holy Ghost, and began to speak with other tongues, as the Spirit gave them utterance. And there were dwelling at Jerusalem, Jews, and devout men out of every nation under heaven. Now when this sound was heard, a crowd formed and were confounded, because every man heard them speak in his own language. And they were all amazed and marveled, saying one to another, Behold, are not all these which speak Galileans?*" She paused. There is also another scripture, First Corinthians 14—"

"That's okay. I went to church today and heard plenty of scriptures."

"Wait, it's only one verse. Number four says, '*He that speaks in an unknown tongue edifies himself; but he that prophecies edifies the church.*'"

"Hmm, that's interesting that God would have a personal message."

"It is, and Rossi says—"

"Rossi again," Layla teased. "Are you sure you don't like him a little?"

Jet frowned. "Girl, I was over that girl crush stage not long after he began to annoy me with his big-brother routine."

"Umm-hmm. Maybe the tables have turned, and it's him who has the man crush on you," she continued to rib her.

"I doubt it. And before you ask, no he's not gay. Although, throughout the years I have wondered what's kept him from tying the knot."

"Maybe it's been a 'who.' So will this change things between you and Karyn?"

"God is truly going to have to help me on that," she added, "big time."

Chapter 8

The next morning, the only counseling Rossi planned to give Jet was marital. He had waited so long for a wife...for Jet. With her salvation complete, he was ready to move forward to be equally yoked.

Feed my sheep, he heard God whisper as he patted his face dry in the bathroom.

Removing the towel, he stared at his reflection until he blinked. "Lord, haven't I been doing that all this time?" For years he had been the go-to man or minister for witnessing, praying, and settling disputes.

As he combed through the fine hairs on his chin, Rossi silently pleaded with God to open Jet's eyes to see the attraction and love he had for her. "Not only as Your servant, but a man who desires her."

Feed my sheep, Jesus repeated, dropping Habakkuk 2:3 in his heart: *For still the vision awaits its appointed time; it hastens to the end—it will not lie. If it seems slow, wait for it; it will surely come.*

He fought against frustration until he finally submitted, "Yes, Lord." God's work had to take precedent in his life, and Rossi had best remember that. Therefore, he shifted his thoughts to meetings he had to attend the upcoming week at church and what was on his agenda at work. At the right time, God would stir Jet's heart and lead her to him.

His phone rang as he was about to leave for the office. Recognizing the number, he smirked. While he was trying to keep his mind off Jet, evidently he was on her mind. "Hey."

"Hey, yourself. Have you had your morning java?" She sounded happy and carefree.

"Nah. I'll grab a cup at work." He swiped his keys off the nightstand, grabbed his briefcase, and headed for the door.

"Well, since we're neighbors, I thought I'd make you a cup."

"Really?" Yes, God's timing was perfect and fast. "Well, although I would love to take you up on your offer, I don't visit women in hotel rooms, not even my Jesetta."

She laughed. "I'm at Starbucks around the corner. I made you an espresso."

He chuckled too. Now that God had cleansed Jet from her sins, her heart was pure. She didn't have an ulterior motive like some other women he had met. "You mean you had the barista make it," he corrected. After locking the door, he strolled to the end of the hall. He pushed the elevator button to take him to the building garage.

"Almost the same thing," she countered, and he imagined her lifting her chin at him in defiance.

"Woman, I'm so glad you're back home, you know that?"

"I'm glad too. So are you taking me up on my offer? If not, you owe me five bucks."

"Five bucks? Is that what they cost?" He slid behind the wheel of his SUV, laughing, then started the engine.

"Including tip."

"Well, I can't have the lady wasting her money. I'm on my way." When they ended the call, he whispered, "Thank you, Lord."

He double-checked his appearance in the rearview mirror. His recent barber visit was still noticeable, his cologne was subtle, and his mouthwash boasted freshness up to four hours. He grinned and showcased his killer dimples. While some men attracted women with their light-colored eyes, his dimples drew women in whether he tried or not. Jet was no exception. She might not give him compliments freely, but her brown eyes seemed to dance when he smiled at her.

He spied the knot in his tie. Jet was a perfectionist when it came to clothes. She was a fashionable dresser whether she wore a T-shirt and jeans or an evening gown. She was one pretty woman. "Ready or not, here I come, Miss Hutchens."

Exiting the parking garage, he turned right on Washington Avenue and drove the three short blocks to Eighth Street near the convention center. After parking, he strolled to the entrance. Glancing through the large windows, he saw Jet. Instead of watching for him, she was reading her tablet. Her hair was swept back up into a ball and hooped earrings adorned her earlobes. He opened the door and walked quietly to her table, then slid into the chair.

Looking up, she greeted him softly, then slid a coffee cup in front of him. "Good morning."

He whispered his grace and took a sip. "Umm. This is good."

As she beamed, he studied her face as he took another sip, although he had memorized her every soft feature the first day they were introduced. He just didn't react to the seduction of her pouty lips. She tilted her head to the side and lifted an eyebrow.

"What's wrong?"

"Nothing." Whether she had on makeup or not, she was naturally beautiful. "I'm glad Jesus saved you."

Her eyes widened in excitement, and that seemed to open the door before she exploded with giddiness. "Me too! Last night, I prayed until I spoke in tongues again, and I could feel God's presence. I've never prayed so long. An hour had passed without me thinking about it," she rambled on, and Rossi breathed in her hunger for God.

"I was so keyed up, I couldn't sleep, so I went online and signed up for Joyce Meyer's daily devotional." She leaned across the table as if she was about to share a secret. "Monday's devotion is Hebrews 12:14: *Follow peace with all men, and holiness, without which no man shall see the Lord.*"

She paused, frowning. "I think I can do that. I mean what's the point in God saving us and not living right until I see Him?"

"I love how you think." He wanted to flirt with a wink, but he was the wiser saint who had to be on guard to tame any carnal gestures around her.

"But I don't know how I can be peaceful around the Tollivers. Levi alone stirs up too much tension. I'll endure as much as I can for the sake of my late sister and Dori, but God may need to put a muzzle on my mouth to keep me from saying the wrong thing."

She reached across the table and rested her soft hand atop his. He sucked in his breath, but she didn't seem to be affected from the contact. Rossi knew something was wrong when Jet's shoulders slumped at the same time she lowered her lashes. Headstrong and confident, she believed in fighting until the end if she believed in a cause. Her tenacity put her at odds with Levi, because she questioned Karyn's mental ability around Dori. Jet had every right to be concerned, but she went about it the wrong way. She glanced up, and her eyes were misty.

He panicked. By nature Jet wasn't a crier, but on the flip side, she had her moments after Diane's death. Jet would bawl in a minute if something reminded her of her late sister. "Talk to me." He placed his hand over hers.

"I really need you to pray for me on this. I don't want to lose what I have with God."

The sincerity in her eyes tugged at his heartstrings.

Blessed are the pure in heart, for they will see Me. God whispered Matthew 5:8.

"You know I will pray and..." He wanted to choose his words carefully as he planted seeds of his attraction without planting carnal thoughts. This was going to be a balancing act for sure. "And I'm more committed than ever to be there for you—in every way."

He squeezed her soft hand and released his deadly weapon. He smiled until his dimples had her attention.

She blushed, then bounced back with a smile that had a pin-size dimple of her own above her lip.

"By the way, you look nice, Jesetta." Her white shirt was free from wrinkles and her jeans were pressed. Despite her five-ten height, she was never without heels. Once she thanked him, he asked, "Where are you off to today?"

"House or condo hunting. This time I'm going to stay on the Missouri side. I only followed Levi to Illinois because of Dori. I think it would be fun to have her help me choose."

Whatever Rossi had to do at the office, he could put on hold. If something came up, Levi could handle it. As a matter of fact, his cousin had stood him up for an important meeting with a client the day he met Diane. Why not return the favor? "Want some company? I do know a thing or two about structures. That is what I do for a living."

She gave him a cute scrunch with her nose, then rolled her eyes. "How could I forget? You micromanaged the builders on my home construction in Fairview Heights, remember? You had them crossing T's that weren't there."

"I wasn't that bad." He bowed his head, knowing that when it came to business, he was the master of it.

"So go to work and be the boss." She lifted an eyebrow and scanned his attire as if it was the first time she was noticing him. "Nice suit, by the way."

"Thanks." He glanced around and checked the time. Being the co-boss did have its benefits, even though he liked being punctual. If he started to act out of routine, someone would probably call the presiding bishop of their religious organization to come and lay hands on him. "I guess I do have to make an appearance." After draining the rest of his coffee, Rossi got to his feet, then gathered his trash. Jet also stood while tucking her tablet back in her oversized purse.

"If you're ready, I'll give you a lift back to your hotel."

She shrugged. "I can walk."

"And I can drive you." He reached for her hand, and she took it without hesitation. One day soon, he planned to put a ring on it.

***

Why wasn't Rossi married? Jet asked herself as she cleared the hotel's revolving doors minutes later. Besides being a nice guy, he was handsome, built, and sincere with the Lord Jesus. It wasn't the first time she'd asked the question over the years. She would marry a man like him in a minute.

She was glad for his one-on-one attention as she attempted to navigate through the scriptures. She'd better get all the spiritual instruction while she could because when the next woman captured Rossi's attention, Jet would have to take a backseat or be put out of the car.

Once she was in her suite, she said a quick prayer before calling the Tollivers' home. She was relieved when Dori answered. "Hi, Auntie."

"Hi, Sweetie, would you like to go house shopping with me?"

Give honor where honor is due. God immediately chastened her for sidestepping Karyn's position in Dori's life.

"Yeah!"

But didn't she still have rights? *Sorry, Lord, I'm not going to fight You,* she conceded as she corrected her bad manners. "Let me speak with Karyn, please." Baby steps. She couldn't bring herself to say "your mommy."

Karyn came on the line, and Jet explained her request.

"We're on our way out the door to Crowning Glory, if you don't mind picking her up from there. Dori likes spending her summer vacations at the shop."

She did mind because the woman's salon was another battlefield. Levi had given his wife a prime business location in a re-developed area in Tolliver Town.

Local politicians, community leaders, and sponsors who thought it was a good idea to give ex-felons meaningful employment were behind the business.

On paper, it sounded honorable, but criminals had gunned down sixteen people, including her sister, so Jet wasn't sold on the idea and had denied the application for funding when she received Karyn's loan request at the banking institution where she happened to work.

Her protest fell on deaf ears, even when she showed up on grand opening day with protesters warning against felons near neighborhoods. In the end, Crowning Glory opened, businesses flourished, and everyone seemed to have a happy ending but her. "Ah, I thought I wasn't allowed on the premises." She might as well be upfront.

"That was before God saved you. Mom Tolliver gave us your salvation report. Congratulations on your new life in Christ." Karyn paused. "Now that we are one body in Christ, I hope we can learn to be friends."

Friends? Out of nowhere, something rose up inside of Jet, and before she could trap it, the words spilled out. "You're pushing it."

"I know," Karyn said softly, "but fair warning, the devil is going down."

What does she mean by that? Jet wondered as they said their goodbyes. Was Karyn calling her a devil?

If it be possible, as much as lies in you, live peaceably with all men, God whispered, *Read Romans 12:1.*

Refusing to leave without reading it, she tapped her Bible app on her tablet, then searched for it. *"I beseech you therefore, brethren, by the mercies of God, that ye present your bodies a living sacrifice, holy, acceptable unto God, which is your reasonable service."* There was that word *holy* again. In no rush to get Dori, she continued reading until she found verse eighteen God quoted, but she didn't stop there, and read the entire chapter, which ended with, *Be not overcome of evil, but overcome evil with good.*

Okay. She took a deep breath. She was armed now with scriptures. Jet refused to let anyone cause her to lose her holiness. After a silent prayer, she pulled up a few home listings she and Dori could check out before leaving.

During the short drive across the Poplar Street Bridge over the Mississippi River to East St. Louis, Illinois, she thought about Rossi. At times, she wished they were more than friends, but then he didn't have a good track record when it came to dating. Even Karyn's sister, Nalani, didn't make the cut, so Jet would keep her girl crush to herself.

In no time, she exited at the first Illinois exit and wormed her way through the streets that bore no street names and empty lots. Literally, a couple blocks ahead, she could see the handiwork of the Tollivers. Newly constructed buildings were intertwined with the historic ones to create the picture-perfect Tolliver Town made up of commercial and residential occupants.

She smiled, proud of Rossi and Levi. They were the brightest Black men she knew. She parked in the lot behind the restored Majestic Theatre in a historic area in downtown East St. Louis, where Crowning Glory had a grand entrance. The Tollivers had spared no expense on the pillars and the outside cafe for pedicures. *Interesting concept*, she thought. Jet never imagined a day when she would actually walk through these doors without venom boiling in her veins. She was barely redeemed twenty-four hours, so she knew she had better guard her words carefully.

She stepped out of her car and activated her alarm. The area seemed safe enough, but it was still East St. Louis where poverty was a haven for criminal activity that didn't draw lines between rich and poor.

Taking long struts, she cleared the door and was in awe of the sleekness of the beauty salon and barbershop combo. The individual stations appeared to be chic and decorated with warm colors.

Dori raced to her with her arms open and a giddy grin. The warmth from her hug did nothing to ward off the chill from the staff—some were former convicts. She prayed none of them were sex offenders around her niece. She would do an online search herself to be sure. *Lord, please protect her from demons.*

The groomers and stylists stared at her without saying as much as hello or welcome. Jet shivered from their cold reception, but gave them her own stare down. She made a judgment call. She didn't like them.

How can you say you love Me, and hate your brother? God scolded. *You lie if you can't love the brother you see and haven't seen Me. Read 1 John 4:20.*

Jet lowered her lashes, conceding the staff as the winners of the stare down contest. She had failed the Lord Jesus already. She took a deep breath to repent and recover. After kissing Dori on the head, she grinned at her niece. "Ready to go, sweetie?"

"Can I paint your nails first?" Dori jumped up and down. "Please, please, please."

Her mouth was so ready to say no, but her heart couldn't deny her. "Okay, but then we have to hurry because you're supposed to help me find a house, remember?"

"Umm-hmm." Dori nodded and latched onto her hand, then dragged Jet into an area separated from the other stylists by a glass wall. Dori had a miniature salon with two pink vanity stands and accessories. So cute. However, the manicurist table looked real with a tower of nail polish. "Wow."

She and Diane would have had a play day with this stuff when they were younger. "Auntie, have a seat at my station," Dori said in a tone that mimicked a licensed nail technician.

The innocence of pretending was precious, so Jet ignored her audience and did as she was instructed. She was adjusting the chair when Karyn appeared with Little Levi propped on her hip.

"Hey. You made it. Welcome to my salon." She waved her free hand in the air, twirling her son from side to side. That's when Jet heard the gospel music playing from the overhead speakers.

Chastened earlier, Jet was determined to be cordial. "This is nice."

"Dori," Karyn frowned and eyed the little girl, "I thought you were going with your aunt?"

"I am," she answered without making eye contact as she busied herself setting up her lotion, dish, and polish. "I'm giving her a free medicure before we go." That's when she looked at Karyn. "It's okay if I give Auntie a free service, isn't it, Mommy?" She looked worried.

Hearing Dori call Karyn mommy messed with Jet's mind. It was heartbreaking that her sister never heard those words from her daughter's mouth. She blinked to keep her eyes from watering.

After correcting Dori to say manicure, Karyn smoothed back the loose strands from Dori's ponytail. "Of course, sweetie. Your auntie gets free service any time she comes in."

That earned Karyn the biggest smile Jet had ever seen on her niece's face.

"Be neat, okay?"

"Okay, Mommy. Aunt Buttercup showed me how to do it," Dori reassured her.

Aunt? Where was the reverence in using those titles? Dori was born with one mother and one aunt, yet she used the endearment too freely for Jet's taste. But she guessed with a new mom came new "aunties." The sadness began to drape her. It seemed as if she didn't have anything she could call her own anymore.

Karyn walked away and whispered something to the staff who immediately returned to their duties, except Buttercup who was anything but a sweet little buttercup. The ex-felon was an Amazon-plus–size woman, at least six feet tall, with long multicolored hair that seemed to be styled in half locks and half braids. Judging from the size of her station compared to the others, Miss Buttercup had to be the head stylist—and a trendsetter in fusing crazy with strange.

A couple of times in the past, Jet and Buttercup had faced off when it came to Karyn. It was no secret they didn't like each other. Correction: Jet would have to pray hard and dig deep in her heart in order to love this woman, so she could see Jesus.

The barber across from her was buffed, and he nodded to whatever Karyn said, but not without giving Jet one last side eye.

Jesus! I'm trying to hold my tongue and keep my composure because you know I don't back down from anyone, but help me to love my enemies.

I can keep you from falling, God whispered. *Read Jude 1.*

Believing God, she relaxed and sat on an uncomfortable kid's stool while her niece got comfortable in her chair. She unwrapped a piece of bubblegum and began to chomp on it until it began to pop.

Jet cringed at the annoying gesture. "Dori, where did you pick up that bad habit?"

"That's what Aunt Buttercup does when she gives service."

"Umm-hmm." She nodded and crafted her words carefully. "Sweetie, that isn't a good thing to do. Plus, gum isn't good for your teeth. You don't want rotten teeth, do you?"

Dori shook her head frantically, removed the gum, and threw it in her polka-dot pink trash can. Hopefully, the horror on Dori's face had done the trick. The real auntie superseded the other aunts, and Jet wouldn't allow her niece to mimic bad behavior. She smiled to herself. With the right balance of love and direction, Dori Lovanne Tolliver would grow up to be an exceptional woman.

"Auntie, you really have to take care of your nails," Dori said as she concentrated on shaping each nail with an emery board. "Mommy says our hands need moisture like our hair…"

Impressed, Jet smiled at the confident little girl.

"When I go to second grade, I'm going to do all the girls' nails in my class."

"All little girls don't wear polish, so they have to ask their mommies first."

"Okay." Dori switched the topic to pets. "I asked Mommy and Daddy for a puppy, and they said to wait until Little Levi is older. Can I have a puppy at your house?"

She considered the request. A dog would definitely be some company. "Maybe." She winked, and Dori grinned, probably knowing that her "maybe" would likely end in a "yes."

At the moment, despite her surroundings, Jet was in a good place. She was with the one person in the world who truly loved her. Her nails were barely dry when Karyn reappeared.

"Look, Mommy!" Dori showed off her handiwork.

"You did a nice job, but I thought before you both leave, I could give you a pedicure," Karyn said with a smile on her face that Jet didn't trust.

The excitement seemed to explode from Dori's mouth. "Yay. Come on, Auntie." Dori stood and yanked on the hand she had just polished.

"Sweetie, we don't have time…" Jet said, but it fell on deaf ears, so she eyed Karyn. "Thanks, but we really need to be going."

Her protests were ignored as Dori and Karyn continued to usher her to the chair. Jet was used to having the final word, even with Dori who had her wrapped around her finger, yet it appeared that God was holding her tongue. Before she knew it, she was stepping up and flopping down into a massage chair.

Dori had already removed her sandals. She slipped her feet into the bubbling water and giggled. "It tickles."

Jet smiled, and Karyn chuckled. "Be still."

"Your turn, Auntie."

Lord, You know I don't want this lady touching me.
Reluctantly, Jet pulled off her ankle boots style sandals.
Wiggling her toes, Jet was ashamed that she was overdue for
service.

Karyn gently guided her feet into the tub at the same time
Buttercup stood over Karyn's shoulder.

"I'll be glad to give you a complimentary color and cut."
She grinned and snapped the blades on her shears.

"Buttercup, this is God's business here," Karyn scolded
in a hushed voice.

Jet frowned. *This is a bad idea.*

"What?" the woman said with a feigned innocent tone. "I
was just going to trim her ends."

Dori shook her head. "I don't want you to cut Auntie's
hair. She looks like a princess," she said with such awe in her
voice. "Mommy, I want my hair like Auntie's."

"Sure, baby. I'll do it later," Karyn said in a sweet voice
while giving her Amazon friend a frown.

"I want Auntie to do it."

Jet's heart fluttered with pride that Dori would prefer her.

Karyn nodded and looked at Jet. "If you don't mind. She
has as much hair as you."

Of course Dori did, because Jet had been combing her
niece's hair since birth. "Sure."

Turning to Dori, Karyn gave her a mini pedicure and
topped it off with some banana-yellow polish. Minutes later,
Karyn helped her down, and Dori walked on the back of her
heels with the foam separators between her toes to the
machine to dry.

Once alone, Karyn went to work on Jet's feet. Her
strokes were soothing and gentle. She didn't offer
conversation, and Jet was glad.

Once her feet were scrubbed, dried, and nails trimmed,
Karyn placed them on a towel. "Have you decided on a
color?"

"The same as my niece."

Karyn grinned. "Good choice, Auntie."

Okay, Lord, I know I shouldn't be irked, but I am. Lord, help me not to be so offended by this woman.

"Before I polish your nails, I'm going to anoint your feet with holy oil," Karyn stated and proceeded without waiting for a response.

What was this woman about to do? Jet watched with curiosity. She was ready to snatch her feet back, but Karyn began to pray.

"Jesus, thank You for saving Jet. Thank You for loving her when she didn't feel loved..."

What makes this woman think I didn't feel loved?

"Lord, please help her to forgive me." As she continued to pray, Karyn began to cry.

Why? And why was Karyn asking her forgiveness?

Karyn whispered, "In Jesus' name. Amen," at the same time she squeezed Jet's feet. After sniffing and dabbing her eyes, Karyn reached for the polish, then glanced up at her. "Jesus is the Lord of second chances. I hope I will get a second chance with you."

Jet didn't have an answer for Dori's stepmother. She was too stunned as she watched the woman meticulously paint her toenails.

When she finished, Jet was about to join Dori whose toenails had to be dry, but curiosity got the best of her. "Why did you ask for forgiveness? Did you do something to my niece?" She lifted her eyebrow this time instead of her fist.

"I officially adopted Dori."

Why did that piece of information sting. Why wasn't she consulted?

"Your sister gave me a second chance to be a good mother with Dori and our son, and I will protect them to my last breath."

"That's good to know, but please answer my question."

"Auntie," Dori shouted from across the salon, waving her arm, "come on."

"Stop yelling," she and Karyn yelled in unison. Both smiled.

"I don't need your forgiveness to get to heaven, but I sure need it for my daughter to be happy. You might not be able to forgive me this day, but one day…I hope."

Now who was asking too much of her, the Lord Jesus or Karyn? Jet didn't know. One thing for sure, her toes could air dry because she was getting out of there. "Thanks." She walked over to Dori, ready to go. She had her own flip flops in the backseat. Her niece didn't question her command to leave, but not before she gave her "mother" a hug goodbye.

Chapter 9

Rossi enjoyed the brief time he'd shared a cup of coffee with Jet that morning. Not only was the brew refreshing, but her invitation didn't have an underlying agenda to snag him like some of the women had done.

The combination of Jet's beauty and her newfound salvation had him in a good mood when he walked into the office. He was even humming a tune. Stepping off the elevator to the third floor where the Tolliver offices were located, he expected Levi to rib him about being late since Rossi gave it to him all the time.

Levi always had a ready response: "I have a family. There's no such thing as 'on time' at my house."

Too bad his cousin missed the opportunity because a foreman needed him on a job site to make a judgment call. Rossi greeted his staff and strolled into his executive office.

An hour later, he was still grinning as he reviewed a list of potential sites near Tolliver Town for development. He couldn't keep his mind off the glow on Jet's flawless skin. *Lord, thank You for saving Jesetta...for me.*

Levi strolled in wearing a suit and carrying his white worn hardhat under his arm. He didn't even stop to speak.

Craning his neck, Rossi yelled after him, "Hey, did you hear the good news about Jet?"

Backtracking, Levi popped his head in the doorway. "Yeah, Mom told me," he said as if they were discussing what to order for lunch instead of a life-changing event that even the angels were celebrating.

"Finally." Rossi exhaled. "I'll never forget how God stirred the water, filling every candidate with His Holy Spirit. All of us in the pool were rejoicing." He paused and considered sharing what God had confirmed about Jet being his wife, but he decided to wait.

Leaning against the door frame, Levi folded his arms. "I'm from Missouri, even though I now live in Illinois, show me," he said, mocking the state's motto. "When it comes to Jet, I can't help but wonder if God's seed will fall by the wayside on rocky ground or be choked out by thorns."

Shocked, Rossi couldn't believe what was coming out of his cousin's mouth. "I happen to know that God's Word is taking root in her spirit, so you forgot to mention Matthew 13:8: *'Some fell onto good ground, and brought forth fruit, some a hundredfold, some sixty-fold, some thirty-fold.'* I believe she will be a good witness for God." He squinted. "Maybe it's an increase of your faith I should be praying for."

Pushing back from his desk, Rossi crossed an ankle over his knee and watched Levi. "Our Christian walk is a process. Don't you trust God to forgive sins and change a person's life?"

"Absolutely, but all I know is she disrespected my wife more than once. I won't give her another chance. I don't care if she is Dori's aunt."

"Or your first love's precious sister," Rossi added, trying to keep the edge out of his voice. "Don't be surprised if God calls her into the ministry and she preaches a revival at your current church. The Lord does have a sense of humor."

Levi came into his office and flopped in a nearby chair. He released his hard hat and bowed his head. "I love my wife. She's had it rough, and I want to make sure she's happy until my last breath," he mumbled. "I am happy for Jet, but I can't help having a wait-and-see attitude concerning her." His phone chimed with a "Your Wife is on the Phone" ringtone, and Levi perked up instantly. "Hey, babe," he greeted with a smile.

Rossi shook his head. There was no doubt his cousin had found true love twice.

A frown wiped away Levi's smile. "Jet's there? I'm on my way." He leaped up, his nostrils flaring.

Rossi got to his feet, his heart pounding at the mention of Jet's name. "What's going on?"

"Jet..." He shook his head. "See, that woman is trouble." He stormed out of Rossi's office, heading for the exit. Grabbing his keys, Rossi followed. Whatever Jet was doing at the salon, he doubted it was anything sinister, but just in case the enemy was trying to dig up the seeds God had planted, he began to pray. His cousin was about to meet his match when it came to defending the woman a man loves. Rossi would not allow anyone to disrespect Jet—anyone.

The good news was Tolliver Town was only fifteen minutes from their office. The bad news was Levi was driving over the speed limit to get there. *Lord, command the storm to cease,* Rossi prayed.

Double parking, Levi rushed toward Crowning Glory's entrance. Pitiful. Rossi shook his head, wondering if his cousin remembered to take his car keys. At least there was no sign of Jet's Lexus. Rossi parked legally, took a deep breath, and hurried to catch up.

"Where is she?" Levi stormed through the double doors like a madman as patrons and the staff stopped what they were doing and looked their way.

Karyn came to him, fussing. "What is your problem, Levi Thomas Tolliver?"

"You said Jet was on the premises. She has a restraining order and shouldn't be..."

"It expired. She was here at my invitation." She planted her fists on her hips. "She and Dori went house hunting. Why are you two here?" She eyed her husband then Rossi.

"I'm trying to keep the peace evidently your husband wants to break." Rossi folded his arms.

"You called and said Jet was here—"

She cut him off. "If you had let me finished instead of hanging up on me, you would have heard me say," she paused and lowered her voice from her staff, "Dori is with Jet, so you only have to bring me and the baby lunch."

"Did she come here and take Dori against her will, without your permission?"

Now, Rossi was irked. "Watch it, cuz. Jesetta isn't the enemy. She never has been."

Jesus, we're going to need a dozen angels, a couple of doses of patience, and a lot of love to get through this day.

Judging by the scowl on Karyn's face, his cousin could be in the doghouse for days. Rossi took that as his cue to leave. He waved at the staff and walked to the exit without looking back. Levi was on his own.

Once in the privacy of his SUV, he called Jet to gauge if there had been a problem as his cousin wanted to convince himself.

"Hey, Rossi," she answered, sounding cheerful.

He relaxed and smiled as he heard Dori in the background. "Tell Cousin Rossi I painted your nails."

Jet chuckled. "I think he heard that. So what's up?"

"Just wanted to hear your voice and make sure you were having a great day." *And safe,* he didn't add.

"I am." She giggled. "I have my favorite niece, and I love Jesus."

"I'm your only niece, Auntie!"

"Then I guess I'll let my favorite ladies enjoy their day." Rossi disconnected, rebuked the devil, and thanked God that it was only a false alarm. He went on his merry way back to the office, praying, *Lord, You're not the Author of confusion, so whatever it takes to get on one accord, please help us. In Jesus' name. Amen.*

***

Lord, how are the saints supposed to judge the world when we can't even judge our thoughts and actions? Karyn thought as she led her husband to the back office where she had laid their son down for his nap. When Levi designed her office, he made sure it was roomy with a kitchenette, sitting area, and even a small play area for Dori who decided she wanted a play area out in the salon.

She closed the door quietly and peeped at their son, still napping in the playpen. Karyn took a seat and crossed one leg over a knee. She stared at the man who only knew how to love hard and faithfully. Now that Jet had surrendered to the Lord, why was Levi still tortured?

He came to a stop, then took a seat beside her. He reached out and took her hand.

Timing was everything, so before he could open his mouth, she lit into him. "I'm confused. What is your problem? What has Jet done to you?"

"Me?" He squinted. "It's the way she treats you I'm leery of. Remember when…" Levi began to count off Jet's past indiscretions. "She's a hurricane and earthquake in one."

Karyn understood Jet's pain. She had lived through her own nightmare. She was solely responsible for the death of her infant. The shame and guilt had been unbearable, but God had restored her.

She couldn't fathom the sudden loss of a sister because she and Nalani were extremely close. Without God, Karyn would have probably snapped too. "That's in the past. God is the Lord of second chances. We should be having a Holy Ghost party because Jesus saved her. Babe, I also have a past and regrets. She didn't kill anybody, I did." She choked it out. And his expression softened.

"You and I know it was an accident," he tried to reassure her.

"Yes, but please give Jet the benefit of the doubt—for me," she pleaded with her husband. "I think we need to pray." When they bowed their heads and Levi opened his mouth, Karyn interrupted, "Lord, You know what is really going on here. None of us deserved You taking our place on the cross, but You did. Help us to love one another and show Jet our love." She paused and waited for her husband to join in. Instead, he listened, and when she said Amen, so did he. Something was definitely wrong. Levi always mingled his petitions with hers in prayer. This time he didn't. *Lord, whatever is torturing my husband, please break the yoke, in Jesus' name,* she asked silently.

Chapter 10

Jet was in love. All this time she thought she was happy, but it was all superficial. She really loved Jesus. Although she still missed Diane, she somehow felt complete. Plus, she had passed her first test a few hours ago at the salon.

Waiting at a traffic light, she glanced at her nails. Although Dori needed practice with the emery board, she was flawless with the nail polish—neon green.

"Auntie, I didn't like the other house." Dori scrunched up her nose.

"Awww, I did." The cozy bungalow in Webster Groves was perfect for Jet. Granted, the ones she liked were pricey. Not only did she have the money, but it was only her. Why not splurge?

Jet knew how to save money as well as spend it. She could see herself frequenting neighborhood shops and cafes. She could take in a play at the Repertory Theatre or return to school and get her MBA from Webster University. She might even apply for a teacher's assistantship. Yes, her life was going to be different with Jesus.

"It stinks and wasn't pretty like your other house."

"That's because my other house was new, and these are historic gems." Her niece was right about the odor. She thought maybe because it was vacant. "Let's take a break and grab lunch."

"Can we eat at your hotel?" Dori's eyes were bright with hope as she bounced in her seat.

The fascination with hotel food was beyond her. Jet was eying the sidewalk cafés. But time with her niece was precious, so she gave in. "Sure, sweetie."

"Can we order room servants?"

"Room service," Jet corrected and laughed. Oh, how being with her niece was the best medicine.

Getting on I-44 Eastbound, Jet exited on South Jefferson to take the scenic route back to Magnolia Hotel.

"Oooh. They look like my doll houses!" Dori pointed.

That's nice. Jet didn't look. She had no intention of living in the city. She was born and reared in the suburbs, and as a single woman, she felt safer. "They do?"

"Umm-hmm." Dori nodded. "A park! Can we go, Auntie?"

"That's Lafayette Square. Not today."

"It looks like a park." The confusion was clearly in Dori's voice.

"It is a park, but that's the name of it. We can't go today."

"Can we at least drive by it? Please." Dori grinned and put her hands together in a praying manner.

"You're silly. Okay." Jet made a right and drove slowly down Lafayette Street, the park's namesake. "If I remember my history, the land was given to the city in the mid-1800s."

"You're smart. I want to be like you when I grow up."

The compliment made Jet's day. She choked out, "Thank you."

"Are those flowers that old too?"

Jet frowned. A botanist she wasn't, so her simple answer was no as she admired the cluster of red, purple, and yellow foliage near a gazebo. It was a nice day for a walk through the small park, but then that would be the end of her house hunting expedition because Dori wouldn't want to leave.

Turning left on Mississippi Avenue, which bordered the other side of the square, she saw a few for sale signs in the yards.

"Turn back, Auntie!" Dori yelled. "I saw it—my doll house. Turn back."

"Hold on. Wait a minute. I'll circle the block." When she came to Kennett Place, Jet saw why the second house from the corner caught Dori's eye.

Condos were intermingled with homes, but the double doors at the top of the gray stone steps hinted this Victorian structure housed two or more condos, if the third level with the dormers was livable.

Parking in front, Jet pulled the house up on her tablet. Together, she and Dori scanned the interior pictures. The price was affordable, much less than Webster Groves, but it was the city. Okay, the neighborhood did have character. Besides the park for a jog, she did spy a cafe nearby.

It had updated appliances and gorgeous hardwood floors. "Nice." When they saw a photo of the bedroom, she and Dori *ooh*ed and *ahh*ed together. The exposed brick wall sold her.

"Let's go inside."

"Let me see if we can get in." Jet called the number on the site, and spoke to the listing agent. Within ten minutes, the agent pulled up behind her.

An older white woman stepped out of the car and tapped on Jet's window. "Jesetta Hutchens. I'm Mrs. Rand."

After brief introductions, Jet and Dori got out and followed the woman to the house. Dori skipped up the steps, counting each one while holding on to Jet's hand. Thanks to her niece, Jet knew there were two steps to the first landing, ten more to reach the second landing and another five to the doorstep. Such energy, she mused, keeping a steady hand on the girl.

Immaculate was Jet's first impression once she crossed the threshold. Trendy was her second thought.

"This is a single family dwelling. The high ceilings give this nine-hundred-square-foot home character. The kitchen features stainless-steel appliances."

Jet politely listened while she admired the walls. "I like the exposed brick." She reached out and brushed her hand against it."

Mrs. Rand's heels clicked on the hardwood floors as came to Jet's side. "Yes, that's also part of the charm. This home was built in 1888—"

"Wow, that's old like the park," Dori said, spinning around.

"Shh." Jet placed her finger on her lips. "It's rude to interrupt, young lady."

"Sorry." Dori halted.

"You're fine." Mrs. Rand smiled at Dori, then turned her attention back to Jet. I have three rambunctious granddaughters. Her personality is blossoming. It's three bedrooms and two baths," Mrs. Rand said. "Perfect for you and your daughter."

"She's my auntie." Dori paused and lowered her lashes before looking at Jet again. "Did I interrupt?"

"Yes, young lady."

"Sorry." Dori pouted.

Jet exchanged a knowing glance with the agent. "She's excited."

"Well, she could definitely be your daughter."

"Thank you." Jet beamed at the compliment and pulled Dori closer and gave her a hug.

The tour continued to the lower level with an open floor plan, which could be used as a large master bedroom or a big game room. On the second floor, she and Dori almost squealed at the sight of the front bedroom. The walls had exposed bricks and long bay windows.

"This could be my room, Auntie." Dori took off to explore every nook and space in the bedroom. Jet thought it would be perfect as a home office or sitting room.

"I don't know. I may have to fight you on this one."

"Uh-uh." Dori shook her head. "And you said I can have a dog, and she can sleep in the bed with me."

"You can sleep with a stuffed toy, not a real animal."

Mrs. Rand intervened, "There is a nice garden area outside your back door for pet lovers."

If Jet could have moved the house to the suburbs, she would have whipped out her checkbook and made an offer. The trio retraced their steps back downstairs to the main level, lower, then upstairs to the bedrooms again. Mrs. Rand sounded like a recorded tutorial as she highlighted perks in the neighborhood, proximity to downtown events, utility costs. "So what do you think?"

"Buy it, buy it. I can give you my allowance from Mommy and Daddy." When Dori folded her hands and grinned, Jet knew what she had to do.

"I like it, but let me pray on it and get back to you."

The woman nodded and handed over her card.

"We can pray right now," Dori suggested.

Tugging on her niece's ponytail, Jet smiled. She had a lot of things to pray for, but buying this house wasn't at the top of her list. Dealing with the Tollivers was number one.

***

By the end of the work day, Rossi felt he had been in the dark about what happened earlier at the shop. Levi hadn't returned to the office after barging into his wife's salon. He smirked, imagining Karyn giving his cousin a tongue lashing for his behavior. But he hadn't heard from Jet anymore. He frowned on that because he welcomed her phone calls about scripture.

Now, he was back at home, dressing for church service. As if Jet could sense he was thinking about her, her ringtone chimed on his phone. "Hey." He sighed.

"Can I ask you a question?"

She sounded serious. He immediately went on alert. "Always." He tried to act calm when he wanted to say, "What happened?" Instead of slipping his feet into his shoes to complete his attire, Rossi sat on his bed and waited.

"Something strange happened earlier at Crowning Glory when I went to pick up Dori."

He exhaled slowly. "O-okay."

"Karyn insisted on giving me a pedicure. I only did it, because Dori thought it would be fun. While prepping my toes to be polished, Karyn rubbed holy oil on them and started praying, crying, and asking me to forgive her."

Rossi sighed his relief, immediately understanding Karyn's gesture. "She was probably washing your feet as a sign of humility."

"I think anyone giving pedicures is in a humbling business, especially if they are handling someone who has less than desirable feet. Rossi, I'm not trying to be difficult, but help me understand."

"I will," he said softly. Never before had he appreciated one-on-one counseling with a new convert. But this was personal. She was his future wife. "To be a Christian is more than confessing with your mouth. It's about humility and holy living. I would guess Karyn washing your feet had nothing to do with business."

He paused and checked the time. Rossi didn't believe in arriving at church late, so he stood. "There are two instances mentioned in the Bible. One is Luke 7:28. I'll paraphrase it. A sinful woman, not worthy of any goodness or respect from others goes to Jesus in humility crying, and with her tears, she washed his feet, dried them with her hair and anointed them with perfume. Sometimes God takes the lowest people in society to show the upper class how to live for Christ."

"That's so deep. What's the other scripture?"

He grabbed his keys. "I can share the other when I return from church. I have to meet with a group of our teenagers. School is out, and we started a program at church to mentor students to keep them safe this summer by keeping God first."

"Since I don't have Dori, do you want some company?"

"If it's for one Jesetta Hutchens, she has preferred seating, but I'm leaving now. How fast can you get ready?"

"Find out when you get here." *Click.*

"Lord, I know You have a plan to mend fences among Levi, Karyn, and Jet...please keep me in the loop." He left his loft and headed to the elevator.

It wasn't ten minutes later when Rossi drove in front of the hotel. Before he could park his SUV, Jet strutted through the automatic doors. She had exchanged her jeans for a denim skirt but wore the same white blouse that looked as fresh as she had earlier.

Putting his vehicle in gear, he hurried to open her door. The seconds it took for him to get back inside, Jet was strapped in and waiting for him. He smiled. "You look pretty."

"Thank you. So what's the other scripture about feet washing?" she asked, not wasting any time.

A woman who was focused. He liked that about her. Matthew 5:6 came to mind: *Blessed are they which do hunger and thirst after righteousness for they shall be filled.* Jet was thirsty for the Lord, so who was he to starve her? "I want you to read John, the thirteenth chapter to get a better understanding of how Jesus has set our example to humble ourselves and serve others."

Jet was tapping notes on her iPhone.

"In verse eight Jesus said to Peter who refused Jesus of washing his feet, *'Unless I wash you, you have no part with me'*. I think that was Karyn's peace offering to you."

He glanced at her when he stopped at a light. Rossi could tell she was in deep concentration as she stared out the window for the longest time.

"This whole salvation thing is going to take some getting used to. I don't know how my sister did it. Not once did I ever hear her complain about living in holiness. I miss her so much." She sighed.

Rossi grabbed her hand and squeezed it, then rubbed his thumb against her soft skin. "I know," he said softly.

She chuckled. "I've resisted the urge to go to the cemetery. I know she's not there, but it's a ritual. We shared everything—happy times and sad times. I miss that."

"I'm here, Jesetta. I always have been here for you. We've laughed together and cried together when your sister passed. I've always been a part of your life from the day you sashayed into my uncle's birthday party in that yellow sundress." He whistled. The woman reminded him of a goddess.

Her mouth dropped. "You remember what I was wearing?" Her stunned expression was priceless before her sass kicked in. "And it was gold, not yellow, but I'm impressed."

"I was too." He was beyond ready to have a heart-to-heart talk, but more than anything, Jet belonged to God first, and Rossi had to feed her spiritually until she could stand on her own two feet. He also recalled glances at her toes. She had the prettiest feet. He could only imagine how beautiful they were after Karyn's ministration.

"Anyway, my little manicurist-in-training painted my nails." She wiggled her long fingers. "I must be getting old because my niece sucked all the energy out of me as we went house hunting, before this condo won us over."

Rossi gave her a side-eye. He imagined Jesetta would age gracefully. "We're the same age, and I'm not old."

"Speak for yourself. You don't have children, nieces, or nephews."

"True, but when my wife has children, I plan to be very active with them and my wife."

Jet gave him an odd expression as she folded her arms. "Your wife, huh? Tell me about this imaginary love of your life because you don't act like you're in a hurry to tie the knot. In all honesty, I thought Nalani was the one." She looked away and mumbled, "Two cousins marrying two sisters."

Nalani. Beautiful—yes, yet she wasn't the one his heart yearned for. He wanted to tell Jet that she had captured his heart years ago, but he didn't want to distract her from building a relationship with the Lord.

"I believe in being selective about a life-long mate. Don't get me wrong, I want to be married like yesterday, but I have to be patient until the woman I want is ready for me." Whether Jet sensed that she was the object of his affections or not, she didn't respond as she turned and faced the window. He changed the subject. "Tell me about the condo you like."

"Actually, Dori saw it first." She chuckled. "She said it reminded her of a doll house…"

Rossi was well aware of the architecture and culture of the Lafayette Square neighborhood that wasn't not far from the trendy Soulard area. "Why do *you* like it?" he asked and exited on the interstate.

She shrugged. "Dori likes it. Plus, it's affordable and has a cozy feel to it."

He didn't interrupt. What he was listening for was her likes that didn't involve her niece.

When they arrived at the church parking lot, Rossi turned off the engine and studied her. "I know you love Dori and she's the center of your world, but I want you to live a life where Christ is your center. God is going to bless you with a man who is going to be crazy about you." His breathing deepened, and he couldn't help adding, "He'll give you as many little girls like Dori."

Jet swallowed and lowered her long lashes. "I hope so," she said softly.

"He's closer than you think." He squeezed her hand and got out. Close quarters with Jet was just what the devil ordered. He had walked with God too long to fall before the rapture. When he stepped out, Rossi took deep breaths to regulate his hormones before opening her door.

Thanking him, she smiled. He grinned, making sure his dimples winked at her.

Once they strolled inside, Rossi steered her toward the small chapel. From his peripheral vision, he noticed Jet smiling. He faced her and witnessed a glow radiating from her eyes.

"It seems as if I can feel God's presence." Her eyes were wide. "No one can make me doubt God—ever."

He pumped his fist in the air. "Spoken like a true saint of God. We are the true Jehovah's Witnesses because we know Jehovah of the Old Testament is Jesus Christ in the New."

"Amen."

As they drew closer to the room down the short hall, he could hear his students. Once they appeared in the doorway, they went rigid, but all eyes were on Jet. He smirked. Yep, she had a commanding presence with her beauty and height. Rossi made the introductions. "This is Sister Jesetta Hutchens. She recently received the Holy Ghost."

"I remember," said Tiara, a tenth grader with a Mohawk haircut. She seemed star struck.

There were about fifteen teenagers, mostly girls.

"You don't mind if I sit in, do you?" Jet asked before she proceeded in the room.

Their response was indifferent. There were a few nods and shrugs, but mostly stares. To keep Jet from feeling unwelcomed, he invited her to sit up front with him.

This would be the first time she would attend a group discussion Rossi led, and it was a little intimidating. While he had seen hero worship in other dates' eyes, he longed to see the attraction in hers. For some odd reason, he wanted to impress her—convince her that he was the perfect man for her.

Turning away, he silently prayed for focus as he took his seat in front of the students. "Our summer scripture this year is Jude 1:24. *Now unto Him that is able to keep you from falling, and to present you faultless before the presence of His glory with exceeding joy.*" After he read the scripture, one by one, he had all his students read it out loud for themselves, then he turned to Jet for her to be the last one to read aloud. He loved hearing her sultry voice.

Once everyone had finished the assignment, he leaned forward. "Recall this scripture when you come up against temptation this summer. If you don't have anything planned now that school is out, then the devil has options to occupy your time and mind. If you need a summer job, I have friends who can help. There is a drug epidemic in the country—you can't get hooked if you don't try. You don't need an artificial escape when you can be in the presence of God through prayer. Don't rob your future with teenage pregnancies—that goes both ways, young men and young ladies. Most of you are fourteen and fifteen, but not too young to know about sex. If you say you love someone that means you care about where they spend eternity if they were to die tomorrow..." He paused.

"God can keep you from falling, even when you're up against seducing spirits trying to lure you into fornication from the opposite sex or same sex. God forbids both. Don't let curiosity be the cause of your spiritual death."

A few times he glanced at Jet. She was either jotting notes or watching him with an awed expression, then she raised her hand.

"Minister Rossi," she said with a touch of mischief in her voice. He was amused. "Are you saying Jesus can keep us from sinning?"

There were yeahs and nods among the group before he answered. "That's exactly what *God* is saying. When we sin, we are rejecting God's intervention."

That prompted a round of questions until Rossi ended their meeting with prayer. When he heard Jet's whispered prayer explode into the heavenly tongues, Rossi knew they were in the presence of God, and before long praises, and worship filled the room.

Once God had gotten His glory and quieted their spirits, everyone walked out of the chapel into a small break room where there were light refreshments to share.

Jet's eyes sparkled with excitement. "I never knew prayer could be so satisfying, peaceful..." She seemed lost for words as she shook her head. "One day I hope to know more of my Bible."

"You will. Come on."

Once they were in the break room, she nudged him as they watched teenagers help themselves. "Why didn't you tell me I had to bring something?"

He admired her under-hooded lashes. "Because you don't. This is voluntary."

"Definitely, next time." She walked away to help supervise the group.

Folding his arms, he watched the nurturer in action as she assisted the girls. He looked forward to their next time.

Sixteen-year-old Byron Miller strolled up beside him, sipping on a soda. "Sister Hutchens is pretty."

"Very," Rossi agreed without taking his eyes off her.

"Does she have a boyfriend?" He grinned.

"Yep. Waiting in the wings." Let the teenager think what he wanted, but Rossi had nothing more to say. He had known Jet for years, and never had she looked so at peace.

Although it had been a long day—physically, mentally, and spiritually—he didn't want to rush the youth fellowship. He stifled a yawn. He needed rest to deal with his cousin's mood in the morning. Jet held court with a few of the girls as she shared her experience when she was baptized.

A few times, she caught him staring at her. As if sensing his exhaustion, Jet gathered the ladies to help restore the room, then strongly suggested the young men sweep the floor. Rossi didn't intervene, but let Jet do her thing. When Deacon Session walked in, he gave Rossi a mock salute. "I'll lock up when you're finished."

The tasks were done soon after that, and finally, Rossi waved goodnight before covering another yawn. As he and Jet strolled across the parking lot to his SUV, Jet opened her hand.

"Hey, give me your keys. I'll drive," she offered.

He immediately perked up. "Why?"

"You're tired, dude. I watched as you answered their questions, even the same ones asked three times." She chuckled. "You have a lot of patience with them. I admire you."

He stopped and faced her. "And I'm in awe of you, Jesetta, so please don't wreck my vehicle. I know how you drive," he taunted, placing the keys in her hand a few times until she snatched them.

After opening the driver's side door for her, he got in the passenger seat. Closing his eyes, he had drifted off, smiling. This was a first, a woman driving him home.

Too soon, a whisper caressed his ear. "Hey."

Then someone nudged him in the shoulder. "Rossi, wake up. I'm at my hotel. At least you don't have far to drive."

Forcing himself awake, he blinked until his surroundings came into focus. "Wow. I can't believe I was knocked out."

"Yeah, snoring and all," she teased.

After helping her out, he escorted her to the door. Towering over her, he wanted nothing more than to kiss her. He had dated off and on throughout the years, but he never knew temptation until Jesetta Hutchens returned to town. "Thanks for going with me tonight and being my chauffeur home. I would like to check out that property, if you don't mind. I have tomorrow afternoon open."

"I'll call the agent." In the blink of an eye, Jet wrapped her arms around his waist and hugged him. Without thinking, he hugged her back until a text forced him to release her.

He stepped back and pulled his phone from its holder and read the message: My parents have been drinking and arguing. I'm scared, Minister Rossi. Please call and pray for me. Gerard. He sighed. "I've got a teen in need, so I'd better say good night."

As he turned to leave, Jet grabbed his hand. A concerned look marred her face. "Who takes care of Minister Rossi?"

He shrugged. "The Lord Jesus always gives me strength." He had to go. The sooner he spoke with Gerard and prayed for him, the sooner he could get to bed. Rossi mustered up a smile for Jet and squeezed her hand. "Night, babe." As he walked back to his SUV, he wondered if Jet caught his endearment.

Chapter 11

*D*id he just call me babe? "The man must be tired." Jet chuckled to herself, stepped into the elevator, then pushed the button for her floor. Rossi had called her many things throughout the years—sometimes, it was little sister just to annoy her. When he was annoyed with her, it was Jet. But babe?

Now she understood other women's attraction to Rossi. If his good looks, dimples, and charisma didn't make them starstruck, then it was his sincerity about the Lord.

How sexy was that package? Rossi was a caring and giving person. She had been the recipient many times in the past. If he couldn't give his all, Rossi didn't bother. She pouted as the doors opened, and she exited to her floor, musing about the exhaustion clinging to him as they left church. How much sleep would he get that night? He needed a wife to take care of him.

And she needed the same thing—a mate. Jet was done with casual dating. At thirty-five, it was time to start the interviewing process for a husband. The first requirement was he had to be a godly man.

Once she was in her suite and had prepared for bed, Jet thought about the scripture Rossi shared with the teenagers about temptation: Jude 1:24. She opened her Bible and read all twenty-five verses. She noted the consequences of sin, and she wanted to be like the saints in verse twenty-three: *And others save with fear, pulling them out of the fire; hating even the garment spotted by the flesh.*

Closing her Bible, she thought about Diane. Her sister had been saved. Jet sniffed when she reflected on how Diane had met her end, but the fact remained that her sister had a godly reward waiting for her.

Had God kept her from falling earlier at the salon with Karyn and the others? If so, she had to let the Lord lead her spirit to hold her peace whenever she picked up Dori and not linger there when she dropped her off. The whole feet washing ritual had thrown her off. Could she do the same to Karyn or Levi's feet in the spirit of humility? She wondered.

Jet frowned at her reflection before scrubbing her makeup off. She had no qualms about getting professional pedicures, yet she was a bit embarrassed when Karyn began to pray for her. Then Karyn apologized to her. Why?

Karyn is doing My will, God whispered. *Read Matthew 18:15.*

Curious, Jet hurried and finished her nighttime routine before returning to the bedroom. Picking up her Bible, she flipped through the pages until she found the chapter and scanned the verses, pausing at verse fifteen: *"If thy brother shall trespass against you, go and tell him his fault between you and him alone. If he shall hear thee, thou hast gained thy brother."* Jet sighed and looked toward heaven. She was offended by the horrible act Karyn had done and was concerned about her niece's well-being around her. "How can I get past what she did, Lord Jesus? Her deed is the first thing that comes to mind when I see her."

Jet hadn't killed anyone, but God had forgiven both of their sins. Their slates were wiped clean, right? She closed her eyes and reminisced about the pedicure and how Karyn had prayed softly, not making a big production out of it. Yes, the Holy Ghost made it easier for her to forgive. The forget part was a burden only God could lift.

The Lord Jesus didn't answer. With silence as her backdrop, her thoughts drifted back to Rossi. Was he at home asleep or on the phone trying to resolve another conflict?

Before she climbed into bed, Jet said another prayer: "God, please send him a good wife." Immediately, Jet wondered would she approve of her.

***

The next morning, hunger woke Jet. Getting up, she immediately slid to her knees, eager to pray. Since receiving the Holy Ghost on Sunday, Jet could feel the Lord's presence like she never had before her baptism, so she poured out her heart. She prayed for Rossi, Dori, even Karyn and Levi. She prayed that she could live up to the standards as a true Christian. She felt refreshed even before she stepped into the shower.

Thinking of Rossi, she wondered if he was already at work making business decisions. Jet had some decisions of her own to contemplate. Finance positions, including the banking industry, were in her blood, but after a short stint in hospitality, Jet was ready for a career move. The money was still important, but she was open to new possibilities. She would call Layla later, and they could brainstorm together.

Jet dressed so she could go downstairs to eat breakfast. As she grabbed her key card, her phone chimed Rossi's ringtone.

"You up, Jesetta?"

The way he pronounced her name made her reconsider introducing herself as Jet. Maybe it was because of the tenor of his voice. However he said it, on his lips, it was beautiful.

"Did you get any rest?" she asked like a mother hen. "Did that call keep you up all night?"

"I have learned to ask God to increase my sleep since He is the giver of time, so to answer your question, I am well rested."

"Good." She was relieved. Not wanting to overburden him with more demands, she said, "If you get too busy to break away, I'll understand."

"That's why I'm calling."

Despite her declaration, her heart dropped with disappointment.

"Text me the address."

Jet grinned, almost skipping to the elevator. "Mornin'." She nodded to a couple getting in with her. "Done." They said their goodbyes too soon. She tapped his name on her phone instead of texting him.

"Jesetta," he answered as if he was smiling.

"Give me a scripture," she said as she walked out of the elevator.

He did without hesitation. "First Peter 4:8." He paused, then added, "*And above all things have fervent charity among yourselves: for charity shall cover the multitude of sins.*"

Her lips curved upward. "You and your love scriptures."

"There's nothing like being in love." Rossi chuckled.

He said it in a way that made her wonder if he had a secret—like a sweetheart. Or maybe, the man was truly in love with Christ. "I'll study it. See you later."

After breakfast, Jet searched the Internet for job leads, reaching out to headhunters and updating her profile on LinkedIn. Before she knew it, it was time to meet Rossi and the agent at Kennett Place. She drove the short distance from her hotel and was surprised to see Rossi had beaten her there. She parked and watched him climb out of his SUV with a bouquet.

A man with flowers sparked dreamy thoughts, but their relationship was anything but romantic. She smirked, wishing for the possibility of a man's unwavering love. He quickened his swagger as she was about to open her door and assisted her.

His dimples, bright eyes, and the flowers greeted her. "Flowers?"

"For you."

Accepting them, she closed her eyes and took a whiff. "Why?" she asked, getting out.

"I didn't know a man needed a reason." Standing on the sidewalk, they stared at the place that could be her next home. Finally, he nodded as he squeezed her hand. "This is you."

"You think so?" She faced him. Before he answered, the Realtor walked up to them. Introducing herself, Mrs. Rand shook Rossi's free hand.

Her eyes twinkled when she glanced at the bouquet, then she led the way to the door.

Rossi still hadn't released her hand. As a matter of fact, he tightened his grip as they hiked the stairs. "Do you know Dori actually counted them? Seventeen from curbside to the door. I'll definitely stay in shape."

"You already are," he mumbled without looking at her.

The man gave his compliments too freely, which only made her fight the crush she was developing on him. But she needed to stay focused because Rossi's interest in her wasn't romantic. Watching Rossi fire off one question after another at the agent as if he was buying it, Jet entertained thoughts about what-ifs: if they liked each other more than friends.

"I understand you don't have any children, so the lower level would be perfect for a game room until you need it for a master bedroom."

She saw Rossi flinch. "Mrs. Rand, we're not married—"

"We're just friends," Jet added.

"We're more than friends," Rossi corrected, giving her a side glance. "To share a bedroom, Jesetta and I would have to marry first. God's law."

Nodding, the woman's face turned red. "Yes. I apologize for my assumption."

"Accepted," he stated. "I would like to see the back of the house."

Once outside, he studied the perimeter of the property while Mrs. Rand stood nervously nearby. The woman probably thought Rossi was hard to read, but Jet understand his response. He didn't sleep around, and now that she had surrendered to Jesus, he expected her to have that same conviction, which she did now. She didn't know if he was a virgin or not, but she hadn't walked with God as long as he had, so mistakes—or sins—were made. Praise God she wasn't a single mother.

He headed back inside. She and Mrs. Rand trailed him. He scrutinized the windows, heating systems, asked more questions, then turned to her.

Slipping his hands in his pockets, he rocked back on his heels. "Jesetta—" her heart fluttered in anticipation of his determination—"if you like it, then this is a good investment."

Squealing, Jet flew into his arms with such a force, he staggered back, laughing. He returned her hug, then released her. "Plus, you'll be close by for me to check on you." He lowered his voice. "Do you have enough for the down payment?" His brows knitted in concern.

"I haven't worked fifteen years in finance without saving money." She spun around to Mrs. Rand. "I'll take it."

The agent seemed to exhale as she looked from Rossi's unreadable expression to Jet who was grinning from ear to ear. They discussed the time to begin the paperwork.

"It looks like my job here is done," Rossi whispered in her ear, and the rich tone in his voice made her shiver. She thought about his comment earlier: *"To share a bedroom, Jesetta and I would have to marry first."* She couldn't see that happening, although Rossi had set the standard for what to look for in a godly candidate for a husband. Plus, she wasn't a minister's wife or girlfriend material.

With Me all things are possible, God whispered.

Chapter 12

Rossi fell into a comfortable routine with Jet. They shared a scripture every morning and a cup of coffee a couple days a week. He preferred her company hands down, but other obligations tugged at him.

He had just returned to his office after a meeting when she called one day. "Do you think you'll feel up to a bike ride after work?"

The image of them racing through the park and the wind blowing through her hair played in his mind. How many times had he imagined that scenario from staring out the window from his loft?

"I took Dori shopping and bought her a new bike. I got me one too…along with elbow and knees pads. Let's race."

Rossi hooted until a few of his workers peeped into his office. He waved them off as tears formed in his eyes. "Jesetta, Jesetta, Jesetta." He shook his head as he composed himself. "If I could play hooky from work, I'd accept your challenge now. And I wish I could later, but I can't."

"Oh."

He didn't like to hear the disappointment in her voice. "I told one of the young boys at church I would stop by the hospital to see his mother."

"That's okay. Tomorrow perhaps?"

"I have a meeting at church with the teens about college choices."

She sighed. "I'm feeling tired for you. I had no idea you were so busy. Want some company?"

"I would love your company." Judging from the number of positions she had applied for, Rossi knew it was a matter of time before she would return to the workforce and have other distractions and commitments. He would miss her terribly, so he was making the most out of their time. Of course, if they were married, she wouldn't have to work.

"You want to come with me today or tomorrow?"

"Both."

Although he protested that she didn't have to tag along for his boring talks, her combative replies only made him more attracted to her. Rossi was falling more in love with her and desperately wanted to tell her his feelings, but the nagging thought in the back of his mind told him to hold back—he would only be a distraction.

This is your ministry for Me. Take her with you, God whispered.

"I'll pick you up at six and take care of God's business."

"Amen."

***

Their routine included working in the ministry. Sitting in his office, Rossi reflected on how Jet actively prayed beside him for those who were sick or in situations beyond their control. She never overshadowed him, but waited to add her input. Instead of making more demands, she seemed to sense when he was burning candles on both ends. If he had a ministry-related event to attend, she invited herself.

He chuckled. "I never knew the woman could fuss so much," he jested. Distracted from his work, he shook his head.

"What?" Levi stepped into his office.

"Nothing. Thinking to myself and saying it out loud. What's up?" Rossi straightened in his chair. "Any word on that Freeman contract?"

"Nope. Not yet." His cousin took a seat near his desk and pushed up his glasses on his nose. "You haven't stopped by the house lately. What have you been up to?"

"Ministry," Rossi replied. Besides speaking engagements and mentoring the young people, he was ministering to his future wife. Levi didn't need to know that. Not only did he keep his feelings for Jet from her, but he kept them under wraps from everyone else too.

Jet was still a sensitive subject between him and his cousin. Levi wasn't one hundred percent persuaded of Jet's conversion. He had thought she had an underlying conspiracy to hurt his wife's feelings. If only his cousin would remove the wall and see Jet's spiritual growth.

"Got plans for Friday? Karyn's making Nalani's favorite since she's back from out of town." He winked and Rossi smiled.

"Sorry. I've already got dinner plans."

And movie plans with Jet on Saturday evening despite her protests that he should rest. The woman was unselfish, which made him selfish with her. On Sunday after service, he planned to take her to brunch with some other saints from the church. His cousin didn't need to know his itinerary.

"Oh?" Levi squinted.

"You remember Landon and Octavia Thomas?"

"You mean the guy who used to be homeless, then married the real estate agent?" That couple seemed to amuse his cousin.

"Yep." He and Landon bonded when he found himself stranded in St. Louis. Their friendship developed into a Christian brotherhood, and Rossi was a groomsman in his wedding. Since, he had known Octavia for years, he was credited with matchmaking. "We've been trying to get together for months. Sorry. Rain check."

Levi stood. "Okay, but I think family should trump friends." He twisted his mouth in displeasure. He opened his mouth and seemed to struggle with his next statement as he slipped his hands into his pockets. "How's Jet coming along?"

"See, you can ask about her without scowling." Rossi smirked.

"Karyn hasn't mentioned any problems when she picks up Dori at the salon for an outing, but then my wife wouldn't tell me if there was a problem anyway. So what's your take? You've been taking her under your wing since the day you baptized her."

"Salvation is good for the soul. Walking with God is a process, and Jet is moving at a steady pace. I'm a witness people do change."

He had seen it countless times in the ministry. Landon Thomas had been a ruthless man when it came to women and money, then he abused his blessings from the Lord Jesus. God had rebuked him and taken away his riches and left him in rags. "God gave Landon a repenting heart to be redeemed. If God could save him, Jet is a piece of cake."

"Umm-hmm." Levi twisted his lips. "I'm watching and praying."

Rossi stared as his cousin walked out of his office. *Lord, although Jesetta has nothing to prove to my cousin, let him see the new Jet.*

***

On Friday, Rossi waved good night to his staff as he left early for his dinner date. He called Jet while en route to his loft. When she answered, he could hear noise in the background.

"It sounds like you're out and about."

"Shopping. I have a couple of promising interviews lined up. Plus, I wanted to buy something nice to wear for tonight. I haven't met any of your friends, so I want to look my best."

He grunted. She was probably a sleeping beauty. "You don't have to impress anyone—me or my friends. You're a class act." And soon everybody would see what he and the Lord saw in her.

"Aww, thank you." He could hear the smile in her voice.

"Pick you up in a couple of hours."

***

"Finally, you and Minister Rossi are going on a date instead of healing the sick, and raising the dead expeditions," Layla teased on loud speaker while Jet dressed.

"Stop it," Jet fussed. "Going with him has been good for me to see what it's really like to be a Christian, and for the record, healing the sick and raising the dead belongs to God. Rossi has taught me to pray God's will in every situation."

"Right."

"Plus, this isn't a date. His friends invited him to dinner and to bring someone, so tag, I'm that someone." Jet smiled eying her reflection in the full-length mirror. The dress was lightweight and airy with splits to the waist and matching wide-leg pants underneath. With a fresh pedicure—not from Karyn—her toes stood out in strappy wedged scandals. "When I think of a date, I think of flowers—"

"Which he has given you."

"True, but I imagine a candlelight dinner for two in a nice restaurant—the works. I'm not saying Rossi doesn't have a romantic bone in his body, but I doubt I'll ever see a glimpse of it." Diane and Levi had showed Jet what romance looked like. What would her sister say about Layla's claims?

"Girl, you're blind. A man doesn't spend that much time with a woman unless he has feelings for her. Since you're clueless, I'll get answers when I come down to your housewarming next month. No questions will be off the table."

Jet laughed and gave herself another twirl. "Rossi has the protective big brother thing going on." Her phone clicked. "Hey, speaking of my big brother."

"Who you have a crush on—" Layla interrupted.

"Bye. He's calling."

"Talk to you after the dinner date," her friend demanded before ending their call, and Jet answered the other line.

"Well, hello, my dining companion." Rossi chuckled. "I'm leaving my place now."

"Then I'm heading downstairs." She disconnected and took a deep breath. Jet wasn't about to let Layla get in her head. Rossi had rejected so many women in the past as "the one." She had seen first-hand the longing in their faces for him to choose them. Jet knew her place in his life, and regardless of the growing attraction she had for him, she was going to stay rooted on the other side of the friendship line.

She was one step out the door when she double-checked her purse for room key, but didn't see it. Going back inside, she glanced at the bedside table—not there. Then she frantically searched for it until she spied the card under her makeup in the bathroom of all places.

After making sure she had everything this time, Jet rushed to the elevator, so not to keep Rossi waiting. Too late. When she stepped out of the elevator, he was standing in the lobby. Turning his head in her direction, his jaw dropped, and she giggled.

"You're stunning, Jesetta Hutchens." He reached for her hand. She took it, and as if they were dancers, he twirled her under his arm.

When he held her steady, she glanced into his eyes. Absent was the mischievous glint. He had an almost trance-like expression. She did her best not to stare. He had shaved and his cologne was intoxicating. The black polo shirt he wore showcased his muscles. Even in her three-inch heels, he still towered over her. "I guess I pass."

Slipping her hand into his, he nodded. "I guess there was a reason I wore black, because you're killing it in your black and white. Love the look—" he glanced at her feet and traveled up to her eyes—"shoes, and the pretty lady wearing it." He paused. "Even though I like your hair down, I'm feeling the ball on top of your head. You're truly a princess."

She couldn't stop from blushing. Rossi was ruining it for another man to steal her heart. At that moment, Jet believed in fairytales, and what if Rossi was her prince? *Whoa*, she blinked and exhaled. Every woman on God's Earth wanted Minister Rossi Tolliver, and she dare say, she was included. Jet needed to get a grip on her mind. It was running crazy.

"We'd better go. There's still traffic going westbound on I-70."

That wasn't surprising. Motorists had to cross over the Missouri River to St. Charles County via the Blanchette Bridge. St. Louis was a river town, stuck between the Missouri going west and the Mississippi going east. During the drive, Jet felt chatty, and Rossi listened.

"Today, I was thinking how much I miss Diane. We talked about things, did everything together—"

"You have me now," he stated, reaching for her hand without taking his eyes off the road.

For safety, she slipped her hand in his, so he would stop searching for it. "I know." He seemed to work overtime to fill in the gap, but some things were reserved for sisters, like shopping, spas, and relationship advice. "If she could look down from where she is, I'm sure my salvation would make her proud. Do you think she knows?"

Rossi shrugged. "Paradise, like hell, is a place where souls are aware of their surroundings. Read Luke 16. In verses nineteen through thirty-one, Jesus describes consciousness of a beggar who died and angels carried him away and a rich man who died and was buried."

Her mind clicked and suddenly, she understood. "Angels came for my sister's soul."

"I believe that. While we buried her remains, the Bible says the rich man lifted his eyes in torment from hell. He saw Lazarus—the beggar—resting in Abraham's bosom or paradise and called out for Lazarus to tip his finger in water to cool his tongue."

Shaking her head, Jet couldn't believe that despite being in hell, the rich man held on to his arrogance. She pulled her phone out of her purse and tapped in the passage. "Thanks for answering me with scripture so I can read and study them for myself."

"It's my honor to do so." In her peripheral vision, she saw the tender glance he gave her, which made her feel more special. "It's a powerful passage. The Bible says hell was enlarged because of sin, and verse twenty-six says, '*There is a great gulf fixed: so that they which would pass from hence to you cannot; neither can they pass to us that would come from thence.*"

The verse struck her with such fear, Jet couldn't wait until later to read it for herself. Her spirit rejoiced that she had made the decision to repent of her sins. What if she hadn't rejected her evil ways? She could have ended up in hell, separated from her sister—or more importantly, separated from the Lord.

Closing her eyes, she escaped to a secret place with God. As she silently prayed, she heard Rossi petition God on her behalf as if he knew she was praying. Suddenly, the heavenly language burst forth from her mouth as she worshiped Jesus in tongues. Rossi didn't interrupt, even when he stopped and parked.

Taking her hand, he ended her prayer with "Thank You, Jesus," "Amen," and "We love You, Lord."

They were quiet as Jet breathed until her heart rate regulated. When she fluttered her lids open, Rossi was watching her. His lips were poised to say something, but he didn't. It didn't matter. She was too full of God at the moment—her spiritual cup was running over.

They sat in front of a tan-colored brick ranch house. The yard was meticulously landscaped, and an arch entryway with stone-covered double pillars gave the house a grandeur welcome. "Are we here?"

He nodded.

"Why didn't you say something?" she scolded, feeling embarrassed.

"Because God always comes first—always. I could wait." He shifted his body. "Ready?"

"Yes." As she unstrapped her seatbelt, Rossi got out and came around to her door. When they stepped on the curb, the front door to the lovely house opened. The couple standing in the doorway complemented each other. He was tall, built, and almost "pretty boy handsome," and she was short, curvy, and could catch a man's eye. Once they reached the porch, the husband stepped out to shake Rossi's hand and slap him on the back. His wife who had an adorable little boy anchored on her hip and clinging to her top, opened one arm and embraced Jet.

"'Bout time you got here. I thought you were going to stand us up. Now Tavia and I see the reason for the delay." He extended his hand to Jet. "Landon Thomas; my wife, Octavia; and our son, Landon Junior."

"We were in traffic," Rossi said.

His friend grunted. "Right."

Inside the open-floor plan, Jet complimented Octavia on her home decor. "This is spacious. It reminds me of a house I had built in Fairview Heights years ago—twenty-five hundred square feet. Now, I'm buying a historic home in the Lafayette Square neighborhood." Living in the city versus in the Metro East meant Jet wouldn't be less than a couple of miles from Dori as before, but I-64 from downtown could put her at Dori's doorsteps in fifteen minutes tops. "As a matter of fact, I should close in about two weeks."

Octavia's eyes widened. "I'm an agent. Didn't Rossi tell you?" She gave her guest a frown.

He shrugged. "I forgot."

Shaking their heads, she and Octavia said in unison, "Men." She gave Landon their son. "Come on, Jesetta."

"Please call me Jet." Only one person could say her name the way she liked to hear it.

Although the dining room table was set, Jet and Octavia chatted as they brought the food from the kitchen. "After I feed Little Landon, I'll lay him down for a short nap while you visit."

Little Landon, Little Levi. Would Rossi want to have a Little Rossi, making him a fifth-generation namesake?

Soon, they were gathered at the table. Landon said grace, then they dug in. True to Octavia's word, their child was dozing before he finished eating. Landon stood, gathered his son, and took him into the bedroom. When he returned to the table, they finished eating with a lively discussion.

"Did Rossi tell you how Landon and I met?"

Jet shook her head. As a matter of fact, he had told her very little about the couple except that he and Landon became fast friends when the man was at a low point in his life with God.

"I was about to show a property," she began.

"And I was sleeping in it," her husband added, laughing. "I'm not ashamed to say I was homeless."

Jet blinked. How? She wanted to ask, but didn't.

Landon stuffed mashed potatoes in his mouth and swallowed. "That's how I met the minister here. He came to a shelter Octavia had found for me." He paused and looked away. Octavia rubbed his shoulder as if to give him strength. "You see, I come from generations of strong Apostolic families, but I rejected God and anything that resembled holiness. I committed sins that are unspeakable. I was the prodigal son, cousin, and father. I lost my six-figure job, pricey condo in Boston, luxury car, and basically all my worldly possessions. When I got on the Amtrak train headed to Texas, I had no idea I would lose most of the belongings when I wound up stranded in St. Louis at a Greyhound bus terminal."

Jet didn't interrupt his abbreviated version, but she was sure there was an incredible story she wanted to hear one day.

"My husband was a wounded soul," Octavia said with a smile as Jet's eyes watered.

Evidently, Rossi knew all this as he ate as if he didn't have a care in the world.

"I am living proof," Landon said, patting his chest, "that God can save anybody. I fathered four children by three women outside of marriage. Besides my son here, I have two daughters and twin boys."

Whoa. Jet glanced at Octavia, and his wife nodded.

"I didn't have a good track record, but somehow God gave me another chance with this beautiful, incredible woman." He lifted her hand and rubbed his lips on it as if they didn't have an audience. Again, Rossi, seemingly unfazed, kept eating.

After the touching moment, they turned to Jet and Rossi. "So how long have you two been dating?' Octavia asked.

"Oh, we're just friends," Jet said, choking on air.

Only then did Rossi rest his glass on the table and command their attention. "We're more than friends," he corrected in a no-nonsense tone.

In what way? she wanted to ask, but she played it off. If he didn't stop saying the sweetest things, she would fall in love with him. Not only would that surprise him, but her too. So keeping her wayward thoughts to herself, she focused the remainder of her visit watching Landon and Octavia's love story play out before her eyes.

Chapter 13

Since leaving Landon and Octavia's house more than a week ago, Rossi had been dropping so many love seeds that he could feed a field of birds. Jet had to see the love beaming from his eyes like a lighthouse. God wasn't helping either, because Jet seemed oblivious to his intentions. Her focus was on getting things ready to move.

How long had he been staring at the same email from the development and planning committee? He had to stop zoning out like that. It was mid-morning, and he was trying to crunch the figures on a proposed site not far from downtown East St. Louis. While the Tollivers wanted tax breaks to expand, the committee was pushing for repairs to infrastructures outside of the proposed building area.

He closed his email. Work was not on his mind at the moment. Getting up from behind his desk, he crossed the room to his mini fridge and retrieved a bottled water. He and Jet had yet to take to the bike trail. Maybe that was something they could do this weekend. His phone rang and interrupted his musings.

"Hey, son. I was sitting here thinking about you. If I didn't see you at church, I wouldn't see you at all." She *tsk*ed. Why don't you come over for dinner on Sunday and bring Jet? You two are practically joined at the hip anyway. Don't think I haven't noticed if you're not with her, you're talking to her, or you're about to see or talk to her." She chuckled. "Like Mark 10:9 says, *What God has joined together*. I like Jet—always have. When are you going to propose?"

Yep, next to God, it seemed like nothing slipped by his mother. Rossi grunted. "I can't propose if the woman doesn't love me and know I love her."

Laura Tolliver's laugh irked him. "Son, it doesn't take the Holy Ghost to see you love her. I can see it without my glasses. Jet is a true example of sweetly saved. She really loves God, and I'm so glad that Jesus has healed her pain."

"Mom, she's embraced her salvation walk a hundred percent. Outside of the ministry, I don't think she realizes I exist as a regular man. She definitely doesn't seem to know how I feel."

This time his mother grunted. "Then she's as blind as you thought I was."

"So when is the right time to tell a woman you love her?" He got up and closed the door, then returned to his desk.

"Trust me, son, sooner rather than later. You've been attracted to Jet for a long time. Now that Jesus has saved her, there should be no stopping you. God created a woman to belong to a man and a man to belong to one wife. Women may act independent, but a woman isn't complete without a husband, and a man isn't complete without a wife."

Tugging on the hairs on his chin, he listened to his mother. For almost a month, Rossi had held back, not wanting to compete with God for Jet's affections, but maybe it was time and God had sent his mother to deliver the message. Jet was finally at peace since Diane's death. Loving each other would only cause their love for God to grow. "You're right. When I spoke with her this morning, she was hyped about closing on her house. I'm sure she'll want to celebrate, and I can tell her how I feel."

"I'm getting a daughter-in-law," Laura Tolliver said in a sing-song manner, "and a pretty one at that." She paused when a series of beeps blared in the background.

"What's that?" He strained to hear.

She didn't answer right away, so Rossi repeated his question. "These people are going crazy. There's a shooter at Bank of America, and he has hostages."

Not another shooting. His heart sank. *Lord Jesus, help us.* "Where is it this time?"

"Right here. It looks like the one in the Central West End on Lindell…"

Rossi stopped breathing—or maybe he was breathing. He couldn't tell. Jet was going to the bank to get a cashier's check for her closing. Not only was that her bank, but it was the closest branch to her hotel. He exhaled, not wanting to jump to conclusions and alarm his mother. He ended the call and called Jet—no answer. Okay, no big deal. If she was driving or conducting business, she wouldn't answer, so he sent her a text.

Call or text me when you get a chance. If he said it *wasn't* an emergency, he would be lying, because it was. If she wasn't affected, then that would alarm her. Closing his eyes, he dropped his head in his hands. His heart pounded against his chest. *Lord, help me not to be afraid.*

Peace. Be still, God whispered.

After series of deep breaths to digest God's Word, Rossi opened his eyes. Turning to his computer, he tapped in ksdk.com on his browser to see live coverage. The news chopper was in the air circling the bank and zooming in. As he was about to check his phone, a cameraperson caught a glimpse of the parking lot, and he spotted a blue car—the same model as Jet's. If he wasn't already sitting, Rossi would have collapsed to the floor. So many outcomes began to play in his mind. He pushed back from his desk, rushing to get to her. Instead of walking out the door, his knees buckled, and he cried out to the Lord, "Jesus!"

Levi stormed into his office, and their small staff trailed him. "What's going on? I think the angels in heaven heard you."

"There's a standoff at the Bank of America. Jet may be there."

His cousin froze. The color seemed to drain from his face. "You're kidding?" A news junkie, Levi's hand shook as he reached for the remote. He used his right hand to help his left one point it to the flat screen across the room. After Levi's three failed attempts to turn on the TV, images finally flashed across the screen.

"Sources tell News Channel Five that the bank's silent alarm was tripped. We know there are hostages, and at least one person has been shot. As you can see from Skyzoom 5, police have cordoned off the area. We'll bring you more details as police provide them. Reporting live..."

When the chopper camera zoomed again, Rossi couldn't blink. "Levi," he said with a shaky voice. "Levi."

"Huh?" He didn't turn around.

"I'm pretty sure that is Jet's car." His voice echoed. He grabbed his phone and called her again. Voicemail. He disconnected without leaving another message.

This time, his cousin spun around. "Not again." Levi rubbed the back of his neck. "Not again. I'm getting Karyn on the phone to start praying and to keep our daughter from the TV." He hurried out the office.

Rossi nodded and called his mother back as he gathered his keys. "Are you still watching the breaking news?"

"Yeah, son, and it's a shame. I'm praying to God that crazy man doesn't shoot up those people. I don't think we can take another mass shooting."

He swallowed before delivering the bad news. "I think Jet may be one of those hostages." His mother gasped and began to wail.

Rossi, of all people, had to be strong for everybody else, yet his faith was shaken. Once he calmed his mother down, he gave her instructions. "Call the prayer warriors." He disconnected, shaking his head. "Not this time."

Your God didn't save the children, church folks, or homosexuals. This will be no different, Satan taunted him.

I am not a man that I should lie! God thundered before Rossi could walk out the door. *Peace. Pray.*

Rossi froze and waited for Jesus to say more, but the Lord had said enough. Hallelujah. It was a spiritual battle, and Rossi was on the winning team. He searched the scriptures for ammunition to fight the devil. Closing his office door, Rossi began to speak to God. Tongues of flames seemed to shoot from his mouth, emitting words in powerful phrases. No interpretation was necessary. It was a private conversation between him and the Lord Jesus.

Remember the promise I made to Abraham that he would be the father of many nations. Did I not show you Jesetta as the woman after your own heart? Did I not test Abraham's faith when I told him to sacrifice Isaac? Is this not a test of your faith that Jesetta will live?

Immediately, Rossi repented and praised God. Once he composed himself, he walked into his private bathroom and freshened up. He had peace, and he was ready.

Levi passed him on the way to the elevators. "Where are you going?"

"To the bank. I want to be there when Jesetta and the other hostages are released alive today."

***

Jet had plans for a busy day after the closing. She parked in the Bank of America parking lot just as her daily Bible in Your Ear podcast finished. The passage for the day was Jude. She was becoming familiar with that one-chapter book. Verse twenty seemed to stick to her bones: *Beloved, building up yourselves on your most holy faith, praying in the Holy Ghost.*

Grabbing her purse, she stepped out and almost glided through the bank doors. It was a good thing most of her furniture from her house was in storage in St. Louis. Painters would arrive in the morning and new carpet for the lower level would be installed on Monday.

Next week, she planned to take Dori shopping for bedroom furniture for when she stayed overnight. Also, next week held promise for a second interview with American Poolplayers Association. At least that was the timeframe the human resources manager told her during a phone interview. When she told Rossi about the company, he had joked, "How much do you know about pool?"

"Enough to be entertaining." She had laughed, but in all honesty, what attracted her about the company was it was headquartered locally in Lake St. Louis.

Her mind was still on tasks when she got in line. She was two customers away from the teller when the hair on her neck alerted her something was afoot, then someone shouted, "He's got a gun!"

In slow motion, she turned and saw a man in army gear exchange fire with a security guard. The guard went down. Amidst the screams, Jet prayed as a tear slid down her cheek. All her plans were for naught. She wouldn't live to see them come to pass.

"Everybody line up," the man shouted, pointing a large gun.

Jet couldn't move as she stood frozen in shock. Someone shoved her, and she fell on the floor.

"Don't shoot, don't shoot," the manager pleaded with his hands up. "Take the money, but please don't hurt anybody."

"Shut up." The gunman's laugh sent chills down Jet's spine. Lifting his rifle, gun, or whatever the killing machine was called, he shot up in the air, causing debris to fall.

Sirens blared in the background, but by the time they would arrive, she and the others could be dead. Jet swallowed back her tears. Huddled with the others, she began to silently pray. *God, why? Did you save me to die like my sister?*

"Slide all purses and cell phones to me. If anybody tries to be a hero today, you'll be the second to die," the gunman ordered.

The security guard was dead? Was Diane taunted like this before she was killed? Did the murderer look her in the eyes before firing two shots into her chest? "Jesus, help us," Jet whispered as a tear blurred her vision. The mass shootings at the North Carolina church; Newton, Connecticut grade school; and Florida nightclub didn't have happy endings. "Lord, if this is my end, I thank you for saving me. I've forgiven all those who have trespassed me. She paused. Had she forgiven Karyn, really? Please take care of Dori…"

Her lips ceased from continuing as Miss Clara, the character in *War Room*, flashed before her eyes. Rossi had taken her to the cinema to see it, but he was so tired he had fallen asleep. Even knocked out, he would not let go of her hand. She smiled at the memory until a voice from the outside grabbed all of their attention.

"This is the St. Louis Police. Release the hostages and then we'll negotiate."

The man's response was peppering the front entrance with a firestorm of bullets.

This deranged man wasn't looking for a happy ending. Jet thought about Miss Clara again and how she called on the name of Jesus when confronted with the would-be thief. God had told her to build up her most holy faith. Was her faith big enough? *Rossi, I hope you're praying for me.* He probably had no idea she was facing death.

Peace be still, God whispered. And just like the passage she read in Mark 4:39, the atmosphere around her seemed to literally freeze. Even the gunman stopped pacing, but the brief reprieve seemed to recharge him. He pointed his weapon at his hostages and fired.

The bullets ripped apart the walls above them and the floor in front of them. Jet cringed with every shot he fired, but she and the dozens of others were untouched. God had created a spiritual barrier that the robber couldn't penetrate.

Oh that men would praise Me for My goodness, and My wonderful works to the children of men, God whispered. *That's My Word in Psalms 107:31.*

Unbelievable. Jet blinked, not believing what she had just witnessed. Others appeared just as stunned as their shooter, although he seemed more frustrated. She would give anything to read her Bible at the moment, but she couldn't, so she opened her mouth and began to praise God. It angered the gunman, and he pointed the barrel directly at her, yet she couldn't contain the praise. More gunfire erupted, but this time, it came the SWAT team. When the gunman turned toward them, they fired away until he dropped.

Chapter 14

There were benefits to trusting God, Rossi reminded himself as the SWAT team entered the bank. If Jet didn't come out alive, then God would be a liar, and He wasn't.

With a clear view from a block away, he watched as hostages were escorted outside. One man, covered in blood, was wheeled out on a gurney. Some walked out on their own, others needed assistance. Where was Jet? He gritted his teeth, shifting from one leg to the other.

Peering through the crowd, he kept his eyes trained on the entrance for the woman who would be his wife. Another gurney appeared, but the woman lying on it was pregnant. He exhaled. What was taking Jet so long? He blinked. Paramedics were escorting her out on a stretcher. Losing it, Rossi took off across the street. Everything he'd mastered in track and field came rushing forth as his long legs leaped over the police tape like a hurdle.

He didn't see any blood. *Thank You, Jesus.* Good sign. "Wait!" He forced the paramedics to stop as he peered over Jet. When her lids fluttered open, she appeared dazed.

"God," she whispered as a tear streamed down her face.

Rossi's thumb absorbed the moisture. "No," he said, chuckling. "It's me, Rossi."

"Rossi?" she repeated and blinked.

He turned and looked at the medic for answers. "Is she injured?"

"More like in shock. She fainted."

He felt like fainting from relief. Rossi smirked. They could be on stretchers together, holding hands. "Jesetta," he called softly, holding up a couple of fingers. "How many fingers do you see?" Her eyes crossed before she mumbled two. "How many gray strands do you see?"

She blinked rapidly, then squinted. "Two on your mustache, one on your beard, and two in your hair."

His eyes widened. "I had one in my head this morning. You gave me the other one." He and the medic chuckled, Jet looked too exhausted to be amused.

"Rossi." She sat up too fast and became dizzy. He gathered her in his arms and held on to her while she gripped his shirt.

The paramedic asked her a series of questions, took her blood pressure, and pulse. "We can transport you to the emergency room to get thoroughly checked out."

Getting to her feet, Jet shook her head. "Can't. I'm closing on my house."

Rossi grunted. "Not today."

"Madam, I would suggest you relax and take it easy the rest of the day. You could've been killed."

"Yes, but my God said no." She looked up at Rossi. "I was so scared. All I could think about was I was going to die like Diane…" she said as he guided her to his car across the street.

Once he helped her inside, she cried, and Rossi held her. Although he didn't say a word to her, he silently praised God for her safety and increasing his faith a little more.

One moment, Jet seemed to relax. The next, she was in panic mode. "My phone, my purse!"

"I'll go back and get them. I want you to stay here and lock the doors," he instructed, hurrying back to the bank. He didn't want to leave her too long. He called his mother. "I've got Jet," he said with such relief. "Please tell the prayer warriors they are relieved of their duties and can now have a praise party."

"Praise God. How is she?"

"In shock, but God gave her an incredible testimony. I do believe without the prayers of the saints, they all would have been dead." He paused. "Mom, I don't want her by herself, and I can't physically check on her in the hotel. Do you mind if she stays with you and Dad a few days?"

"The invitation is always open. In the meantime, stay by her side."

Rossi nodded. "For better or worse…"

"Richer and poorer," his mother added. "Take care of her."

"For the rest of our lives," he said and disconnected, giving God a second round of praise.

***

"I saw evil today, and it wasn't human." Jet needed to hear herself talk. That was the only way she would know that not only was she alive, but she wasn't dreaming. Sitting on a park bench in Lafayette Square with her head on Rossi's shoulder, she stared at the Victorian house. If she had closed today, she would be on the inside, peeping out. The madman had ruined her plans, so the best she could do was look from the outside.

Rossi didn't interrupt as she rambled on. Every few minutes he would remind her of his presence by squeezing her shoulder.

Jet was mentally, physically, and spiritually drained. She hadn't been this shaken up since the night she got the call that Diane had been killed. It had been Rossi who kept her from a total breakdown then. Seven years later, Rossi was by her side again, and so was Jesus.

Tears trickled down her cheeks, and she sniffed. Rossi had cleared his schedule at work for her. She listened quietly as he called and asked another minister to fill in for him at a commitment that evening.

She whispered, "I appreciate you."

"And I love you." He kissed the top of her head.

He had loved her as a sister since the day they met. She understood that and appreciated it more and more. "I know."

"I don't think you do, Jesetta." He shifted and forced her to look at him. "I'm in love with you, and if anything had happened to you…" He paused, and the horror on his face was unmistakable. "I think I would have been worse off than Levi."

Everything seemed to move in slow motion as Jet rewound the conversation. Did he just say he was in love with her? "You're in love with me?" She blinked. "As in a romantic relationship?"

He nodded, but his expression never changed as he watched her. Then he reached inside his suit pocket and retrieved a velvet box. She gasped, but couldn't speak. The day she almost died was the day he was proposing? Jet was about to faint for the second time.

As Rossi got down on one knee and opened the box, she regained her strength. She reached out and brushed her hand against his five o'clock shadow. "It's beautiful." The prisms of the diamond blinked as light touched it from different angles. She looked at him. "Of all the women you've dated, how do you know I'm the one?"

He smiled and tilted his head. He began to finger comb her hair. "My sweet woman, because you love the scriptures so much, this is how I know. Just like Ephesians 4:5 says, *One Lord, one faith, and one baptism,* there is only one woman for me. The other women were only imitations. Just like Jesus is the real thing for salvation, you are real one for Rossi Tolliver."

The man was stirring emotions that she had suppressed when she learned he was a minister and she wasn't a churchgoer. Was he going to kiss her? Should she close her eyes and pucker up? She blinked to clear her head. "When did you buy this ring?"

"The day after you were baptized. So are you going to let me propose?" His dimples winked at her.

Her heart said, "Continue," while her mind said, "Your timing is lousy." She knew he was waiting on her. "I don't know what to say," she whispered, looking into his eyes.

He looked worried. "Babe, we've wasted time, and I want you to know my feelings are only going to get more intense. It's hard to handle the attraction as a saved man."

Wow. It just got intense, and no doubt Layla would smack her for saying this, but there was no stopping her now. "Can you propose to me on a different day?"

Confusion marred his face, then he stood and lifted her in the air as if she was a toddler. He barked out a laugh that seemed to echo through the trees. "My Jesetta is back."

Not so fast. She loved Rossi, she really did and was flattered by his declaration, but at the moment, she needed some quiet time—alone. She had a lot to process. "I'm really drained. Do you mind taking me back to my hotel?"

He lowered her to the ground. "Didn't Mom invite you to stay a couple of days there?"

Right. There were texts she needed to read and phone calls she'd sent to voicemail—one had been from his mother. Jet had been too drained to argue. "Yes, it was sweet of her to offer. Why don't you come back and get me in a few hours?"

Rossi looked as if he was about to protest, but maybe she looked too tired, and he conceded. "Ninety minutes. That's all I'm giving you." Taking her hand, he guided her back to his SUV and drove away from the house that was almost home.

Less than ten minutes later, he parked in front of the Magnolia Hotel and helped her out. "Are you sure you're going to be okay?"

"Yes, Minister Rossi."

"I'm more than that to you," he said softly, "and you know it. Trust me, I'm coming back in full force with another proposal, so you'd best be ready."

Jet couldn't keep herself from giggling. She had never seen this side of him, and she loved it. Layla had known something she didn't. Jet waved and walked through the revolving door to the elevators. All around her everything seemed normal, like when she had entered the bank. Just in a blink of an eye things changed.

Be sober, be vigilant; because your adversary the devil, as a roaring lion, walks about, seeking whom he may devour, God whispered.

Recognizing the scripture as 1 Peter 5:8 from Sunday's sermon on spiritual warfare, Jet shivered. She never imagined Satan's next move would involve her. She stepped off the elevator, and forcing one foot in front of another, she made her way to her suite.

Seconds after closing her door, Jet collapsed on the floor. The day's events before and after the robbery swiveled in her head. At the bank, the man's eyes seemed wild as they moved back and forth in a trancelike state. When he spoke, he scowled. Without God intervening, all of them would have been killed for what? Money?

She cried out to Jesus and praised Him through her tears. "Lord, I could have died, but You spared me and the others." The more she worshiped, the greater God's presence could be felt until He filled her mouth with heavenly tongues. She poured out her soul to Him. When she was able to take charge of her tongue again, she thanked Him. She paused and thought about Rossi. He had proposed? That didn't seem real either. She gathered some clothes and toiletries as she called Layla.

"Are you calling me from inside your new abode?" she answered in a cheery voice.

"No, I'm calling you from inside my hotel," she choked. "Otherwise, I might be in a morgue."

"What?" her friend screamed.

Rossi would have to wait because she planned to tell Layla every detail. "It was like special effects we see in movies, but it was so real that if I hadn't seen it and lived through it, I wouldn't even believe it myself."

"I'm booking my flight as soon as I hang up." Layla sniffed. She sounded so scared. "You shouldn't be alone."

"I won't. I'm spending a few days at Mrs. Tolliver's house."

"Ah…uh-huh, so what happened?"

Shaking her head, Jet didn't answer right away. "I was in the bank line to get my cashier's check to close on the house. One minute everything is fine, the next my life is in danger. It's one thing to have a gun pointing at your face. It's another thing to see it fire at you, to hear the popping sound, and see the sparks." She paused. "This morning it seemed as if God was telling me to build up my holy faith. Well, after today…" The blank stare of the gunman flashed in her mind. "I'm sticking with Jesus."

"Did you tell this to the police?"

"Girl, once I realized the ordeal was over, I fainted. There were enough witnesses to talk to the police because we all survived."

"Wow…wow. I'm so glad nothing happened to you." She was quiet, so Jet's mind wandered until Layla spoke again. "So what did Minister Rossi have to say about all this?"

"He said a lot, but mainly he proposed." She got up and continued her packing.

Layla screamed in Jet's ear. "Proposed! And you're just now telling me this? Girl, this is 'the news'… I mean after you lived of course, but he proposed. Yeah, baby, so when is the wedding?"

Now Jet laughed as she rolled her eyes. "I didn't say yes." She pulled tops from hangers and quickly folded them before placing them in the suitcase. She didn't know how long she would stay—maybe a few days—but she always believed in over packing, even if it was for an overnight stay.

"Please tell me you didn't say no because, Jesetta Hutchens, I will personally strangle you. I've been waiting for this news ever since you first mentioned Rossi's name three times in a sentence."

"Honestly, I can't remember. Nothing seemed real."

"You may be alive, but you're brain dead if you don't say yes." Layla paused. "Sorry, bad choice of words, but you know what I mean. So when are you closing on the house?"

"I don't know. Right now, I feel like I'm frozen in time."

"Well, you'd better thaw out real soon because Rossi isn't the kind of man who has to beg a woman to marry him."

*Hmph*ed. "He has met his match." If her sister could have a fairytale romance and wedding, Jet wasn't going to settle for anything less. "When we first met, I had hoped he would have flirted with me, but after a while, I accepted our friendship." Her phone vibrated. "Hey, that's my Prince Charming calling now."

"I'm the maid of honor!" Layla yelled before Jet hit End and answered the other line.

"Are you okay?" He sounded worried. "It's been one hour and thirty-two minutes."

"I was talking to Layla. Give me ten minutes."

When she disconnected, numerous texts flashed on her screen. Besides the three from Rossi, her heart warmed at the messages from church members she hadn't interacted with regularly. She smiled.

Praise the Lord for protection, Sister Hutchens. It was from the mother who helped her dress for the baptism.

I was so scared, Sister Jet, but Minister Rossi taught us 2 pray not faint. I'm glad Jesus heard our prayers. Jet's eyes misted at Erica's text, from the youth ministry. How did she know, or did Rossi send out a group text? She hoped the girl would never find out she had fainted.

It would take her hours to go through all of the messages. A tear fell. Jet had no idea so many people cared about her.

She noted the number of voicemails: five from unrecognizable numbers. She played the first one.

"Sweetie, Rossi called me, and we began to pray. Hallelujah, Jesus answered and gave you a testimony..." Laura Tolliver. She had called a second time. She had decided to get in touch with Jet through Rossi, and that's when she invited Jet to stay a few days with her.

"Jet, this is Karyn. Everyone at Crowning Glory is glad you're safe. We shut the door and had a prayer vigil during the standoff. Levi was beside himself. We kept Dori away from the television so as not to upset her." There was a pause. "You're important to us, Jet. Even if I didn't know you personally, because of Dori, we're part of one body of Christ. Well, I guess that's it." She disconnected.

Jet choked. "Lord, I'm starting to see how being among the believers is so different." It could rival a sorority, social club, or sports team. When it came to the saints of Christ, it was hard to be on opposing teams." The last message was from American Poolplayers Association. She had been invited for a second interview. Jet took a deep breath and grinned. Somehow the devil had mixed mischief in with God's blessings. But she had the victory. The house, the man, the possible job, and Karyn—a friend?

Chapter 15

Karyn had to be strong. That's what she kept telling herself. She had to be there for her husband. The reality was she was scared for Jet when Levi called her.

He arrived at the salon with a cheerful façade for Dori and bribed their children with videos and video games to occupy them in the office as the storm brewed outside. She had never seen her husband so shaken.

She had immediately called a staff meeting and included the customers that were in the salon. "There's a bank robbery in St. Louis. The gunman has hostages and… Dori's aunt is inside."

Although Jet wasn't Halo and Buttercup's favorite person, Karyn saw the horror in her friends' eyes. Buttercup gasped. Her hands shook as she covered her mouth. The others looked to one another. An elderly man who Halo was servicing spoke first. "When we committed crimes, it was for the money—"

"Or drugs," said Percy, another ex-offender who worked at Crowning Glory.

Halo growled. "Now, it's for blood. The devil's on a rampage and it's time for us to stop him."

"Yep." Karyn nodded. "Want to pray?"

Levi locked the door and turned off the Open for Business sign in the window. They joined hands and lifted their voices to God, calling on the name of Jesus to protect everybody.

At one point, Dori and Little Levi joined them as they enjoyed "playing church," without knowing they were interceding on Jet's behalf. Once they got tired, they retreated back into Karyn's office.

When Rossi notified Levi the gunman was dead, the security guard was in stable condition, and the other hostages were unharmed and released, the group turned their petitions into praise.

"That could have been me," Percy said, followed by murmurs from other staff workers.

"Yes, any of us could have been hostages," Karyn said.

"Correction, any of us with felony records could have been that gunman who was shot dead. Thank You, Jesus, for second chances," Halo said.

There was a unanimous Amen throughout the group. The doors were unlocked, the open light was flickered on, and it was business as usual—not really.

Now, hours later at home, Karyn and Levi snuggled under the covers after putting the children to bed, no wiser of the drama earlier. Levi held onto her tight—so tightly that she had to wiggle out of his embrace. "Are you okay, babe?"

"I don't know." He stared at the ceiling. "I just relived seven years ago. I feel like I lost Diane twice today." He sighed and shook his head as if he was tangling with a dentist over a tooth extraction.

Scooting up, she watched the tormented expression on Levi's face. She kissed his forehead and soothed away his frown lines. "The most important thing is Jet and the other hostages are safe."

"I know. You're right." He closed his eyes. "Our little girl could have lost her aunt."

"But God said no, and Rossi took Jet to his mother's house. She was pretty shaken up." Karyn couldn't help but wonder how Jet was really faring. Even if she never called Karyn back, Dori's aunt would know of her concern.

Soon, she heard her husband's light snore. Before closing her eyes, Karyn prayed Jet would see her as a saint on the Lord's side and not a sinner on the gunman's. However, if Jet wanted to lash out at Karyn again because of the actions of another person, God help them both. Karyn didn't know if she would turn the other cheek this time.

***

The next morning, Jet woke to the smell of biscuits. Sitting up in bed, she adjusted her eyes to the light peeping through the curtains and surveyed the room to get her bearings. Instead of her hotel room or the Victorian home, she was a guest of the elder Tollivers. She had spent the night in Rossi's childhood bedroom, which had been converted to a guest room.

"I'm alive," she whispered as the bank robbery ordeal flashed before her. *It is My mercies men are not consumed,* God whispered back.

Lamentations 3:22–23. Rossi had shared those verses with her more than once. "Because His compassions fail not," he had told her. "They are new every morning: great is thy faithfulness."

"Thank You, Lord, for showing me the magnitude of Your power." After throwing the covers back, she slid to her knees. "If I never see another miracle, I know that scripture is true. Thank You for saving me and sparing me…"

Over the past month she had learned to take her time petitioning the Lord. When she concluded with "Amen," she smiled. One thing was for certain, she loved Jesus…and surprisingly Rossi, and she didn't see that coming. When did and what made her attraction for him change? The man was one of a kind for sure. After making her bed, she pushed the horror of the day before aside and reached for her phone to call the manager at American Poolplayers Association. "Good morning. This is Jesetta Hutchens."

"Thanks for calling us back. If you're still interested in the position, I have an opening next Wednesday,"

"That works for me." They ended the call minutes later after the woman told her what to bring to the interview. Next, Jet showered, dressed, then followed the aroma downstairs to the kitchen. To her amazement, Rossi sat at the table with his parents and Chaz. His youngest brother was home from college for the summer. At twenty-five, Chaz had changed his major several times from medicine to business and now dentistry. Of all the Tolliver sons, Chaz seemed the least serious about life and God, according to Rossi.

Everyone but Chaz looked up.

"Good morning," Rossi and his mother said in unison.

"How did you sleep, dear?" Laura asked.

"Surprisingly well. Thank you." Jet was about to grab on to the back on the chair across from Rossi, but he stood and pulled out the one next to him. He winked.

"Thanks," she mumbled to keep from blushing. "What are you doing here?" she asked him, reaching for a plate. She piled it with a biscuit, bacon, fruit, and a scoop of eggs.

"You're here, so I'm here." He seemed to puff out his chest while their audience snickered. "I wanted to make sure you were alright." His tender expression softened her heart.

I'm in the house with your parents. You stayed last night until I yawned. What did you expect? Me to escape? Those musings she held to herself.

The elder Rossi cleared his throat. "I guess my eldest son doesn't think Chaz and I can fend off intruders." His brother nodded but kept eating. No wonder he was the thickest of all the Tollivers sons, but it didn't take away from his attractiveness.

"I'm backup." Rossi grinned. "What are your plans for the day?"

She paused to say her grace before answering. "Besides rescheduling my closing date, I have to go see Dori—give her a hug and kiss." *And thank Karyn for calling yesterday,* she thought, then shrugged. "There are a few other things to do." She switched the subject. "I do have good news, I have a second job interview next week."

"You can stop with the interview process altogether," Rossi said in a serious tone. "I'll hire you in a minute—create whatever position you need. With your background in finance, we can use you."

Touched by his generous offer, she smiled. "You're the chief financial officer, and you have an accounting manager. You don't need to make room for me, but thank you. I have a good feeling about the American Poolplayers Association."

Chaz looked up. "You play?"

When she advised him no, he reached for another helping of grits. "I've played for two years in college. I was good too. It looks easier than it is—"

Rossi commanded her attention. "If you change your mind about…the job or my other offer, say the word," he said, then took a sip of his juice, watching her. "It will be a done deal."

His gaze made her shiver. She was glad when his mother changed the subject, even if it was revisiting yesterday's events.

"You sure have a testimony, dear," Laura stated, then grasped her hands. "I'm so glad God spared your life."

What made my life more special than my sister's? she wondered, but didn't ask. Who could answer that but the Lord Himself. She exhaled. "Me too, but that's a test I don't want to re-take." She shivered. "I think about the evil on that man's face and wonder if this was what my sister saw her last minutes on this earth." She choked, and Rossi's strong hand softly massaged her back.

"The human psyche is unpredictable. Maybe I should switch to psychology," Chaz stated, breaking the moment of silence.

"No!" the Tollivers snapped in unison. Even Jet chuckled.

Rossi checked the time on his phone. "I guess I'd better get to the office before Levi sends out a search party for me."

He didn't move right away. "Yep, I'd better go." Seconds ticked off before he stood, gathered his dishes, and took them to the kitchen.

Returning to the dining room, Rossi slapped his brother on his back, shook hands with his father, kissed his mother, then turned his attention to her. His eyes sparkled with mischief.

What was this man about to do in front of his parents? He planted a kiss on Jet's head. When she shifted in her chair to hide the shivers he caused, she caught sight of his mother's pleased expression.

His dad was the next to leave for the golf course, his new pastime since retirement. Jet helped Laura tidy the kitchen after Chaz left to do whatever he was going to do. "You are welcome to stay here as long as you want."

"Thank you, but I don't want to be a bother. I feel like a nomad since moving away. I lived with my best friend, and I've been at the hotel for a month...I'm ready for the next chapter of my life."

Laura nodded, then gave Jet her full attention. "I was sad when you moved away, and I kept you on my prayer list."

The revelation brought tears to Jet's eyes, and she swallowed. "I felt invisible, like no one would notice my absence."

"No, sweetie. You were missed. C'mon, let's have some girl time now all the men are gone." She wandered into the sunroom and Jet followed. She loved the openness of the room and the plants strategically angled for the best sunlight. Jet couldn't wait to get her place decorated.

"You see, I didn't have any sisters. When I married into the Tolliver family, wives became my sisters. Although there has never been any real competition, I watched Sharon welcome Diane into the family for Levi and then Tia for Seth..." she faded off with a whimsical expression. "I prayed and asked God to send me some daughters, not daughters-in-law, but daughters."

Jet felt a kindred spirit. She was touched. Choking back her own emotions, she scooted next to Laura and hugged her.

"When you returned, I claimed you for myself, so I'm here to talk, shop, and lunch with."

"I'd like that." They began to discuss decorating websites, losing track of time until Jet's phone chimed Rossi's ringtone.

"Whatcha doin'?" he asked in a playful manner that made her chuckle.

"I've been sitting here talking to your mom, but I'm about to head out to run errands."

"Where?"

She frowned. Since when did she need to account for every minute of her day? "You don't have to track my whereabouts." She rolled her eyes.

That's a Tolliver, his mother mouthed, *I married one,* then stood and walked out of the room.

"Maybe I want to take you to lunch at someplace near wherever you're going."

"We just ate a few hours ago, and you're hungry already?" She laughed.

"Okay, maybe I just want to see you, hold your hand…"

"Holding hands, huh?" She smirked.

"Yes...we could pray, or just hold hands."

This man wasn't backing down. At the moment, Jet was craving some 'me' time. "Name a place, and I'll meet you."

"You're not going to tell me where you're going?"

"No, big brother, I'm not," she said, annoyed and ready to end the call.

"One day, Jesetta, you will call me another term of endearment. Goodbye." He disconnected.

"Oooh." She squeezed her lips. Not only did he hang up on her, but he had the nerve to tell her what she was going to do, which only made her more determined not to do it.

She found his mother in the kitchen, watching the news. The reporter was giving updates on the shooter from yesterday. "Laura," she interrupted, "thanks for the bed and breakfast. I'll be back in a couple of hours." She gave her a hug, then went upstairs and grabbed her purse.

At least Rossi and his father had gone back to get her car. Otherwise, she would have been held hostage at his parents' house. Once she was strapped in, she looked over her shoulder to see if Rossi had her under surveillance or something.

As she was about to drive eastbound on the highway to take her to the Metro East, she suddenly found herself going in the opposite direction. She was heading to St. Peter's Cemetery. Laura's longing for a daughter only ignited Jet's longing for Diane. Soon, she turned into the grand entrance and followed the winding road.

She parked and strolled slowly to the headstone. Death seemed more real now as she read the inscription. Since her last visit, Jet accepted her practice of speaking to Diane was fruitless, but the place was comforting, surreal, and gave her solitude to think. "Sis, I don't know if you can hear me, but Lord, I know You can hear and know my thoughts. Diane, I get now how you must have felt the day you died. I almost died yesterday. I was so scared, then something happened before my eyes. It was so real, yet unbelievable. If I weren't there I wouldn't believe the people trying to describe what they saw to the reporters. Jesus spared my life," she choked out and patted her chest as tears formed. "I don't know why—maybe for Dori's sake, but I don't know why."

She smiled. "But the good news is I'm saved!" She did a happy dance in place. "If I would have died, I would have a promise in Christ—like you."

Jet paused and stood at attention as she watched a funeral procession wind its way to the other side of the cemetery. *God, now I know You can give them comfort.*

Closing her eyes, she exhaled. Opening them, Jet began to release emotions from a secret place inside of her. "There is a new development: Rossi. Yes, your cousin-in-law told me he's in love with me. Can you believe that?" She laughed, hardly believing it herself. "I thought two cousins would marry two sisters, Karyn and Nalani. I never imagined the sisters would be me and you. After years of accepting my place as a sister, how do I tear down this wall?"

When she first met Rossi, the attraction was instant, and it lingered off and on. Then she observed his dating choices and figured she wasn't church material to compete.

"I wish I could hear your thoughts." She paused and listened. "He's handsome, kind, and he's always been here for me, but—" she gnawed on her lips—"I guess I'm surprised that he's attracted to me. How do I know he didn't buy the ring for another woman, but he was so scared that he gave it to me?"

"Because I had your name inscribed inside." The unmistakable voice made her jump.

Twirling around, Jet patted her chest. Not only did he know where she was, but he had overheard her thoughts. Planting a fist on her hip, she frowned at him. "Do you have a GPS on my car or something?"

For the first time since knowing him, Rossi didn't have a comeback. Folding her arms, she lifted an eyebrow. "Well, do you?"

"My actions toward you are led by my heart. When you were evasive about where you were going, I took a guess." He walked closer, invading her space.

Either out of defiance or fear of stepping on a soft spot in the ground, she didn't move. Then Jet realized, she didn't want to. She stared into his brown eyes and waited.

She relinquished her hands to him without resistance. "I believe that our hearts have been in sync for years, but neither of us knew it or was willing to admit it. I am—now. While you were away, my heart ached for you. "His voice became a whisper. "I want to say I'm a patient man and I can wait for you to come around—" he smirked until his dimples winked at her—"but considering I'm in love with a stubborn woman, I have no choice."

He tugged on her hand and led her away from Diane's headstone without letting her say goodbye. As if sensing her hesitation, he stopped. "You know she isn't in the grave, right?"

"I do." She bowed her head in embarrassment. He lifted her chin with his finger.

"It's okay to visit her graveside as long as you know Diane won't rise until Jesus comes back with a new body for her as described in 1 Thessalonians 4:14. That will be a great day for the dead and those living with the Holy Ghost."

He glanced back at the grave as if giving Jet the go-ahead to do the same. She waved and turned around, her hand linked with his.

Chapter 16

Rossi had served God all his life. He had seen miracles and misery. He had been the constant in the midst of turmoil, but the thought of losing Jet put him in unchartered territory.

He was overpowering her, but it was as if he couldn't help himself. On Saturday, he tagged along with her and his mother as they shopped for furniture for Jet's home. He wasn't even scared of her sharp tongue when she put him out of his own mother's house Saturday night because she was tired and ready for bed. Sunday at church, he praised God the loudest after she gave her testimony to the congregation.

Now, it was a new week, and he accompanied Jet to the bank so she could get the cashier's check to close on her house. She didn't argue, but it wouldn't matter if she had. Jet wasn't going to win that round. Rossi returned to his office with the promise of helping her move in the next day. He had barely slid in behind his desk when Levi strolled in.

"So Jet is taken care of?"

Rossi nodded. "The Victorian house is a good investment, so even when she sells it in a short period of time, she should make a profit."

"Oh, she's not planning to stay there long?" Levi took a seat and crossed his ankle over his knee.

After the bank shooting, Levi spoke kind words about Jet and seemed to have removed the hostile barrier he'd erected. It took this scare for everyone to let go of misunderstandings. Having missed confiding in each other about matters of the heart, Rossi welcomed their closeness again. He grinned. "Well, I'm going to marry Jet and—"

"What?" Levi seemed to roar as he leaned forward. "You're kidding me, right? I know you've always had a soft spot for her, as you do others, but to marry her?" Levi stood and began to pace the office. "Really think about this, cuz. Jet isn't a good fit for you. Did you forget that you're a minister and your choice for wife could go ballistic, snapping without warning? I could see it now, a sister in the church needs your counseling, and Jet thinks the woman is flirting. Cut your losses before they start. Walk away—no run—as far as you can."

"Enough." Rossi got to his feet. He balled his fists, but kept them on his desk where they wouldn't do any harm. "My love for Jesetta was led by the Spirit. She is perfect for me."

"What about Nalani? She's pretty and has a good head on her shoulders. She would complement you as a minister."

"Nalani? Why bring her up? We were never meant to be."

"And you and Jet are?" Levi threw his arms in the air.

Lord, help me not to do tit for tat, Rossi prayed and waited for spiritual guidance. He took a series of deep breaths while squinting at his cousin. Since repenting wasn't something people—including him—performed with zeal, he guarded his words. "Not once did I tell you not to marry the woman you loved—either one of them. I supported you all the way. I strongly suggest you give me the same respect, Tolliver."

"Jet is part of the family as a distant in-law. I think the hostage situation tugged at your common sense," Levi shot back. "Plus, I don't trust her around Karyn and my family. Karyn has repaid her debt to society." He patted his chest.

Rossi grunted. "That's too bad, cuz, because Christ paid Jesetta's, yours, mine, and this world's debt. You need to get over it. She will be my wife—" He looked up and Jet was standing in the doorway with a few of their staff peeping from behind her.

Judging from her pointed glare at his cousin, Jet had overheard their heated words and had some to deliver of her own. He groaned, then began to pray faster and harder. She had been progressing steadily in her faith, and he didn't want this to be a setback. *Lord, in the name of Jesus, we need you now!*

"Levi Thomas Tolliver Senior," she bit out.

Not good. Middle names were never meant to be used in a good way except on birth certificates. This wasn't going to be pretty.

"You have a lot of nerve. Yes, I slapped Karyn before she was your wife when she confessed to killing her son, but I apologized because it was a knee-jerk—or hand-jerk—reaction. When I returned home, my mindset was to restore my relationship with God and build one with Karyn because of Dori. We're not friends, but I do think we respect each other. You know what? You need more prayer than Rossi can give you."

Her nostrils flared when she faced him. Not good. What did he do? "I guess I'll never know if you were the man for me. One thing for sure is the Tollivers are not the family for me. *Hmph*ed." She twisted her lips. "I'll get my things from your mother's house."

He could see the tears forming in her eyes, and his heart tore. He came from behind his desk to comfort her, but she stepped back. Now would be a good time to sock his cousin in the jaw. But there wouldn't be enough repenting on his part to erase his actions from the mind of those that would witness him sin against God. "Jesetta, I love you. This is between you and me…"

She shook her head. "No. Levi's right, I'm not a good fit to become a Tolliver. I'm not a jerk enough." She spun around and stormed out of his office with his staff stepping aside for her departure.

"This isn't over, Tolliver," Rossi said and gritted his teeth. "I'll contact our attorneys in the morning. It's time we go our separate ways. Be prepared to buy out my shares in this company."

He hurried after Jet, but not without hearing Levi counter, "We can sell it, because you're no longer fit to co-own it."

***

Jet refused to cry, so why were the tears blinding her? What possessed her to surprise Rossi at the office with lunch? Maybe it was Layla's tongue-lashing after she complained about how Rossi had smothered her since the shooting.

"The man loves you, and we all were scared."

Of course her friend had been right, and Jet began to tear down the walls because she was afraid she couldn't be what Rossi needed. Evidently, based on what she'd overheard, Jet wasn't the only one. Why couldn't everything in her life be on the same page?

"Jesetta, wait up," Rossi shouted.

She had no intention of responding, then changed her mind. Whirling around, she hurled the lunch box filled with sandwiches and stuff at him, then raced to her car. She was done. Marriage was a package deal—husband and in-laws. All Jet wanted was a family who genuinely would love her as a daughter. She swallowed and thought about Rossi's mother. *Sorry, Laura.*

She drove off, peeling rubber without looking back. As she crossed over the Mississippi River into St. Louis, Jet's heart was aching. She and Levi had their differences, but she had no idea he thought she was unfit to legally be a Tolliver.

For by what judgment you judge, by the same measure you will be judged, God whispered Matthew 7, but no verses.

Did that mean she had to read the entire chapter to get the message? Sniffing, she sat dumbfounded. What had she done? Hadn't she repented of everything before her sins were buried in water? "I don't understand, Lord."

As she exited downtown, she didn't know where to go. Usually, when something bothered her, she went to the cemetery. She had checked out from the hotel. Going to Mrs. Tolliver's house for her things was out of the question at the moment. Rossi would eventually find her at either place. She was trying to understand how she—the victim—had become the perpetrator in the argument between two cousins.

Furniture or not, with the keys to her new house, Jet opted to go there. If she parked in the garage and Rossi came snooping, she didn't have to answer the door. Hiding in the upstairs bedroom, she pulled out her iPad and found the scripture God led her to read.

She frowned. How had she judged? God answered, giving her a flashback when she gave Levi a hard time about Karyn not being good enough for anything—a mother or a wife. Jet had been pretty adamant. But hadn't she apologized?

Words inflict wounds that only I can heal, the Lord Jesus whispered as tears streamed down her face.

She had no idea Levi was still holding that against her. "Lord, don't I deserve mercy?"

How would she know a happy day in her life would turn into her heartbreaking? She had the keys to her house and the interview for the next day. That's when it hit her that her clothes, toiletries, and computer were at Mrs. Tolliver's house. "Noooooo."

Although that would give her a reason to go shopping, she was too crushed to go anywhere. She wanted to be alone. Her phone alerted her to a text.

`You're not at the cemetery or Mom's house. I know you don't shop when you're stressed, so where are you? I'm sorry, Jesetta, for the things my cousin said and what you heard. This doesn't change how I feel. Call me.`

No, she texted Rossi back and called Layla instead.

"Hey," she said, trying to sound upbeat.

"What's wrong?" Layla evidently didn't buy it.

"When I woke up hyped about my house—nothing. When I decided to take your advice and be thoughtful and take Rossi a boxed lunch at his office—mind you with enough food for us to share—everything. A day I wouldn't wish on anybody. I've never felt so hated, worthless, and hurt."

"Ooh. What did he do?" Layla practically growled. "He defended me to his cousin."

"Levi?"

Jet shook her head as if her friend could see at the same time she was alerted of a text. "You're hurting. I'm hurting. Let's work this out," she mumbled.

"Huh?"

"Oh. Rossi texted me."

"Start from the beginning and tell me exactly what Levi said. I'm starting not to like that guy."

"Get in line," Jet said and went on to repeat what she'd heard. "I don't remember him being this crazy about Diane."

I don't know what his problem is, but you are my concern. Are you okay? Rossi sent another text.

She read it while Layla ranted on her behalf. I'm fine, she texted while trying to calm her friend down, which was a joke. "I thought turning my life over to Christ would make me lovable to others. I guess Levi didn't see a difference. I got my sins washed away, but I guess it doesn't mean anything." She swallowed.

Christians' allegiance should be to Me for I died for all. Don't cause Layla to pledge allegiance to you as Levi has done to Karyn. Recognize the adversary as the author of this confusion, God didn't whisper. It was a rebuke.

Jet thought about her next words carefully. She didn't want to expand the circle of confusion. "Don't mind me, I'm venting."

You may not need me…I need you.

That gave her pause. "Rossi says he needs me," she repeated slowly. She had never heard him ask for anything, and pride didn't have anything to do with it. Jet knew he was content as a man and as a minister.

"You two are still texting? Will you talk to the man," Layla demanded. "You've got too much crossfire going on for me not to be there. I'm flying in tomorrow. You need backup. Rossi may not throw a punch, but I ain't saved like that. I'm a Sunday-only churchgoer, so I'll pack a pistol. Missouri is 'a conceal and carry' gun state, right?"

"Don't pack anything but your clothes, and pray. God's going to work this out."

"Okay. I'll pray. I'll text you my flight info. Now call your man." She disconnected. Closing her eyes, Jet bowed her head to pray, "Lord, please forgive me for whatever I've done to cause this division. Please lead all of us to love and reconciliation, in Jesus' name. Amen."

She stood and rubbed her backside. She loved hardwood floors, but at the moment, she was going to the lower level where there was carpet. Then she called Rossi. "Jesetta," he answered in a low voice filled with desperation.

"You have everything," she said with sadness. "You don't need me."

"I need you for several reasons. The more pressing is to share all this food you were sweet enough to bring me."

She laughed out loud. "We're trying to have a serious conversation, and all you can think about is food?" She shook her head. "Besides, I've seen you eat, so I know you can put away that foot-long deli sandwich I brought you."

"Any other time that would be true. When you walked out the door, I lost my appetite. Now, hearing your voice, it's coming back. But the sandwich will taste better if you'll share it with me."

Did God give him the right words to say? "Okay. I'm at my house. You know I don't have my furniture, but I have carpet."

"I figured as much, but I do need you in the purest way God intended for a man and his wife. We're not there, considering you don't even love me yet..."

Let him fish. Jet bit her lip to hold her amusement. She wasn't going to profess her love until she was good and ready. "I don't want you to entertain me unchaperoned," he continued. "I'll be there in a few minutes, and we can have a picnic lunch in the park across the street."

"Okay," she said softly. His thoughtfulness made her good and ready. "Rossi, I do love you."

Chapter 17

"Jesetta, don't ever run away from me again," he scolded, standing outside her front door with the boxed lunch and a bouquet of flowers. His puppy-dog expression tugged at her heartstrings until she wanted to wrap him in her arms and kiss him to make him feel better. "All you have to do is call my name once. I would stop whatever I'm doing for you." His eyes reflected the love behind his words.

"I won't." She took the flowers he offered and sniffed them. The aroma immediately seeped into her senses, calming her nerves. Holding hands, they walked across the street together.

Once Rossi spread the blanket he had in his SUV, they sat, gave thanks, and ate. Between bites they discussed what happened.

"I feel like a drama queen, and I'm not trying to be." She shrugged and looked away. "I thought coming to Christ, my life would be better."

"Don't let the devil play mind games with you," Rossi said with a stern expression, then he smiled. "And don't change the subject—please. I have never told another woman I loved her, not even puppy love when I was growing up because I was afraid it was probably lust. I love you, and I need you in my life permanently."

"And I love you, too, Rossi, but I've watched the Tollivers over the years. You're a tight-knit bunch, and no woman should come between that."

"Levi and I will always be family and eventually shake hands and make up, but I'm not backing down when it comes to you. Maybe, it's time for Levi and me to go our separate ways."

"What are you saying?" she asked cautiously, hoping he wasn't about to do anything drastic. "I contacted the attorney to draw up the paperwork for Levi to buy out my shares. I'm done with our business partnership. You're not the only one who needs a career change."

"What?" She frowned. "There's a difference between leaving the finance or banking industry for another job and walking away from a business you helped build from the ground up," she tried to reason with him.

The set of his jaw made her wonder if he was trying to convince her or himself. Regardless of his bold declaration, Jet held the copyright on hurt, and she recognized it on Rossi. "Did you pray about this?"

He didn't answer right away. When he finally said no, that worried Jet. Rossi prayed about everything.

Even in the midst of the storm, Rossi was concerned about her clearing her head and getting rest for her interview. Once he felt they were both okay, he trailed her back to his mother's house.

Despite their declarations of love, Rossi didn't kiss her good night. Instead, he engulfed her in a hug. "Good night," he whispered, made sure she was inside his parents' house, then walked back to his car.

"What a hot mess." Jet went straight to the guest bedroom, showered, prayed, and willed herself to wake up in the morning and hope the day had been a nightmare.

The next morning, Jet hadn't slept well and barely had enough energy to pray or dazzle on an interview. But she slid to her knees anyway. She prayed for forgiveness, favor, and peace. "Thank You, Jesus, for everything. Lord, let Your perfect will be done in our lives. Rossi says he needs me, but I know he needs You." By the time she whispered, "Amen," she knew she was willing to walk away from Rossi so as not to be the cause of breaking up the Tollivers. Family was too important. She knew firsthand.

Her day was too busy to dwell on her woes from yesterday. She had to prepare herself for the interview, and the movers would arrive at her new home with her furniture that afternoon. Plus, Layla would be in town and they could have some girl talk in person. One thing was for sure, she wouldn't badmouth Levi.

Before she dressed, Jet stripped the sheets from the bed and wiped down the bathroom. Next, she packed her belongings in her three suitcases and garment bag. She showered and applied her full makeup, something she hadn't done in months, then she tackled her hair. Accustomed to her princess ball on top of her hair, she combed it down. She donned her blue power suit and slipped her feet into her stilettos. She never let her height keep her from wearing the fashion trends. After grabbing her portfolio and purse, she headed downstairs.

"Good morning," Jet said as she walked into the kitchen and froze. Instead of Laura, Rossi was wielding a spatula as he tossed a pancake.

He turned and whistled. His eyes seemed to smile before he said a word. "Good morning, Miss Hutchens. Ready for your big day?"

"I should be asking you the same thing." She rested her head on his shoulder and stole a piece of bacon. She could feel him flex his muscle. "I'm praying for you." She moved away, asked for blessings over her food, then chewed on the crispy strip. "Where is everybody?"

"Dad's in the garage, checking the oil in Mom's car while she ran to the store for something. I'm sure Chaz is still sleeping, so I'm your chef. Sit and I'll fix your plate, then I'll get your luggage from upstairs. How much time do we have?"

She checked the time. "Half hour. Lake St. Louis is forty-five minutes with traffic." She paused. "Ah, don't you think leaving the business is a bit drastic? I mean it was one argument."

"No, babe, it was one of many. I need to focus on you and me."

"What does God want you to do?" Reaching across the table, she rested her hand on top of his. "You're so in tuned with me. Help me to return the favor. What aren't you sharing?"

He filled her plate and then his before looking at her. Not only did he evade her questions, he switched the subject. Stubborn, but she let him as they ate rice, scrambled eggs, turkey sausage and of course, Laura's biscuits.

"How do you feel about the interview this morning?" The smile tugged on his lips until his dimples appeared and the smile reached his eyes.

"Excited. I've always wanted to learn to play pool, so working for the American Poolplayers Association will teach me that and more."

Jet checked the time. For a month, she had no job or other commitments to keep her from being with Rossi. Now, on the day of her big interview, he had a crisis, and she wasn't available to hold his hand. It seemed like their timing was always off. "Well, I'd better leave. The traffic should have thinned, but I wanted to give myself an hour to Lake St. Louis." She stood and gathered her portfolio and purse.

He stood too and gathered their plates. He looked so domesticated with an apron tied around his waist. "I'll run upstairs and get your luggage."

Rossi returned within minutes, and they walked out the door together. Once he stored her things in the trunk, he faced her. "I still can't believe this company is headquartered in St. Louis for the U.S. and Canadian association. Go win them over, Jesetta." He winked.

"I wish I could win you over to confide in me." She kissed him on the cheek. His eyes twinkled.

During the drive, she prayed for Rossi and Levi, asking the Lord what she could do.

Pray, was the Lord's response.

So she did until she pulled into the business parking lot some fifty minutes later. *Jesus, I want this job, but Rossi warned me against claiming something that wasn't Your will. So Lord, please let me find favor. In Jesus' name. Amen.*

She had enough experience to land the finance manager position. If she was offered the job, her commute could be a nightmare from Lafayette Square to St. Charles County. In hindsight, she could have purchased a house closer.

The American Poolplayers Association was on the top floor of a five-story building. After introducing herself to the receptionist, Jet took a seat as instructed. While waiting, she wondered what Rossi was doing. Before she could think more, the vice president of the company strolled into the lobby. She stood as he introduced himself as Mark Scull.

"Jesetta Hutchens." She gave him a firm handshake. Her height usually intimidated shorter men, but he didn't appear affected.

Following him to his office, she listened as he pointed out the various departments behind open, closed, and cracked doors. What caught her eye was the impressive number of plaques that stretched from one end of the wall to the other. She caught a glimpse of some of the awards: *Forbes, Entrepreneur, GI Jobs, Franchise Business Reviews,* and other magazines had featured American Poolplayers Association on their cover for various honors: Low Cost Franchise for three years; Franchise 500; Best of the Best Overall Top 50 Franchises, and on. Even speed-reading she couldn't read fast enough.

The company wanted team players; Jet definitely wanted to be on this team. That meant stability. After offering her a seat, Mark sat behind the desk and scanned her résumé, then folded his hands.

"Your phone interview was with my colleague, Dan Risen." He paused. "I'm curious. With your background and experience with federal agencies and national banking companies, what attracted you to APA?"

"I think your wall of fame is number one." She pointed to the plaques outside his door. "I wanted a working environment where success is not only recognized within, but outside too. The *St. Louis Post* listed your company as this year's top work places, plus you're the headquarters for the U.S. and Canadian association, right here in my backyard. That's impressive." She grinned. That was just the tip of the research she had uncovered.

"And Japan," he added. "Yes, the franchises are a big part of our association's growth."

Okay, so she missed one. "I was also surprised to learn billiards started as a lawn game, like croquet. Eventually the sport found its way inside and confined to a wooden table covered with a green cloth to look like grass." When he nodded, she continued, "In the film *The Color of Money,* Tom Cruise performed all his trick pool shots, except for one."

He nodded. "Do you play?"

"No—" Jet shifted in her chair—"but I can learn." He got her. If she wasn't so busy starting family fires, she could have visited a few pool halls.

"That's not a prerequisite for employment. Even though APA is the world's largest amateur pool league—we boast a quarter of a million members and just under three hundred leagues—believe it or not, we don't even have a pool table on the premises."

He chuckled. "Our focus is to bring amateur pool players together to form leagues. Over the course of time, pool has been tabooed because of gambling ties and other scandals. We run a tight ship to keep our league drama-free. No money is allowed to change hands in our leagues. If players want to win money, they can compete in any of our four annual national tournaments—two in Vegas, Davenport, Iowa for a junior championship and Tampa. Our staff is welcomed to attend if they like. This is not just about skill, but fun. My ten-year-old son can beat me using our Equalizer® handicap system, which basically gives games to a lesser skilled player to even the match with a more skillful opponent."

After Mark gave her a three minute lesson on the art of pool playing, they discussed salary expectations, then he concluded the interview. He escorted Jet back to the bank of elevators with the standard closing: "We'll make our decision in a few days."

Thanking him, Jet didn't exhale until she got behind the wheel of her car and sat there. Did she win him over? Did she seem too eager, come off as too overly qualified? Did she ask for too much money? Did they have any minorities? If not, would being a qualified African-American woman give her an edge? After a few minutes of obsessing about the position, she laughed.

God, how could I forget You are in control of my life? The bank shooting was proof of it. Since she had an hour before Layla's plane landed, she texted Rossi.

`Interview went well. :)`

`I'm sure you wowed them.`

The man seemed to have confidence in her when she didn't have it in herself. `Thank you. Is everything peaceful at the office?`

`Don't know. Working from home.`

Uh-oh. She was about to call him when an unfamiliar number came across her screen. She debated answering, but did anyway.

"Jet, this is Octavia, Rossi's friend…"

"It's nice to hear from you. How are you?" She welcomed the call from the woman whose calm personality made Jet want to emulate. Plus, she possessed an engaging smile.

"Wonderful. I really enjoyed meeting you last week, but you've been on my mind lately, and not because you were supposed to close on your house. How did that go anyway?"

"Ha." Jet explained the bank situation. "My movers are coming later this afternoon."

"You were in that bank? I saw it on the news. Praise God. Isn't it wonderful when God shows up when we need Him and shows off?"

"Amen. Because of that I had to reschedule my closing. Rossi was so scared, he proposed."

Octavia screamed. "I knew it. So when's the wedding?"

"I haven't said yes yet."

"But you will, right?" Octavia asked confidently.

"Maybe." They both laughed. "He's a sweetheart. I'm just not sure I'm the perfect fit for him."

"Huh? Why would you say that? You complement him, and he seemed pretty content to me."

Briefly, Jet debated if she should share her doubts with a woman she had only met once, but there was something about Octavia that made Jet trust her. "Levi and Rossi got into an argument over me."

She sighed. "We've got to do lunch. What are you doing later today?"

"I'm leaving a job interview in Lake St. Louis, and my best friend is flying in from Nashville." She paused and checked the time. She was at least half hour from the airport, so she decided to head toward the city.

"I would love to treat you two to lunch, but if you both want some sister-girl time, I understand."

"I'll let you know." Jet ended the call with a smile. She cruised I-70 east to Lambert Airport without delay and parked in the garage for Southwest Airlines.

Scanning the crowd, she spotted Layla from the slight bounce when she walked. When her friend saw her, they hurried to hug. Stepping back, her friend scrutinized her from head to toe.

"Nice, sister." She smirked. "Please tell me you killed that interview."

"I hope so," Jet said, looping her arm through Layla's and steering her downstairs to the baggage area.

Both women were the same stature at five-ten. Where Jet wouldn't think twice about wearing heels, Layla always said she was more comfortable in flats. Their other contrast was skin tone. Jet was bronze, and Layla's dark skin reminded Jet of the flawless, rich, and pure dirt.

"So how are things between Rossi and his jerk cousin?"

Jet laughed. Despite wanting to be on good behavior, Layla's unbridled tongue was just what she needed to hear. "Be nice. I want you to form your own opinions, not go by what I say when I'm frustrated."

"Umm-hmm." She put her fist on a hip. "I have formed my own opinion. How are things between you and Rossi?"

They stopped in front of the carousel and watched for her luggage. Jet frowned before answering. "I feel like I'm being cheated out of what is supposed to be romance."

She nodded. "You do have a lot of distractions." She pointed to her suitcase coming toward them. "I brought you Goo Goo Clusters."

Jet stepped up and swiped the luggage while her friend snickered. The sweet treat was one of the things she couldn't resist from Nashville.

The accompanying bag was coming toward them. Before Layla could reach for it, a muscular gentleman of Mid-Eastern ethnicity intercepted and grabbed it for her. "Yours?"

"Yes," Layla flirted and blushed.

Jet shook her head and tugged Layla away from the trance the man had put her under and rolled her suitcase toward the parking garage. "I got a call from a woman I met through Rossi. She invited me to lunch. When I told her you were coming in, she invited both of us, but if you just want to catch up, that's cool too."

"I'll be here until the end of the week. I'm hungry, and if you think she's nice, I want to meet my girlfriend competition."

"There is no competition. The people who have touched my life are irreplaceable. If you're my best friend and have claimed the maid of honor spot, I've got to pick up a couple more girlfriends." They snickered, then Jet called Octavia back. "It's a go."

"Great! Let's meet at Bananas Yummies. It's not far from the airport, and I'm just leaving a showing. Say in about twenty minutes?"

"Got it." It was another ten minutes before the pair left the airport and headed to the restaurant.

"Is that her?" Layla asked when they pulled into the parking lot and saw a woman with what could be called wild hair blowing in the wind, a short dress, and tall heels.

Jet smiled. "Yep." She and Octavia had the hair and shoes in common.

Getting out of the car, they met her at the entrance. After the introduction, the trio hugged like old friends.

They made themselves comfortable and scanned the menu.

"So how did you find this place?" Jet asked.

"By accident." Octavia grinned. "I had to meet buyers at a house not far from here. I stumbled upon this place. Now, whenever I come in this area, I stop for a stuffed burger."

"Good choice," Layla said and rubbed her stomach. "I'm hungry."

Octavia and Jet ordered the cheesy cheese stuffed burger while Layla kept changing her mind until deciding on the Gouda apple onion turkey burger.

Once the server brought their drinks and salads, Octavia reached for their hands to bless the food. "Jesus, we thank You for being our Savior and the fellowship with new friends."

Jet smiled, liking the sound of that. Layla gave her hand a quick squeeze, so her thoughts might be aligned with hers.

"Please remove all impurities and sanctify our food, in Jesus' name."

All three of them said, "Amen."

Octavia took a deep breath, tapped her fingers on the table, and stared into Jet's eyes. "If you love Rossi, say yes."

Layla agreed with a high five with Octavia.

"Didn't see that coming. You don't waste any time." Stirring the straw in her glass of water, Jet shrugged. "Blood is thicker than water, and I guess that's what I am to Levi—water." That hurt to admit.

"Levi's happy. Why shouldn't you be?" Layla asked.

Jet eyed her college friend. "I'm not about drama."

Octavia released a melodious laugh and twisted the hoop on her earring. "My husband has four children by three women and one son by his only wife."

Layla's jaw dropped, and it had nothing to do with the big burger placed in front of her. Once the shock seemed to wear off, she closed her mouth. "And you married him anyway? You get woman of the year. I couldn't do that."

Jet had thought the same thing, but withheld her opinion when they first met.

"I'm striving to be a godly woman. Landon had a past I couldn't change. Once he returned to the Lord and I found myself in love with him wholeheartedly, I had to ask God to help me with the children who had no say-so about their birth. You see, Rossi was part of the 'delegation of sorts—'" she made quotes with her fingers—"who traveled with Landon to Boston to bear witness of Landon beginning the steps to restore his relationship with the children and their mothers." She raised her hand. "So now, it's my turn to report for duty. I'm a praying woman, and I'm a witness that God changes hearts."

Layla nudged Jet and grinned. "I like this girlfriend. I'm on board. So what are you suggesting?"

"Fight for Rossi, not only against Levi's opposition, but against demons that rise up against him and you." She nodded at Jet.

It was as if Octavia was breathing strength into Jet's body with every word. "Are you quoting a scripture?" She was ready to take notes.

"Well…" Octavia paused and sampled her burger, chewed, then wiped her mouth. "I kind of tweaked 2 Corinthians 10:5, which talks about bringing thoughts under subjections, but I believe the same principle holds true for evil spirits. 'Casting down imaginations, and every high thing that exalts itself against the knowledge of God, and bringing into captivity every thought to the obedience of Christ.'"

Jet made a mental note to reread the scripture later as they took time out to enjoy their meals. Soon, Octavia's phone whistled, alerting her of a text. She grinned and read it, then looked at the others. "My husband says hi, and to enjoy our lunch."

"Aw, that's sweet." It was hard to believe the wonderful man she had met last week had such an ugly past.

"Landon wanted me to know he picked up our son from daycare and to take my time," Octavia finished as Jet's phone tinged with a text. Reaching inside her purse, she read a message from Rossi.

Let me know when the movers will be at your place. I'm coming over to help. Miss you.

Hearing Octavia's testimony made Jet want to fight for their happiness. She texted back, Miss you too. Love you. Enjoying lunch with Octavia and Layla.

Then you're in good company. Love you more.

Layla cleared her throat and glanced around the restaurant. "Where's my phone call? I wish a hunk would text me." Jet blushed as she put her phone back in her purse and chuckled with Octavia.

"Like I said, Jet, you should fight for Rossi and maybe Karyn can do the same for her husband," Octavia picked up the conversation.

"That would mean we would have to join forces. We've talked—sort of. Karyn called to check up on me after the shooting." Jet shrugged. "I have to admit, she's not as bad as I pictured her to be." Still, that didn't mean she wanted to welcome her into her circle of girlfriends. Still, if Octavia could deal with Landon's children's mothers, Jet could ask for favors. "Okay."

"Great." Octavia signaled for their check, then grabbed her purse. "I'm ready. Let's go."

"Whoa. Go where?" Jet swallowed.

"Yeah?" Layla lifted a brow.

"I've visited Crowning Glory a few times. Since we're your prayer warriors, we have your back." She faced Layla for confirmation.

Jet withheld her grin. Layla was a churchgoer, not necessarily a prayer warrior, but maybe this was what her best friend needed to take her salvation a step beyond "confess with my mouth and believe in my heart" part.

Layla grabbed her purse and was the first to stand. "Don't know about the prayer part, but I'm definitely a warrior when it comes to my girl."

"Excellent!" Octavia got to her feet and headed for the door. "Let's go. I'll lead the way."

As Jet and Layla followed, Jet wondered how this was going to play out.

Chapter 18

Everything was alright in Karyn's world until her husband showed up midday at the salon to deliver a bombshell. "What do you mean you and Rossi are selling the company?" She couldn't believe it. Instead of recognizing her handsome, confident, well-dressed husband sitting before her, Karyn saw a man who looked weary, shoulders slumped, and a tie missing from his suit.

When she and the children left home this morning, there was no hints there were problems at the office. She exchanged looks with her younger sister who was visiting the shop after recently returning from an overseas trip. Nalani frowned as Karyn asked, "Honey, why?"

Closing his eyes, Levi fell back on the sofa as if he were exhausted. As far as she knew, they both had enjoyed a good night's sleep. The office was so quiet, and they could hear their son snoring in his playpen across the room. "Because my chief financial officer has lost his mind."

"Rossi? Is he okay?" Nalani gasped, then lowered her voice when Karyn hushed her not to wake Little Levi. The alarm in her voice made her husband open one eye. Nalani and Rossi had dated off and on for months. Karyn thought Nalani's constant traveling led to their drifting apart because from what she saw, they both were smitten. Now that Nalani's travel was down to once every quarter, they could rekindle their relationship. But it wasn't her business to pry. If her sister didn't share, Karyn respected that.

"Hi, Daddy." Dori busted through the door and raced toward him. Levi perked up right away, leaving her and Nalani on the edge of their seats.

He welcomed his daughter's hug and rocked Dori in his arms as if he was trying to gather strength from her. Now, Karyn was more worried. She wanted to send Dori back in the shop, but she never denied father-daughter time.

Karyn and Nalani had to be patient as Dori told him about her day and the "customers" she serviced, which most times were her dolls and mannequin heads. Once she ran out of breath, she disappeared back into the shop under the watchful eye of Buttercup and her husband, Halo, who ruled the salon with an iron hand. They also spoiled Dori and Little Levi as if they were their own. Halo was the enforcer to make sure nobody looked at Karyn's kids the wrong way.

Nalani repeated her question as Little Levi woke and saw his father. Scrambling to his feet, he tried to climb out of his playpen. Karyn saved him the trouble and picked him up.

The boy stretched out his arms for Levi who stood and took him. "Hey, Buddy." He hugged him and smacked a kiss on his head. "Did you take care of your mommy and sister today?"

The boy nodded and rubbed his ear.

"Hey, don't I count?" Nalani faked a pout.

Little Levi shook his head and all three laughed.

"Enough stalling." Nalani folded her arms. "Talk, brother-in-law."

Levi sat with son bouncing on his legs. "Rossi's delusional, thinking he's in love with Jet."

The shock on Nalani's face was frozen in time until it slipped, and she laughed as if catching the joke. "That is unstable. I thought he was in love with me, too, and it wore off. But of all women, Jet? Did she drug his drink or something?"

Karyn was slow to speak as she processed the news. Every woman she knew had puppy love for her cousin-in-law. Rossi probably didn't even realize it, nor did he encourage their affections. His conviction was winning souls for Christ. There was more to the story. Karyn could see it on her husband's face.

"He plans to marry her." Levi shook his head.

"He's lost his mind. That woman has nothing on me." Nalani performed a catwalk across the room, then posed like a model. "There is no comparison in looks, education, and whatever."

Actually, there was, but Karyn wasn't about to fuel the fire. The Wallace women were petite, averaging between five-one and five-five. Growing up, Karyn was envious of the tall girls, and Jet carried her five-ten height with a confidence that made one take notice. She had a healthy shape—she guessed size fourteen or sixteen—exotic facial features, and silky long hair or naturally wavy without the flat iron to complete the physical package. As far as education, Karyn thought Jet had an MBA. Karyn could see why any man, including Rossi would fall to her charm. But was it just charm or really love?

"Will you two stop it? I'm still trying to connect the dots. What does Rossi's feelings have to do with selling the company?" Karyn scolded.

Levi immediately looked away. That wasn't a good sign. She loved her husband, and he loved his family hard, sometimes, ridiculously overbearingly so. She sensed words had been exchanged between the cousins based on Levi's guilty expression. He swallowed and glanced at Nalani, then her. "I voiced my opinion that I didn't think she was a good choice. She stirs mischief wherever she goes."

Karyn understood her husband's indifference to his sister-in-law when they dated and first married, but she didn't understand his behavior now that Jet walked in the same light of God as them.

Nalani nodded and lifted her hand for a high five, but lowered it when Karyn cut her eyes toward her. "Levi

Thomas, Senior, should I remind you that our heart picks our mates, not other people? Jet has always had a special place in Rossi's heart. I thought it was because of Diane. I didn't see how special."

"She doesn't deserve a man like Rossi." Nalani jutted her chin. Karyn recognized the "I'm right on this one" look. Anyone who came up against her sister better be armed with book sense, common sense, and case studies because Nalani was serious when it came to winning an argument, and seeing Jet as her opponent would give fuel to Nalani's fire.

"My words exactly, and she kinda walked in when Rossi and I were arguing about it. She left first and before Rossi went after her, he taunted he would consult with our attorneys about me buying his shares to the company. Humph. I told him we can sell it."

Karyn flopped next to her husband on the sofa. "God is not the author of confusion, so why are you letting the devil write this chapter?"

Mimicking their daughter, Levi said, "I duh know."

She sighed, then closed her eyes and rubbed her temples. "Lord, help us. You and Rossi need to work this out—" He opened his mouth, but she held up her hand. "Wait, I'm not finished. If for no one else, you owe your daughter's aunt an apology. You have no right to make a judgment call—either of you." She frowned at Levi and Nalani.

"Baby," Levi said, standing and putting their son on the floor. Little Levi raced back to his toys in the play area. "Businesses dissolve all the time, and I think it's time we both find other interests. Who knows, I might open a non-alcoholic sports bar."

His mind seemed made up when he kissed her on the lips, Nalani on her cheek, then strolled out of her office lacking the confident swagger to which she had grown accustom. Not good. She felt sick to her stomach. It was either nerves or nausea, and she doubted their lovemaking the previous night would make her that queasy.

Karyn had to get out of the office and get some fresh air. She turned to Nalani who seemed to be in her own thoughts. "How about a pedicure on the house?"

Nalani hesitated. "Maybe another time. I've got a conference call later, so I'm heading home, but I'll be over for dinner this weekend." She gave her a smile, but it barely curled her lips.

Late afternoon, Karyn was relieving the front receptionist for her break when two familiar faces entered Crowning Glory. Although it had been a while, Octavia's was a friendly face. Jet's expression was tortured. The dark beauty with them had the body language she had seen many times with Buttercup. She had Jet's back.

Uh-oh. What now? Karyn needed this day to end, but then she would have to go home to a sulky man or a repenting husband. *God, can I put in a request for the latter?*

The three ladies split up. Octavia opened her arms. Jet made a beeline to Dori's play station area while the other woman seemed to be admiring her salon—always a good sign.

"How are you?" Octavia asked, exchanging an embrace. After asking about the children, they were quiet.

"Is this a social or business call?" Karyn asked, watching Dori chat away with her aunt.

"Spiritual. You and Jet need to talk while Jet's friend Layla and I see what service we can get." She grinned, and her eyes sparkled.

Karyn liked to give family and close friends discounts, but there was no sense in arguing with Octavia about anything on the house. The few times the woman had frequented her salon, she paid and tipped her staff well. "Thanks."

Heading toward Dori's play area, Karyn gave herself a pep talk. She was no longer Jet's enemy, but more than anything, she wanted her friendship. She waited for Jet to acknowledge her before speaking. "It's nice to see you," she said and stood on her tippy toes to give Jet a hug. She returned it loosely. Karyn faced Dori. "Watch your brother while your aunt and I chat in my office."

"Okay, Mommy, but I wanted to paint Auntie's nails." Dori frowned.

"You will, sweetie," Jet assured her as Layla joined them. "I can't believe this is your niece. Wow, she looks just like you!" Layla wore an awed expression.

Jet's face glowed with the compliment. "Yes, this is Dori." Stepping forward. Karyn introduced herself. "Welcome to Crowning Glory. Please look around, talk to our staff, and see what services you would like."

"You don't have to tell me twice. I'm Layla Keyes, Jet's *best* friend from Nashville," she emphasized.

"Miss Layla, I can do your nails for free." Dori's eyes widened in excitement as she licked her lips in anticipation.

Karyn was amused. She was so glad Levi had come into her life and given her a second chance at being a mother. She would always be thankful and proud to be Dori Lovanne Tolliver's mommy.

Layla shook her head and chuckled. "No, I'll pay you."

Dori looked to Karyn for the okay. When she nodded, Dori began to straighten her mini station and adjust her client chair for Layla's long legs.

"She's happy," Jet whispered.

"Yes, she is," Karyn agreed. "Come on back to my office." She felt like a midget next to Jet. Her heels clicked with each step, trying to keep up with Jet. "By the way, you look stylish. I always wanted to be tall."

Jet chuckled. "Not when you're in grade school and you're taller than the boys by half a foot, but thanks. I had an interview."

"I hope and pray you get it," she said and opened her office door.

"Wow." Jet stepped in and looked around. "If you'd want to run away from home, this would be a hide-out."

"I know. Have a seat." Karyn offered the sofa and sat on the ottoman in front of Jet.

After taking a deep breath, Jet met Karyn's eyes. "I don't know if you know why I'm here."

Karyn swallowed and felt her heart pound with uncertainty on what would be Jet's version. "I'm guessing it's because of Rossi and Levi."

She nodded and bowed her head before meeting Jet's determined expression.

"I can't help but feel like I'm the cause of their discord," she began. "I love Rossi." Jet paused, then shrugged and lowered her voice. "I guess I always have, but I can't be happy if he's not. I need you…"

Karyn blinked and her heart raced. Did she hear right? Jet actually asked something of her. *Lord, thank You!*

Jet swallowed as she struggled to speak, so Karyn reached out and patted her hand. "And I need you too," she repeated, reminding her of an old, but still popular Hezekiah Walker song, "I Need You to Survive."

Releasing a soft *hmph*ed, Jet shook her head. "I never imagined us having this conversation."

"We're in the body of Christ. Because you and I are both sincere about our salvation and walk with Jesus, it was a matter of time before the hip bone would connect with the leg bone, so to speak." Jet was quiet, hopefully reflecting on what Karyn had just said. "I love my husband. I do understand loss, and I'm been praying for complete restoration, even for you, but we have to be on a unified spiritual front to achieve that."

Her eyes watered. "So how do we bring two stubborn men back together?"

Joining in prayer, she heard the Lord speak to her spirit. "Connecting our prayers. Since stubbornness is not a spirit that pleases God, it's time to activate Matthew 17:21."

"I don't know that scripture." Jet looked defeated.

"But you will when we get the victory. Mark 9:29 says the same thing, but Matthew seven, beginning at verse nineteen explains it more. Basically, some situations aren't resolved or people delivered without much fasting and praying. You game?"

"It's a good thing I just had a good lunch." Jet grinned and patted her stomach. "I'm on this."

"Then we agree to be partners in prayer, not only on this, but whatever situation God rests on hearts?" Karyn held her breath, wanting to earn Jet's trust.

Jet gave her a high five. "It's about time." Karyn exhaled.

"Amen."

"We'll pray and fast beginning in the morning until dinner for three days and see if God will give us direction."

"Three days?"

Karyn wondered if she should have suggested one day with Jet being a baby saint in the Lord, but God didn't say otherwise. "Can you hang?"

"For Rossi, yes."

Chapter 19

Rossi knew his behavior with Levi didn't look good to his employees and wasn't acceptable to the Lord, and for that he repented. Didn't Ephesians 4:26 say, *Be angry and sin not?* Well, he had done that much and walked away.

But do not let the sun go down with your wrath. God whispered the completion of the verse.

Yeah, he would work on that, because he was a day late on that one. "God, help me." He had no problem apologizing for the disagreement. It was the subject of the argument that caused Rossi to make his decision. If he and Levi disagreed on personal choices, it was best to cut ties before their difference in opinions spilled over into their business decisions.

He had made his choice for a wife. God gave His stamp of approval, so nobody, including his family, was going to badmouth Jet. Rossi frowned as he stood from behind his desk in his home office. He had no idea that Levi had such a deep-rooted dislike for Jet.

Even his mother sensed something that morning when she returned and Jet had left.

He had cleaned the mess he made in the kitchen and was about to walk out the door. "Everything okay, son?" his mother had asked.

"It will be," he answered cryptically. If his aunt hadn't called about his and Levi's fallout, Rossi wasn't saying anything.

Laura gnawed on her lips. "You and Jet aren't having problems already, are you?"

"Nope. Jet and I are perfect."

He shifted in body in the chair and came back to reality. If Octavia hadn't invited Layla and Jet to lunch, he could have treated them just to be in his lady's presence.

After an hour or so of unproductive work, he opted for the comfort of the scriptures. He was invited to speak Thursday night at a church meeting, so he needed to study anyway and get the message from God.

He began to pray before opening his Bible. Ten minutes into it, Rossi sensed he couldn't get a prayer through. "Not good." He sighed before rubbing his head.

Stuffing his hands in his pants pockets, he strolled from one room to another until he stopped and stared out the floor-to-ceiling window from his spacious loft. Although he designed the interior to have a comfortable and cozy feel to it, the truth was Rossi wasn't a homebody. He enjoyed and thrived being around people. He heard the phone in the other room alert him of a text. He walked back into his home office and picked up his phone. He chuckled as he read the text from Jet.

I got the job! Celebrating with the girls. Dori's spending the night. The movers will be there by four.

He was happy for her. Everything seemed to be working in her favor, while it seemed he was losing God's favor. It was only two o'clock. He couldn't wait to see her, so he could keep his mind off his own issues.

My presence will go with you, and only I can give you rest! God spoke in a forceful whisper.

Finally, a Word from the Lord. Instead of comfort, it sounded more like a reprimand. That scripture was in Exodus 33 when God was encouraging Moses that he would lead him and the Israelites to the Promised Land. Rossi's Promise Land was heaven, and he needed Jesus to make sure he stayed on course to get there.

Minutes later, the Tollivers' corporate attorney returned his call. "I've been in court all morning. Sorry, I just listened to your message, and I'm surprised by your request for your cousin to buy out your stock in the company. I'd rather counsel you and Levi first before making a major decision like this," Daryl Steele said.

"My mind is made up." Rossi would not be swayed.

Daryl was slow in responding. "I see. I have trials the rest of the week. The earliest I can see you is next Tuesday."

Tuesday! That meant be would have to return to the office and work four business days with Levi. Otherwise, he would go stir crazy at home. "Thanks." They agreed on the time and ended the call.

At three forty-five, Jet called. "The movers are here!"

Hearing her voice was like a thirsty man needing a quart of Gatorade "I'm on my way." He swiped his keys off the kitchen counter. "I'll bring some pizza, sodas, and salads."

"Sounds good."

"Do you want to me to grab some breakfast food for you and your guests?" Rossi's hand was on the doorknob, but she hadn't answered. "Jesetta?"

"Uh, no, that's okay."

They said their goodbyes, and he immediately ordered a couple of Imo's pizzas from around the corner. While waiting, he decided to pick up some eggs, turkey sausage, and juice anyway. He chuckled. "She'll thank me in the morning."

Rossi's spirit lifted when Dori greeted him with a warm hug, followed by Jet. He didn't want to let her go, but peering over her shoulder, it appeared Layla was waiting for an introduction. He reluctantly released her.

"Yes, you are fine." Layla grinned, then hugged him too.

"Hush." Jet frowned at her, then turned and blushed at him.

After relieving him of the items, she took them to the kitchen. Rossi whistled at the boxes that lined the counter.

Jet chuckled. "And I gave away a lot of stuff when I sold my house." She shook her head.

It didn't look like she was too generous because there was stuff everywhere. At least her dining room table was clear to eat. Rossi was the first to sit down. He gave thanks for their food and ate. All three of ladies grabbed their slices. While munching on her third slice, Jet scolded him for bringing the extra food.

"It's no trouble," he said between bites.

Afterward, before his eyes, Jet turned into the sergeant telling him where to put things, what should stay in boxes until some rooms were repainted, and what she'd decided she didn't want anymore.

Women. But he didn't complain. They were together, and that's all that mattered. "I'll send painters over tomorrow," he said, offering his contractors at no expense to her. "I'll even be here to offer my services." He grinned.

"You're not going to the office?"

Not as long as his cousin would be there too. "Nah. Whatever I need to do, I can do from my laptop."

Her eyes seemed to plead with him to go, but Rossi ignored her. The next time he saw Levi, it would be with the company lawyer.

Chapter 20

Jet woke the next morning stiff, hungry, and annoyed that Rossi had brought breakfast food, which she'd asked him not to bring. He had no idea the temptation he was causing her, and the fast was for his sake.

She opened one eye to see Layla coming out of her bathroom. While at Crowning Glory the day before, Layla had decided to get a facial. Her face glowed. "Now, explain to me why I can't crack an egg and fry a piece of sausage?"

"You agreed to fast and pray, remember?"

Grrr. "I thought I said that in a dream." She walked back into the bathroom. "I guess I'd better brush my teeth again. At least, I'll have the taste of something in my mouth."

Getting up herself, Jet slid to her knees to pray then read her Bible. Checking her phone, she found Karyn had texted her a scripture: Ephesians 6:18.

Flipping through her Bible, Jet found the passage: *Praying always with all prayer and supplication in the Spirit, and watching thereunto with all perseverance and supplication for all saints.*

"You know I can't go without my coffee in the morning, so I've got to keep busy, otherwise I'll go stir crazy. I'll finish cleaning the kitchen," Layla said.

"Thanks. By the way, here's the scripture Karyn texted me." She repeated it; Layla nodded nonchalantly, then took the stairs to the first floor.

Octavia called. "Be encouraged. God will show up and out."

She hoped so because Rossi didn't seem like his carefree self. Instead of flirting, he was like a lost puppy following her around. Layla noticed that too.

"I'm loving this," Octavia said. "God's army of believers is about to take the devil down. Go, Team Jesus."

For someone fasting, Jet thought she was too hyped up not to be fueled by food. "Thank you for doing this with me. This isn't your problem," Jet said.

"But it is. The Bible says rejoice with those who rejoice, weep with those who weep—Romans 12:15. We'll touch base throughout our prayer and fast day, so we'll stay on one accord." She paused. "Now, I have a showing in a few hours, so let me get dressed."

Dori was hungry when she woke. Karyn had packed dry cereal and fruit, and sent plastic bottles of milk for breakfast. Rossi arrived minutes before the painters. He toted cups of Starbucks coffee and a small hot chocolate for Dori. His laptop bag was hanging off his shoulder. It took all her willpower not to bite his head off.

"How was breakfast?" He kissed her cheek and had the nerve to give her a glimpse of those twin dimples.

The things she was doing for love. "I haven't had a chance yet. Busy." She held her breath so he wouldn't hear her stomach rumble.

"Oh, you want me to cook you something?" He set his things down.

"Oh, no," she said, startling him. "Why don't you go behind the painters and touch up so we can get the bedrooms together?"

"O-okay." He gave her an odd expression.

Keeping Rossi busy was challenging while she tried to keep Layla away from the coffee. Dori was doing her own thing, while Jet took hourly bathroom breaks to read scriptures in quiet and pray. She wondered how the saints mastered fasting and praying on their jobs when it was supposed to be done in secret. It was like the left hand not knowing what the right hand was doing. That's the way she felt keeping this from Rossi, who she had come to depend on for spiritual understanding.

You have Me to teach you the scriptures in Matthew 6:4–6, God whispered. *Did I not teach my disciples?*

Hearing His voice made her giddy with excitement, which made her eager to "use" the bathroom every hour just to hear God's voice. After a few hours, the routine had made her body weak. She did her best not to watch the clock and countdown to four o'clock.

Layla was noting the time and by noon, she told Jet she needed a nap. "I can pray with my eyes closed."

"Hmm-mm." About three-thirty, Jet was pulling pictures out of boxes when Rossi snuck up behind her. "Hey, babe. I need to head home and freshen up before the church meeting tonight. Are you still coming with Layla?"

"Yes, sir."

He winked. "Would you like me to go out and get you something for dinner?"

"Yes!" Layla answered without Jet knowing she was awake and eavesdropping.

How Jesus went without food or water for forty days was unimaginable.

Karyn called and asked if she could pick up Dori to save Jet a trip to bring her home. An hour later, Jet opened her door and Karyn immediately walked in with an "awe" expression as she scanned the first floor. "This is nice. It reminds me of my childhood home in Chicago."

"Would you like a tour?" Jet offered.

"I'll show Mommy, Auntie," Dori said, running to Karyn to give her a hug. Excited, she ran ahead and looked back. "Come on." She disappeared to the lower level.

Karyn smiled. "You see who's the boss at my house—my daughter. She says hurry, and we run."

Jet chuckled, noting she'd never heard Karyn refer to Dori as her step-daughter. She needed to accept that Karyn would be the only mother Diane's baby girl would ever know.

"One day down, two to go?" Karyn gave her a hopeful expression before heading in Dori's direction.

"Absolutely."

At four-fifteen and the fast over, Jet invited Karyn to stay for dinner, but she declined.

"We try to eat as many of our meals together as a family. But let's pray."

Taking her hand, Jet bowed her head and listened as Karyn took the lead. Layla mumbled, Amen first and almost ran into the kitchen.

They chuckled, then Karyn left with Dori. In the kitchen, Layla was getting a third helping of spaghetti, a delivery Rossi had ordered for them instead of dropping it off. "Scoot over." Jet prayed and gave thanks for the fast and food, then indulged.

"Hey, I'm going to shower, then I suggest you do the same so we won't be late. Rossi is speaking to the young adults."

Patting her stomach, Layla exhaled. "Girl, I may need a nap after this."

"Oh no you don't. You're not supposed to go to sleep on a full stomach. Plus, you've seen Rossi, but I want you to hear the wisdom God gives him."

"Umm-hmm." Layla chewed the last bite of garlic bread and stood. "Only thing I've got to say is he better be worth me going without food for hours and now losing sleep."

"You won't regret it!" Jet beamed.

***

Jet was beginning to regret bringing Layla to church. Clearly Rossi wasn't on his game as he seemed distracted. She so desperately wanted to stand next to him and whisper scriptures as if she could recall them like him.

She had to nudge Layla twice to stay awake as Rossi spoke from 2 Timothy 1:9.

"Do you belong to God today?" Rossi paused and looked around the small chapel. "Do you have His seal, which is the Holy Ghost?" He seemed to ponder the question he asked.

Even her mind began to wander as she read the verse several times for herself: *Nevertheless the foundation of God stands sure, having this seal, the Lord knows them that are His. And, let everyone that names the name of Christ depart from iniquity.* She searched her footnotes for any cross references, and found Matthew 7:23 listed. *If we profess God and still sin, the Lord will reject us in the end.*

She flipped to the passage, then glanced around her. Rossi was known for his having people sitting-on-the-edge-of-their-seats wisdom. The young adults loved him at Living for Jesus Church, but today those who weren't on their electronic devices, wore blank stares. Jet frowned. Why wasn't Rossi spitting out scriptures with the breath of the Holy Ghost like he normally did?

Jet gnawed on her lips. She didn't bother to elbow Layla whose head began to bob. From where she was sitting, the fast didn't seem to have any impact. She prayed things would change by the end of fast.

Once My Word comes from My mouth, it will accomplish what I set out for it to do until it is done, God whispered. *Read Isaiah 55:11.*

Jet wished she knew what God's game plan was, because she was sure it wasn't a family scrabble, and Rossi not in tune with God. While Layla dozed, Jet did everything in her power not to join her friend while waiting for the benediction.

Chapter 21

To Layla's relief, the three-day fast ended on Saturday evening. "For all the meals your boyfriend has caused me to miss, I want a steak and potato dinner," she fussed while she and Jet were relaxing on the patio off the living room.

Her friend had missed the purpose. Maybe it was Jet's fault. Spiritual fasting wasn't for the faint. Even after the constant prayers before God's throne, Jet was disappointed that there had been no peace treaty reached between Levi and Rossi.

Plus, Jet had hoped Layla would witness God move by their self-denial and petitions toward heaven before she returned to Nashville. But meditating on Matthew 6:10, Jet realized in the end, the Lord's will would be done. Now, she understood that her prayers should be filled with God's will for their lives.

As if the wind had carried Layla's complaint to his loft miles away, Rossi called. "If you and Layla don't have any plans tonight, I would like to take you both to dinner before she leaves tomorrow."

"That's sweet." She accepted for Layla, especially when he mentioned the pricey Ruth's Chris Steak House.

A few hours later, they sat around the table in the restaurant, touching on topics ranging from church to playing pool.

"We'll have to find a pool hall before you start work," Rossi suggested.

How about reconciling with your cousin before I clock in on Wednesday morning? Jet wanted to say, but went with the flow. "Sounds like fun."

The evening was unrushed as they enjoyed dessert, and Rossi and Layla compared notes about owning their own businesses. When she and Layla returned to her house, they were stuffed as they prepared for their last night hanging out. "Rossi seems genuine. He's fine, loves you, and is employed."

"The last part is debatable." Jet twisted her lips.

"Everything is going to work out," Layla said before drifting off to sleep.

On Sunday morning with her bags packed, Layla accompanied Jet to church before taking her afternoon flight. Jet prayed for a word from the Lord for her friend, Rossi, and herself.

The praise team led the congregation with a medley of worship songs. She and Layla stood and stretched out their arms to heaven. She spied Rossi in the pulpit with a bowed head. Her heart ached, but she believed God's will was working.

Pastor Brown made his way to the podium. "Praise the Lord, Saints of God, and welcome to our visitors." After making a few announcements, he opened his Bible. "My text this morning comes from Matthew, chapter twenty. Sometimes Christians need a reality check."

"Amens" floated around Jet and mingled with hers.

He slipped on his reading glasses and bobbed his head. "Let's see how many Amens I get when God finishes His message." He got a few "alrights," before he continued. "This passage does that. In verse sixteen, 'The last shall be first and the first last. For many are called, but few are chosen.' Pride separates us from God whenever Christians believe one is better than the other, or deserves more than another. We are all invaluable to God, regardless of race or sex. God created us all. My sermon today is entitled, 'Are

You Chosen of God?' The lord of the vineyard called anyone and everyone to work for him. But at the end of the day, who do you think had the right heart or mindset for him to choose? Reality check."

Jet wondered if Rossi was soaking in the message.

"There shouldn't be a competition among the saints to be first, but our hearts should be in tune with God so that we can go back and get that last runner and finish the race together. In the body of Christ, the Bible tells us to humble ourselves. If you don't humble yourself, God will do it for you, and it might not be pretty. In other words, practice humility."

Where the congregation was usually energized, standing on their feet, or shouting hallelujah, today the atmosphere was still. Maybe everyone was doing their self-examination like her. The process was slow, but Jet felt she was changing her attitude, but was it enough to be considered humble? He continued to preach, citing other scriptures and examples for almost an hour.

Closing his Bible, Pastor Brown asked the congregation to stand. "Do you want to be chosen today? This is your moment, for God is calling you to repent of your sins. Tell God how sorry you are. I don't have a prayer for you to repeat, because it needs to come from deep within, then God saves you. Complete your salvation with the baptism in water in Jesus' name, and the Lord promises to baptize you with fire of the Holy Ghost, and He will speak to you through other tongues as evidence."

Jet closed her eyes and prayed, hoping that Layla would want more than simply going to church every Sunday as they had begun to do in Nashville.

"Hey," Layla said, nudging her, "despite the drama, I'm impressed with Octavia and Karyn's sweet spirits, and I've seen how you have changed. I want to tackle my problems in a spiritual way, not just on the surface." She scooted Jet out of the way and glided down the aisle toward the altar. Less than thirty minutes later, she was being baptized in Jesus' name.

"My dear sister, upon the confession of your faith and the confidence we have in the mighty Word of God, concerning His death, burial, and Grand Resurrection, we now baptize you in the name of Jesus for the remission of your sins for there is no other name under heaven by which man can be saved. Amen," the minister proclaimed from his spot in the pool as Rossi looked on from his seat in the pulpit. Layla and other candidates were submerged and came out of the water new creatures.

Unfortunately, their celebration had to be cut short because of Layla's flight. She pouted. "I so wanted those ladies to pray for me to receive the Holy Ghost like on the day of Pentecost."

Rossi joined them in the sanctuary, evidently overhearing her friend's comment. "If your soul is hungry, God will fill it. Some saints have testified, God woke them from their sleep and filled them with the Holy Ghost, so we'll keep praying for you that the power will descend on you."

Layla nodded. "Thank you, and I'll keep praying for *you*."

Jet acted like she accidently bumped her as a hint to quit talking. Their prayers were said in secret, so that God would reward them openly. Slowly, her friend got the hint.

After she and Layla said their tearful goodbye at the airport, Rossi suggested they go bike riding.

They rode for hours, stopping to admire historic sites, sample ice cream from street vendors, or just to relax on park benches like at the moment. She faced Rossi. "The sermon was refreshing today, and to see my best friend want God's complete salvation was heartwarming. Reality check…"

She opened the door for Rossi to share his thoughts on the sermon, but he didn't. Opening her hand, she waited for him to take it. She didn't look at him. "Minister Rossi."

He chuckled. "Sister Jesetta."

"I thought we could talk about anything."

"We can—always."

Jet exhaled and turned to him again. "About you and Levi—"

"Except that." He seemed to grit his teeth.

"But the sermon today—"

Rossi held up his hand and shook his head. "I'm still doing my reality check." He stood and helped her to her feet. "Come on. Let's go another mile."

She didn't hide her disappointment or argue. There had to be a Plan B, and she would contact Karyn to help her work out the details.

Chapter 22

"Well, this is it," Rossi told his reflection as he lined his mustache and beard. His heart remained heavy after the sermon he heard, but the decision had been made. There was nothing sinful about parting ways. As chief financial officer of Tolliver Real Estate and Development Company, Rossi knew he and Levi had earned enough money over the years to buy the other out. Would Levi do it, or would he have a counter offer to sell the company?

When Rossi drove into his parking spot, he stared at the familiar building that had housed their company for seven years before going inside. Minutes later, he strolled into the office to find their attorney waiting in the lobby.

"Has Levi arrived yet?" Rossi asked as the two shook hands.

"I'm here," his cousin answered, walking up to them.

"Good morning, Rossi, Levi, and Attorney Steele," their administrative assistant greeted them hesitantly. "The conference room is ready."

"Thank you, Kelly." Rossi led the way.

Not another word was spoken until they were gathered at the table, and Daryl opened his folder and slid out the documents. "Before we get started, I have to say I'm surprised at both of your requests—Rossi wanting a buyout, and Levi—" he paused—"selling the business."

Levi had a poker face, and Rossi did his best to match it.

"As your legal counselor, I advise you rethink your decision."

There was a knock at the door, then it opened. Karyn appeared. Clearly surprised, Levi stood. "Baby? What are you doing here?"

Amused that his cousin was in trouble, Rossi smirked, then blinked when another surprise walked in behind Karyn. He scrambled to his feet. "Jesetta?"

Stuffing the papers into the folder, Daryl stood and excused himself.

"What's going on?" Levi beat Rossi in asking.

Karyn smiled, then took the seat Daryl had vacated. Jet sat next to her.

Rossi wondered the same thing as he admired his lady's beauty, even when she wasn't smiling, which was now as she glared at him.

"We don't need Daryl to settle this." Karyn squinted at her husband. *"Dare any of you, having a matter against another, go to law before the unjust, and not before the saints?"* She tapped her nail on the table, emphasizing every word of 1 Corinthians 6:1. "The saints shall judge the world, so if the world shall be judged by us, surely we are wise enough to settle these small matters."

Rossi squirmed in his seat. When it came to scriptures, Karyn was a force with which to be reckoned. Karyn read and studied her Word diligently since she had surrendered to Christ in prison.

Folding her arms, Jet lifted her chin. "I know God is the Author of peace, not confusion, so let's put all of our differences on the table, shall we, Levi?"

"Why are you trying to alienate Rossi and Jet?" Karyn asked her husband.

Jet didn't give Levi a chance to answer. "This company is my niece's legacy...and her brother's. If for no other reason, you should pass it on to them."

"I know that!" Levi slapped the table.

"Watch it, Mr. Tolliver," his wife said sweetly, but her expression was stern.

"Jesetta is going to be my wife, so watch your tone," Rossi threatened, and Jet gave him her own version of a stern rebuke.

"You have the floor, dear brother-in-law. Remember, God is our judge before answering. What do you have against me wanting to find the same happiness you found with Karyn?"

Yes, I want to know that myself. Smirking, Rossi would have given her a high five, but he thought better of it and folded his arms.

Levi exhaled and looked away, it seemed at every object in the room but their faces. Whatever he was about to say was a struggle. "Guilt."

Their "huhs?" blended in a chorus.

"Why?" Jet asked softly.

His cousin took a deep breath. "When Diane died, we all lost so much." He paused and reached across the table for Karyn's hand. Her fingers met his halfway. "When this woman came into my life, she took the pain away and gave Dori and me more than I ever thought I would have again." Karyn's eyes watered while Jet had a blank expression. "I'd moved on, but you hadn't. I felt you hated me for that, but truth be told I hated you right back for wanting to take away a happiness I thought I'd never see again."

"Hate?" Karyn repeated.

Nodding, Levi bowed his head. "The Holy Ghost kept warning me to repent at the same time the devil was cheering me on that you were a threat. It was easier for me to believe the worse. I'm truly sorry, God and Jet."

The room grew quiet as all eyes were on Jet. "The truth will make you free to see I'm not the enemy." She squinted. "Let me find my happiness…with whomever I chose."

That's my baby! Rossi wanted to shout, but he contained himself.

Leaning forward, she continued, "You're right. I did struggle when you met Karyn, but after a reality check, I realized it was your life, and I would have to accept your decision. When I learned about her past that made me crazy." Her voice shook, and Karyn released Levi's hand and squeezed Jet's. "I connected her killing her son to the person who killed my sister. That was hard to process."

The sadness in her eyes tugged at Rossi, and he wanted to get up and wrap his arms around her.

Let her be, God whispered.

"The Lord helped me to understand that everyone has a past, and unless we all take the same road to salvation— repenting and the baptism in water and spirit—none of us would be saved." She patted her chest, and her eyes watered, then she choked out, "I wanted God to save me. Karyn and I—mostly me—are working on a friendship. It's slow, but I'm trying."

Shaking his head, it was clear Levi was tortured. "I'm so sorry, Jet. I would welcome you as a Tolliver." Levi's eyes seemed to plead with Jet's.

Karyn cleared her throat. "So, if Jet and I can work together, so can you and Rossi. Enough of this buyout or selling the company business." She stood and grabbed her purse. "That is all, gentlemen."

Jet was right behind Karyn. He and Levi would talk later, but at the moment, they were eager to follow the ladies out of the room. Reaching for Jet's hand, Rossi squeezed it. "So does this mean you're going to marry me?" He grinned and gave her his killer dimples.

"I'm not marrying you." She wasn't smiling.

"B–But you just said," he stuttered, staring at the woman he loved. He was speechless as he replayed "I'm not marrying you" in his head. He opened his mouth and finally "Why?" came out.

She planted her fist on her curvy hip, and Rossi dared to look elsewhere but in her fiery eyes. "If you think I'm going to marry you just because you asked, you have another thing coming. I'm not marrying a man who can't romance me and win my heart…"

Whew. That's all. He exhaled and grabbed her around her waist, startling her. He had enough of her nonsense, so he kissed her. Pulling back too soon, he watched as her lids fluttered before she opened them. He also blinked. Did he just lose control? *Lord, help me.* Her lips were off limits, and he had yielded to temptation, but it wouldn't happen again.

Dazed, Jet straightened her shoulders and walked away. Levi hooped and cackled. He bent over laughing so hard that Rossi sneered at him.

"Good luck, cuz, because that woman is going to get her way." Slapping Rossi on his back was like old times.

"Don't I know," Rossi mumbled as he walked back to his office. Behind closed doors, he looked up and whispered, "Lord, thank You for reconciliation."

Sitting behind his desk, Rossi nodded with a smirk. So his Jesetta wanted romance. "And romance you shall have."

***

Word traveled fast in the family about what almost happened. Rossi's mother called. She and his father were on the speakerphone. Rossi chided himself for his actions. "I'm sorry for disappointing you both and God. Levi and I have already apologized to our staff who were worried about what would happen to their jobs if we sold the company."

"Stop beating yourself up, son. Karyn and Jet interceded for their men," his mother said softly.

"Yeah. She made me proud while I'm sure I disappointed her." Rossi rested his elbow on his desk in his office, a place he hadn't bothered coming to for almost a week. How ridiculous.

"But she's the real deal," his father said. "Any woman who is willing to pray until something happens is the one most cherished. Prayer is the answer to all discord, problems, and other disruptions. We need praying partners in our lives."

"Amen," his mother added. "Now, we'll let you return to running your business—personal and the otherwise."

Chapter 23

Jet meant what she said. She didn't want a man to take her love for granted, even if he was the dark-skinned, deep dimpled, and sculpted Rossi Tolliver IV. She had watched how Levi wooed Karyn and how her sister Diane's eyes had sparkled when her soon-to-be husband was near. If Rossi wanted her, then he was going to have to work for her heart. She smiled, knowing the man already had it, but he didn't have to know that. "We were fierce!" Karyn pumped her hand in the air, and Jet met it with a high five as she cleared the door to the salon. The plan was to meet Octavia there and give her the update then to take Dori to the park before Jet started work the next day.

Dori dropped her dolls and made a beeline toward her. Jet knelt and received her hug as Little Levi ran toward her too. Once her niece stepped back, Little Levi waited his turn. She trapped him against her chest. Although she had never mistreated him, this time she felt an unexplainable sense of connection. "Hey, stranger. How did it go?"

She looked up, and Octavia was standing nearby. Instead of the natural wild style Jet had seen her rock from time to time, Octavia had her hair straightened, curled, and styled. She was gorgeous.

After releasing Little Levi, Jet stood, and the two embraced.

"It went well. You should have seen the look of shock when Karyn and I walked in like drill sergeants. Thanks for directing me to the passage on fasting and praying. Now, I know what to do when I face something unbearable. I see the benefits of adding fasts to my prayer life. Although Layla couldn't hang all three days, one out of three ain't bad." They chuckled. "But…" she paused. Maybe she should keep these thoughts to herself. As they strolled to the seating area, Little Levi trailed them while Dori went back to painting her dolls' nails.

"Go ahead," Octavia encouraged.

"Honestly, I was surprised by Rossi's behavior—a minister acting that way. He knew how his cousin was." She looked to Karyn. "No offense."

"None taken." Karyn grinned and told her son to go play.

Octavia was quiet as she seemed to ponder an answer. "Maybe this whole misunderstanding had nothing to do with Levi and Rossi."

Frowning, Jet squinted. "What do you mean? I walked in on them in the midst of a verbal duel."

"Maybe this was about your spiritual growth."

"Are you saying those men set me up?"

Octavia shook her head, causing her hair to bounce from side to side. "I think the Lord set you up. You had a problem with Karyn initially. That seemed to be your stumbling block. Not that she was your enemy, but what better way to draw people together than prayer? Because of your love for Rossi and hers for Levi, you two—basically, you—were willing to put aside your differences to mend their relationship." She smiled. "That's love."

Jet thought about it. "You really think God did that?"

"Yep. God will use any situation or anybody to help us grow. You, me, and Karyn are soul sisters."

"He got me." Jet chuckled. "The Lord pulled a fast one over on me, but I ain't mad at Him."

They exchanged another round of high fives before Karyn stood. "Is there any service you need while you're here?"

"I could really use a real manicure," Jet whispered.

"Done, but my daughter is going to want to give you a pedicure. She's been practicing on me and Buttercup."

Jet laughed and nodded. "I have the perfect pair of pumps to wear just in case."

***

Thursday morning, a wakeup call from Rossi stirred Jet before her alarm clock. "I just wanted to tell the love of my life good morning and to be blessed on the new job."

"Aww." She scooted up in bed. "Thank you. I'm a little nervous and excited."

"I also want to tell you thank you for sticking by my side, despite my stubbornness."

"My pleasure. For once, I wasn't the drama queen." They shared a laugh and scripture before saying goodbye.

First days on a new job were overrated, Jet thought as she parked her car. She would have to adjust to a new environment, personalities, and responsibilities. What was she thinking going from major corporations to a small business, even though it was taunted as the headquarters? The what-ifs began to burden her as she pushed the elevator button to the third floor.

The receptionist greeted her with a grin as she held a big bouquet of flowers. Jet immediately felt foolish for her doubts.

"Welcome, and these are for you," Shannon said and showed her to her new office where a smaller arrangement was the centerpiece on her desk.

The woman chuckled. "Those are from us." She pointed to the daisies. "And these are from someone with good taste. I'll bring your paperwork in a minute." She winked and backed out of the office, closing the door.

After sniffing the flowers, Jet read the card: *Congratulations on your new journey. Remember I'm in the passenger seat, and God is steering your career. Have a great day. Love, Your Rossi.*

They're beautiful. Thank you. Love you back. Your Jesetta, she texted him.

Her morning was filled with employee introductions, then she settled in her office with a binder that gave a history of the company, which was formed less than fifty years earlier. Jet was impressed by the entrepreneurial spirit of two professional pool players and Billiard Hall of Famers Terry Bell and Larry Hubbart. What a legacy to be credited with a concept that would be copied in Canada, Japan, and she learned, even China.

During her interview, her new boss said franchise operators were the driving force behind the popularity of pool leagues. Rossi and Levi would also leave a legacy for generations to come, thanks to God's intervention. She could imagine their real estate and development company expanding from the bi-state to regional offices. Yes, she saw great things for the Tolliver cousins.

Mark had said knowing the mechanics of pool wasn't a perquisite for the position, but the more she read about the 8-Ball and 9-Ball team formats, the more her interest piqued, especially after seeing that APA's spokesperson was a female professional pool player, Jeanette Lee, nicknamed the Black Widow.

By the end of the day, Jet was convinced she had made a good career move. When she arrived home, she was surprised to see Rossi perched on her porch with a picnic basket and a bouquet of balloons.

He stood and graced her with a smile. "Tired?"

"Yes." She nodded, then accepted his kiss, this time on her cheek. "Want to come in?"

"I'll wait out here, then we can pick a spot across the street." He pointed to the park. "It's a nice day."

She shrugged. "Okay. Let me change." The heels came off after she stepped into her house. Within minutes, she swapped her suit for jeans and a dressy short sleeve top. When she reappeared, Rossi linked his fingers through hers.

They stretched out a checked blanket near the walkway bridge in the park, which boasted colorful foliage in the spring and summer. They barely had opened their basket when a dirty man approached them for spare change.

Jet had to hold her breath, so as not to lose her appetite before taking the first bite. How Rossi could stomach the odor was beyond her.

"Would you prefer a couple of dollars or a hot meal?" Rossi asked the man.

His uncombed wooly natural hair was gray by default with dust and dirt. The tears in his jeans weren't reflective of the latest fashion trend. He looked from Rossi to her.

"Hungry," he said with a bowed head.

Without hesitation, Rossi reached for one of the two large dinners. He handed the beggar one. "Eat, brother." He passed him utensils and one of two bottles of water. "Mind if I pray for you?"

The man took the food and hurried away. "Nah, I'm good. Thanks."

Jet waited for Rossi to be outraged because she certainly was. "That was rude." She huffed. "You're better than me, because if I was going to give up a meal, he was going to have to listen to me pray, and who knows, I could have become long winded. Didn't that bother you?"

"The only thing that bothered me was him interrupting my time with you." His words were just as tender as the look he was giving her. "I'll grab something to eat on the way home."

"No, we'll share." She shut down his protest with a look that said, "Don't even try it." "So come on and give thanks for God to bless our food."

Wrapping his hands around hers, he bowed his head and prayed. "Lord, thank You for the food we are about to receive and even the meal that got away. Please bless it, sanctify it, and help us to remember those who are hungry. In Jesus' name."

As they said "Amen," in unison, Rossi brought her hands to his lips.

"I love you," he whispered in a husky voice that made her eyes water from the tenderness she could feel from his declaration.

"I know, and I love you back."

He smirked. "I know."

Ignoring him, Jet began to portion out the chicken carbona pasta. She wondered if God had multiplied it like the fish and the loaves because there was plenty of food, and she gave Rossi most of the serving.

"Tell me about your first day." He stretched out his long legs and gave her his full attention while she gave him a recap.

"I thought about you and Levi today when I read how two pool players built the business. My company oversees almost three hundred leagues, thanks to the hard work from franchisees."

"Impressive. Sounds like a great opportunity for someone who wants to start a business. Speaking of business—my personal one, I'm getting married as soon as the woman dining with me says yes."

She grinned. "I want a real proposal."

"Who says it wasn't real?"

She jutted her chin and said nothing.

"Now that you're working full-time again, I hope you'll have energy for mid-week services, including youth night. I think we'll go shoot pool in honor of my almost fiancée's new gig."

***

Saturday morning, Rossi's plans to spend the entire day with Jet were dashed, but it was a good thing. He was pleasantly surprised that she was out shopping with Karyn for Dori's school clothes and supplies. "Can you pencil me in for a dinner date this evening?"

"How about I cook you dinner? I've decided on making the lower level a home theater, and I might get a pool table," she said excitedly.

Rossi took a deep breath. Friendship with Jet was easy. The courtship would be challenging because of his strong attraction to her. As Christians, they would have to use much restraint with their affections. "I'd rather take you out to a nice romantic dinner."

"Come on. Let me cook for you," she whined, and Rossi chuckled. "Seriously, you surprised me for breakfast at your parents' house. I can cook, you know." Her voice was defiant.

"I'm well aware of my almost fiancée's culinary skills, but I still have to decline." He braced for her comeback, and she unfortunately didn't disappoint.

"What's your problem?" She sounded beyond irked.

"Trust me." He softened his tone to calm her down. "If you want romance, then let me take the lead. Agreed?"

*Hmph*ed. "You can pick me up at six-thirty." When she disconnected, Rossi chuckled and shook his head. Being a Christian couple with Jesetta Hutchens was going to be challenging. He was beginning to see how his father landed in the doghouse with his mother when he tried to be thoughtful or something and his father's timing was off.

He stayed busy while Jet was out shopping. He even paid Levi a visit for a few hours until it was time to get ready for his date.

Soon, he parked in front of her house and hiked the steps two and three at a time to her door. He rang the bell and waited. She opened seconds later and under the guise of not being ready, Jet opened the front door and disappeared inside, clearly inviting him to follow. Refusing to cross the threshold, Rossi waited on the porch. Five minutes later, she reappeared.

Rossi swallowed. His knees wobbled until he stood straight. The stunning beauty before him had his mind jumbled. He didn't know whether to whistle or speak. Finally, he released, "Wow." He stepped closer—his mistake. Her perfume was teasing. "I am one blessed man." He took her hand and brought it to his lips before escorting her down the steps.

She blushed as he whisked her away to Elaia Restaurant on Tower Grove, not far from Forest Park. The atmosphere was a mixture of casual and chic and came highly recommended by Levi.

Once they ordered appetizers, the staff faded into the background. Reaching across the table, Rossi gathered Jet's hands in his. He admired the precision of the shape of her nails and wondered if this was Dori's handiwork. "You look beautiful. You can make a man lose his appetite."

She leaned across the table. "Not if you taste my pasta. I'm an excellent cook."

"I don't doubt that, but I don't want you to cook for me until after we're married."

Jet gave him a side eye. "What is this really about, because if I invite you one more time for a free meal and you turn me down…?"

"Don't challenge me, Jesetta. We both may lose."

As she tried to pull back, he tightened his hold to trap her long fingers, but measured his strength so not to hurt her. Gazing into her eyes, he was drawn into the brown hue.

"How is a woman wanting to cook for her man a bad thing?" She frowned.

Looking at her, Rossi wondered if this was how King David was smitten with one glance at Bathsheba. Jet was a tease, and he doubted she was trying.

"First off, I'm a minister ordained by God, then by man. I'm in the spotlight at all times like a politician. My shameful behavior in front of my employees was a bad example of acting Christ-like. We have to walk a fine line when it comes to dating the Bible way. I won't skip a beat on the romance."

"What are you saying?" She paused as their server placed their plates before them, asked if they need anything else, and disappeared.

"Our affections aren't for public display."

"I invited you to my house for dinner, and there would be no prying eyes."

"Or private display. Baby—" he lowered his voice and prayed for her to understand—"a lot of sins are committed behind closed doors. Even if our intentions are pure, Romans 14:16 says not to let our good be evil spoken of."

Leaning back in her chair, Jet's eyes wandered as if she was giving some thought to what he was saying. Their dishes arrived before they had finished with the appetizers. She nodded her thanks and bowed her head for him to pray. Once their Amens mingled, Jet picked up their conversation before taking the first bite of food. "We're both practicing Christians and filled with the Holy Ghost."

"And trapped in a sinful body, so I want us to be a team. Let's shame the devil, not God in our love." He held his breath, watching her, praying that she understood.

"Only because I love you, Rossi Tolliver IV—or should I call you Minister Tolliver from now on?"

"Whatever your heart calls me, I'll answer."

Picking up her fork, Jet began to sample her dish, so Rossi followed with his meal. Minutes later, she asked, "Do you like being a minister?"

It wasn't the first time he had been asked that. "It's not so much that I like the title, more so, I like pleasing God."

She nodded, then took a sip from her glass. "What about being a pastor?"

He sighed and wiped his mouth. "That's up to the Lord. If He's not promoting, I'm not trying to climb a corporate—church—ladder. As a youth minister, my focus is on the teens and young adults that are dealing with issues. Counseling that small segment of the church keeps me busy."

"I remember one teenager text you as you were dropping me off at the hotel."

"Yes, and I get those calls from time to time. A pastor would get more. His responsibility is unlimited. Pastor Brown is our regular Bible teacher, Sunday preacher, counselor, public speaker, worship director, prayer warrior, mentor, leadership trainer, and fundraiser."

Jet exhaled. "That sounds stressful."

"That's why it's important that preachers are called by God because He is the One who will give us strength. Some pastors walk away from their congregation because of their criticism, rejection, and betrayal. I was surprised to read that a majority of pastors consider leaving the ministry because of problem people, such as disgruntled elders, deacons, worship leaders, worship teams, board members, and associate pastors. That makes me wonder if God called them."

Resting her fork, Jet reached across the table. "I don't want to add to your stress level. If you say we're on public display while dating, I'll do my best to support you."

Rossi choked back his emotions. "This is why you are the perfect woman for me."

She blushed. "You're going to have to show me how this Christian romance works."

"It will be my pleasure."

***

"Can we talk?" Nalani's call came as a surprise to Rossi the following Monday as he prepared for a meeting in a few hours.

"Always. Is everything okay?"

"How about lunch or dinner?" she asked after a brief silence.

Rossi shook his head before answering. "I'm in a relationship with Jesetta. I don't want her or anyone else to misunderstand seeing me with another woman I once dated.

Is there something we can discuss over the phone or at church?"

"Why Jet, not me?" Nalani's voice was barely above a whisper.

Her wounded heart was evident. Rossi wished he could play dumb, but he couldn't. He formed his words carefully. He and Nalani were friends and in-laws. "When we dated, I went into it wondering if you were the one. I was open to finding love—"

"Did you give us a chance?"

"Did we give us a chance? I believe so, I walked into our relationship with an expectant heart. But our hearts never connected."

She sighed. "Rossi, you're honest and a good minister. I don't want to see Jet bring you down, instead of building you up. It's not like she's a people person."

Nalani had no idea how much Jet had been by his side. Jet loved and respected him, and he her. "I wouldn't say that. You only know her post Diane's death. I knew her before when she was vibrant and glowed with life." He paused. "Levi and Karyn have resolved their issues with her."

Clearing her throat, Nalani's voice grew stronger. "I'm not there yet. First, she messed with my sister and now…"

"Now what?" Rossi prompted her to finish.

"Never mind." She disconnected without saying goodbye.

Chapter 24

With little effort, Jet could seduce any man for the fun of it. Of course, that was before she surrendered to Christ's will for her life. Since she and Rossi were both practicing Christians, and he was stronger than her, surely they could contain their emotions, right?

It saddened her that they wouldn't be able to share an intimate dinner, watch a scary or romantic movie together, or play a silly board game in the privacy of her home. She wanted them to experience so much as they grew as a couple, and they didn't always have to go out to date.

The flesh lusts against the Spirit, and the Spirit against the flesh, God whispered. *Read Galatians 5:17.*

Reaching in her desk drawer, Jet pulled out her tablet and tapped in the scripture and meditated on it before she had to go into a meeting. Shaking her head after reading the verse a couple of times, Jet realized it was foolish thinking that she was in control of the seduction game she played with her dates. It was her flesh in control of her, putting her in situations that could have resulted in diseases or pregnancies. "Thank you, Jesus, for Your spirit."

Minutes later, her phone rang. She smiled when she recognized Layla's number. "Hey, girlfriend. How's my Holy Ghost–filled sister?" Her friend had returned to Nashville unfulfilled about receiving the water baptism in Jesus' name. She had wanted it all.

Layla's hunger for spiritual strength caused her to increase her prayer life until God filled her with tongues of fire. She had been so happy, she couldn't sleep, which meant she woke Jet. Together they had a praise party over the phone until Jet realized the time and had to go to sleep for work. That had been a few days ago. Now, they spoke every day.

"Hey, I need some dating ideas," Jet said, having explained to Layla her and Rossi's restrictions on dating.

"Movie marathon, dinner, picnic, bike riding, shopping..."

"Basically, we've done all of the above."

"What about a couples' painting party. They're popular now."

Jet grinned. "Sounds like Rossi and I are about to paint the town."

***

What did Rossi know about painting, except to plaster colors on a wall? The painting party was Jesetta's idea. He worked with architects on designs, contractors on projects, and painters on color selection, but when it came to a canvas, he did better with a number two pencil. He could sketch for days, although it had been a while. But who was he to deny his lady a date night at Painting with a Twist art studio?

"This should be interesting," he mumbled as he parked in front of Jet's house. She was dolled up in an oversized gray shirt, black pants, and cute cap to mimic an artist. "You look pretty."

"And you look seriously handsome." She grinned. "Come on. This should be exciting. Next time, we should invite Octavia and Landon."

Next time? he repeated to himself. He hoped this wouldn't be a routine date. Left up to him, they would have gone rock climbing. In the end, he didn't care as long as they were together.

When they arrived at the Creve Coeur art studio, Rossi didn't know what to expect as they strolled through the lobby, admiring artwork. They were led to a large classroom where at least a dozen easels were set up. Three couples had already picked their spots.

"Sit anywhere you'd like," their art instructor advised.

Looping her arm through his, Jet leaned into him. "Let's surprise each other."

Her brown eyes were captivating. He didn't respond right away until she bumped him with her hip, then took her place at the easel facing him. As the room filled up, couples introduced themselves until Annie Mims, their instructor, asked for their attention. "Welcome, everyone. Since this is a date night for most of you, I thought creating a romantic scene would put you in the mood." She wiggled her brows.

A few men replied, "That's what I'm talking about," "Alright now," or "Yes."

Rossi didn't need any artificial sparks. Jesetta did that all herself when she walked into a room, smiled, laughed, or concentrated on the message whenever the Word was preached. All he needed was to woo her to say yes, then it was on.

"Hey," Jet said, peeping over her canvas, "Annie said to pull out your brushes."

He complied, but soon the soft background music inspired him to paint another image his mind was seeing rather than following the example that had been provided—two empty chairs on a beach with a soft moon in the night sky. He started forming Jet's lips as the focal point. He manipulated the brush to curl her lips like when she smiled. Her cheekbones came next. He switched to a smaller brush to form them with a gentle hand. Once he added her long lashes to her seductive brown eyes, it was as if her face came alive and blinked back at him. He smirked.

"What are you smiling at?" Jet's voice broke his concentration.

"My artistic ability." He met her stare.

"Let me see." She was about to stand.

"No. We can compare our talents at the end of class," he said as the instructor came and looked over his shoulder. He hoped she wouldn't give him away.

"Interesting," she said, studying it. She moved to the next couple.

Jet laughed. "Umm-hmm. Do I need to come over and show you how to paint?" she teased, then dismissed him to continue her project.

He examined his interpretation of God's masterpiece on his canvas. The only thing left was her hair. It truly was her crowning glory. Should he paint swirls to depict her mass of silky curls, or use long strokes to represent her mane, hanging down her back? He gnawed on his lips. Decisions, decisions. He glanced up and admired her hair swept up in a ball on top of her head. It was a style that even Dori had started to copy.

Rossi wasn't an artist by any means, but looking at his handiwork was proof that his mind had created the image, and he still had it when it came to sketching.

"Let's finish up so you can mingle a few minutes and show off your artwork to your date and others," the instructor told the couples.

He stood from straddling a stool and walked around to the other side. Looking over Jet's shoulder, Rossi couldn't contain his snickers. "Stick to your other God-given talents."

She stuck out her tongue. "Which are?"

"Among others, making me happy just being you, your ability to love hard, and…"

She's My prayer warrior, the Lord Jesus whispered.

"God has given you a spirit to pray," he said softly. "A prayer warrior."

Her eyes misted. "Thank you."

I love you, he mouthed, keeping their moment private. After assisting her from her stool, he guided her around to his easel. She gasped and drew the attention of others in class.

Covering her mouth, she glanced back at him, then peered closer.

"That's how I see you," he said close to her ear, causing her to shiver.

Her hands shook and her eyes watered. Jet's lips puckered, but words were slow in coming. "It's beautiful."

"Just like you." He squeezed her shoulders.

Their private moment was shattered when others crowded around them.

"Jason, why didn't you paint a portrait of me?" one woman demanded of her date.

"Hey, I followed the chick's instructions," a tall dude defended himself then mumbled, "You made us brothers look bad, man."

"Can I have it?" Jet asked with such reverence in her voice.

Rossi was torn. When he created his masterpiece, he hadn't thought about it being a gift, and when he finished, he imagined it on a wall in his house or in his office, but his way of thinking was changing. If Jet wanted anything, he wouldn't deny her. "Yes. We'll swap." Besides, Jet's image was already ingrained in his mind.

She pouted. "Mine isn't as good as yours. You're holding back on your talents, Minister Rossi. "Painting you was easy." He leaned closer. "I started with your lips and went from there."

He was so close to her mouth, his heart begged for a kiss. Then he recalled Romans 6:12: *Let not sin therefore reign in your mortal body, that ye should obey it in the lusts thereof.* Kissing her wasn't a sin, but it wouldn't aid in taming the temptations many men yielded to. Refocusing on Jet's picture instead of her mouth, he took her canvas and examined her artistic ability. "I don't care if it was stick people, it was created by the woman I love. To me, it's invaluable." That earned him a smile from her and applause from others.

***

When Jet returned home, she hung Rossi's artwork on the living room wall and stared at it before taking it to her bedroom and admiring it as if it was the first time she ever laid eyes on it. Finally, Jet snapped a picture and texted it to Layla since it was too late to call her.

The night was more romantic than a candlelight dinner. Rossi had taken her breath away. Besides the gift from his heart, her mind replayed his sweet words—a prayer warrior. Was she that? "I hope so, Lord."

Rossi didn't know behind closed doors, she had prayed for strength to love Levi, strength to let go of Diane, strength to be the woman Rossi thought he saw in her, and to tear down the wall she had boxed Karyn in.

She snuck another peek at her portrait, then opened the Bible. "Lord, guide me through Your Word." She flipped through the pages until she stopped at Proverbs 31. Her heart seemed to open. Is this what she would be to Rossi? When she married, she planned to be a good wife and mother, but verses eleven and twelve made her reread them: *She will do him good and not evil all the days of her life. She seeks wool, and flax, and works willingly with her hands.*

Jet was ready to be Mrs. Rossi Tolliver. She wanted to give her heart completely to him. Now she had to wait on him to propose—again.

As she was about to prepare for bed, her phone chimed Layla's ringtone. "Girl, if you don't say yes to that man, I'll steal him." She laughed. "He's setting the standard for my future hubby."

"I'm ready to become a Mrs., and no other man could be my husband but Rossi." She stared at her reflection. "Don't let me have to ask him to marry me."

Chapter 25

Weeks after Jet started working at APA, Rossi added pool dates with her to their outings. He didn't realize she was so competitive. He withheld his amusement at her serious expression while trying to break the set of balls. She was horrible at getting the cue ball to make any pocket shots.

"Hey, if Jeanette Lee can do this, so can I," she said, referring to the spokeswoman for APA who had won more than thirty international and national pool titles. To Rossi's amazement, Jeanette was ranked number one as an American pool player.

It was as if Jet was trying to emulate the Black Widow's techniques. His lady had a long way to go. He would chuckle at her frustration, but in the end, the beauty was learning the sport together.

Soon, more Tollivers joined them until it became a weekly family affair. He was surprised his brother Chaz was as good as he boasted. Rossi laughed at Levi's expression when Karyn beat him—even Dori did better.

"We can blame the Black Widow for their competitive nature," he told his cousin.

One night as he was driving to Bible class, he asked Jet about her company's franchise opportunities. "That might be a good investment."

"Really?" Her eyes widened. "My boss told me about one employee who went part-time after buying a franchise, then she quit to focus on growing her business."

"I wouldn't want to manage it, but I would be willing to be a silent partner."

When it came to money and business, Rossi earnestly petitioned the Lord for guidance. He did later that night. When a name came to mind, Rossi wasn't sure if it was definitely a yes from God, but he had a strong feeling that this person would be affected in some kind of way.

The next morning, Rossi made a pit stop at Crowning Glory before going to the office. He waved at familiar faces. Bypassing the salon section, he headed to the barber chairs.

"What's up?" Halo the head barber asked, glancing up for a second before finishing up a trim on a customer's mustache. "What brings you in, Minister?"

"You, my friend."

"Let me finish up with Gary here, then you can have a seat in my chair." Halo tilted his head in the direction of the waiting lounge.

"Nah, this is a different type of business call." Rossi lowered his voice so the three other barbers couldn't hear.

Halo paused and straightened slowly, then lifted his brow. "Yeah?" He turned down his lips, thinking. "Everything okay?"

Before Rossi could answer, Buttercup waved at him. Her hands were wrapped in plastic gloves. "Hey, Rossi," she said, her voice muffled behind a surgical mask covering her mouth and nose. The couple had recently announced their pregnancy, and it appeared Halo and Buttercup were taking every precaution to ensure a healthy baby. She wiggled her fingers. "Perm."

He nodded and took a seat to wait. When he and Halo were behind closed doors in the break room, Rossi presented his proposal. "I have a business opportunity that I think you would like. I'll back you financially the first year."

"Whew." Halo shook his head. His eyes watered, and he used his hand to shield his emotions in front of Rossi. Before Christ saved him, the six-five and two hundred fifty-something bulky Latino was considered a threat to society. His criminal activity landed him in prison after being charged with countless felonies. Now, his goal was to witness to others about the consequences of being involved in gangs. Halo was a true ambassador for Christ ninety-nine percent of the time.

Emotions contained, Halo met Rossi's eyes. "Thanks, man," he finally choked out and looked up. Exhaling, he rested his hands on his thighs. "If you're willing to back me, I know I've got the favor of God, so what is it?" He grinned.

"Jet works for—"

Halo frowned and gritted his teeth. "Not her...I mean," he hurried to say, "I know you two got a thing going on, but I'm not going for a repeat with her. When she turned down our business loan for Crowning Glory, I thought Karyn, Buttercup, and my second chances were over. My honey was crushed until Nalani showed up and put Jet in her place. If she's involved, all hope is gone."

Rossi tried to keep a poker face until Halo finished bad-mouthing his almost fiancée. "Bro, we all have a past, including you, me, and Jesetta. She's part of the Body of Christ now, so she's a perfect fit." He waited to give Halo time to consider what he said, before adding, "And for the record, you would protect Buttercup until your last breath. The same goes for me with Jesetta. I love her and will marry her."

"Enough said." Halo folded his hands. "So tell me about this opportunity."

"Now, it has nothing to do with Jet anyway. It's the company she works for—American Poolplayers Association. They're one of the top companies when it comes to investing in a small franchise. I prayed and God sent me to you. You would build your business by forming leagues wherever there's a pool table and players. I don't know all the details, but I'm sure Jet can get you a packet. Are you in?"

He stood, and Rossi did the same. "Definitely." A smile spread across his face until he was as giddy as a kid with his first bicycle. "With the baby on the way, it'll feel good to have something I own—after I pay you back your investment, of course."

"Of course." Rossi chuckled. "I'd better head to work. Talk it over with Buttercup and see what she says."

At the office, Rossi shared his plan with Levi after they concluded a conference call. "Halo was real excited." He paused. "Crowning Glory is about giving back to other felons, but with this franchise, he will be able to build a business."

His cousin pushed back from the table and rested his ankle across his knee. Adjusting his glasses, Levi twisted his mouth in thought. "Instead of Halo going on the hunt to find pool players, why not bring them to him to form leagues?"

"What do you mean?"

"We have that vacant space in the Tolliver Town II development. I'm thinking a recreational center would be a great attraction for sports entertainment. We can call it Halo's Hall and construct, let's say, ten bowling lanes, four to six pool tables, and a game room..."

Levi's suggestion got Rossi thinking. "Besides the pool tables, maybe we have a rock climbing area."

"This is a game changer for Buttercup and Halo. I guess everyone will get their happy ending, including you." Levi nodded.

"You know it."

Chapter 26

Late one Saturday after a day of hanging out with Dori, Jet was dropping off her niece when she noticed Rossi's car in front of Levi's house. Karyn met her at the door. "You're back sooner than I expected with only a couple of bags." She chuckled.

"Yeah." Jet laughed. It felt good to interact with Karyn without any reservations about her intentions. God had washed both their sins away. "Can you imagine I couldn't get Dori to spend my money? So I bought her more books and sweaters for school."

The two exchanged genuine warm hugs before Karyn invited her in, then loud voices from their backyard beckoned Jet to the kitchen.

"Girl, the Tollivers are talking smack about who's the better three-point shooter. They're taking it too seriously."

Jet smirked. "I should go out there just for laughs. With my height, I played in high school."

"But, Auntie, you have on heels and a short skirt," Dori reminded her. They were dressed alike in black skirts and red short-sleeved sweaters.

Although she had been teasing, it sounded like a plan. "Heels are a woman's best friend, honey," Jet said. "If you're going to wear them, then you have to be able to strut, run, and jump rope. Come on, I'll show you."

"This is when I wish I was tall." Karyn led the way. After checking on her son who was napping, she returned and led the way outside.

Jet stood at the top of the deck stairs and put her hands on her hips like she was a superhero as she overlooked the patio. Rossi dropped the ball and his jaw. Levi took advantage of his distraction and grabbed the ball for a layup.

Jet caught her breath too. It wasn't often she could admire Rossi's athletic build. She had grown accustomed to his polo and slacks or suits. Not today. His wife-beater was drenching with sweat from his exertion. Brown shorts matched his brown and orange tennis shoes. Her man was built solid. His sculptured biceps and muscular legs made her blush.

For Dori's sake, she put on her game face as she strutted toward the cousins. "Gentlemen." She nodded at Levi, then Rossi. Snatching the ball from her unsuspecting brother-in-law, she dribbled and took her a shot. "All net." That surprised her, but she kept her game face on. "I've still got it."

"How'd she do that?" Levi huffed as he walked in circles.

"Yay, Auntie." Dori clapped.

Retrieving the ball, Rossi tucked it under his arm and walked toward her. His approach was more like a predator calculating his steps to his prey. He was breathing heavy. They were within inches of each other. Her stilettos made her almost eye level with him. "Jesetta," he said with a twinkle in his eyes, "yeah, how did you do that?" He lowered his eyes and scanned her from head to toe.

She shivered at his scrutiny before grabbing the ball and dribbling it to the basket.

"I got this," he yelled at Levi as he scrambled to block her.

"I don't think so." She elbowed him, moved to the left, then right as Levi called a foul and traveling, but she didn't stop. She was having too much fun. By this time, Karyn and Dori were reciting cheers.

Could she do it again? She leaped to shoot. Rossi jumped higher and blocked her. Then in a surprising moved, he wrapped his arm around her waist so she wouldn't stumble. His strength and gentleness was attractive.

"Like I said, I've got you."

Her heart pounded as his nostrils flared. His eyes left hers and focused on her lips.

"Kiss my auntie, Cousin Rossi," Dori screamed.

Forgetting they had an audience, Jet struggled to be set free as Rossi released her. She exhaled as he dropped the ball and turned from her. His fists were jammed on his waist. Walking in circles, he mumbled to himself, loud enough for her to hear, "Lord, this woman You gave me is torturing me."

It would have been funny if he didn't look so flustered. She glanced at the other Tollivers who were also watching him. After a few seconds, she called his name. "Rossi?"

He turned around and walked to her. His expression was unreadable. "Babe." His husky voice was soft.

"Yes?" She batted her eyes, flirting with him.

"I'll pick up you up for dinner at seven."

Dinner? That was all he had to say? Before she could question him, he lifted her hand, kissed it, and swaggered away. Now who was flirting?

"Play with me, Auntie!" Dori ran down the deck stairs, picked up the ball, and began to dribble.

When her niece missed a third time, Jet did her best to lift Dori in the air to help her make a basket, but the girl wasn't a light-weight anymore. They repeated the stunt four more times at Dori's insistence—because Jet was counting—before she could call it quits. "Whew. You gave me a workout." She winked. Plus, she had to get home and find something to wear. She wanted to dazzle Rossi.

Chapter 27

Rossi slipped behind the wheel of his SUV and drove home, trying to take control of his senses and get his hormones under control. He couldn't get the image of Jet out of his mind. He came dressed for some one-on-one with Levi while Jet was out with Dori. He had no idea she would return early and woo him in her get-up.

She was tall, but wore heels as if she was born with them. Legs were his weakness, and she had them. Instead of her hair up, she and Dori had theirs brushed to the side in one braid. His woman was adorable, youthful, and seductive at the same time.

How did a simple game of one-on-one with her turn into a moment where he had to walk away and repent? He jammed his fist on the steering wheel. "This stops now."

His phone rang through his car Bluetooth. "Hello."

"Hey, bro. You were on my mind," Landon, Octavia's husband, greeted him. "What are you and Jet doing tonight? We have a sitter. Want to double date for a movie or dinner?"

Not tonight, not now. He grunted. "Rain check. We have other plans."

"You two need to go ahead and get married."

"That's exactly what I plan to do." Jesetta was going down—tonight. He and Landon chatted until Rossi made it to his loft. Before showering, he made some calls.

Although they already had dinner plans, Rossi was about to up the stakes. He showered with a different fragrance gel, then shaved with precision. Next, he dressed with the intention of wooing her as she had done him with her appearance earlier. It took a couple of tries, fumbling with his bow tie, but finally he perfected it.

His phone rang at the same time as he lifted his car keys. "Mr. Tolliver, unfortunately, we're one musician short, but we're here, set up, and awaiting for your arrival," the man said.

"I'm sure everything will work out." Rossi grinned. "I'm on my way."

Less than seven minutes later, he parked in front of Jet's house. Across the street, three members of the quartet stood at attention. The catering service his company used for luncheons had set up a table for two with the white linen swaying in the evening wind. A dozen red roses were placed on top between crystal flutes of Sprite and a plate of hors d'oeuvres.

Everything was in place as he began his ascent up her many stairs. After ringing the doorbell, he waited only seconds for her to answer. She was trying to kill him in the dress that draped her well-toned body. The red, brown, or whatever color family was accenting her golden brown skin. It was neither too snug nor loose, but just enough to catch a man's eye while reaffirming that she was a lady.

The violinist began "Sound of An Angel." The cellist followed. His senses were on high alert as he caught the intake of Jet's breath. The music seemed to coax her out the door. Briefly, she glanced at him, then began to glide toward the musicians as he escorted her. A small crowd gathered nearby. Even two motorists stopped to allow them to cross the street.

Once they were at the table, Rossi scooted his chair beside hers instead of facing her. He put his arm around her shoulder, and together they enjoyed the mini concert. When the wind stirred her hair, she resembled an angel in flight. She was so mesmerized by the music that she didn't utter a word until the musicians touched the last note.

"This is so romantic," she whispered, then added, "thank you." Leaning closer, she brushed her soft lips against his cheek, pulled back, and gazed into his eyes with a dreamy expression. "You're going to ask me to marry you again, aren't you?"

"Yes." There was no need for an element of surprise. She knew it was coming. "Do you plan to say yes?"

"Yes," she answered as the trio played another selection. When she rested her head on his shoulder, Rossi relaxed.

She munched on the treats and gave him bites. If only she knew how powerful her simple gestures were as a tease, maybe she wouldn't do them. But Rossi liked it, and as long as he could restrain himself, then they both were safe.

When the musicians finished their final selection, the audience applauded. Looking around, he noticed the crowd had enlarged. Plus, their horse-driven carriage had arrived. "It's time to go," he whispered.

Standing, he helped her to her feet. The wind stirred again, and her fragrance tickled his nose. Reaching into his pocket he pulled out money for the musicians' tips. "Stay as long as you want."

The violinist grinned at the two hundred-dollar bills Rossi placed in his hand. "We'll give them a few more selections, Mr. Tolliver, then we'll pack up."

Some folks clapped and parted a path for their escape to the carriage. As the driver took the scenic route downtown near the riverfront, Jet snuggled closer. "I know you love me," he whispered, then kissed her head.

"And I know you've loved me for a long time and I didn't know it."

The plan was for them to ride around downtown for about an hour and chat, but Jet was so quiet. He looked at her and noticed she was dozing or thinking based on her smile. He didn't disturb her. He smiled too. Rossi wanted them both to cherish their engagement night.

Jet stirred when the carriage came to a stop in front of her house, and he helped her down. Her eyes widened when she saw the limo behind them.

"What's going on?"

"Aren't you hungry?" He grinned. "I'm working up an appetite, and I need my strength tonight."

She lifted an eyebrow, but didn't say anything as the driver opened the door for them to get inside. "You're full of surprises, Mr. Tolliver. So where are we going?"

"Fleming's Steakhouse in Frontenac." Rossi had it on good authority that it was the most romantic place to propose. This time, Jet was chatty about her job, church, and Dori. Every few minutes, he would comment, but he was content to hear her voice, watch her expressions, and admire her beauty.

By the time they arrived at Fleming's, both their stomachs were growling. They were greeted and seated immediately. Keeping a possessive hand on her back, Rossi felt like he was escorting a beauty contestant from the quick glances some men were giving them, in spite of their dining companions.

Once they placed their orders, Rossi reached across the table and took her hands. Looking into her watery eyes, he saw happiness, excitement, and a glimpse of sadness. He squeezed them and brought them to his lips. "My parents have been married for forty-two years, I've officiated more than six weddings. Each time I've asked God, when will it be my turn? I've waited for years, looking for the right person. Then one day, God led my heart to you."

A tear fell, and he touched her face to wipe away another that splashed on his thumb. "Jesetta, when you weren't ignoring me, we got along as friends. We've acted like siblings when you would allow me to give you brotherly advice. Now it's time to let me love you as your husband who will never have any regrets for asking you to be my wife."

Taking a deep breath, he stood, then knelt before her. He pulled out her ring box from his pocket and opened it. "Will you do me the honor of being my girlfriend, my lady love, and my wife?"

She was bawling by the time she mumbled yes. He slipped on the ring, then kissed her hand. *God, help me to be sensitive to her needs and always make her happy,* he silently prayed as he took his seat. While she fumbled in her purse, a woman next to them handed him tissues and congratulated them.

"Thank you," he said, then reached over to dab the moisture off Jet's cheeks before handing the tissues to her.

More congratulations circulated around them. Conversations dulled and their surroundings blurred as Rossi focused on his beloved. One thing he couldn't understand was the sadness in her eyes that didn't go away. "What's wrong, babe?" he asked as he finished his meal.

She shrugged. "I'm fine."

"On the outside, I couldn't agree more, but what's hurting you on the inside?" His question seemed to take her by surprise.

"Nothing." She mustered a smile, but he still wasn't buying it.

"If I'm willing to give you my heart, let me share yours."

"Missing my parents, Diane..." She sniffed, and he thought she was about to cry all over again. *Lord, please don't let her.*

Tend to hers needs, He whispered back.

"I always imagined sharing my news with them. I remember seeing the look of awe on Diane's face when she admitted she had said yes to Levi's proposal. I wonder if I'm wearing that same glow because of loving you." She choked and Rossi moved his chair beside her and gathered her in his arms. He didn't care that they were the center of attention for the second time within hours. As a matter of fact, he and Jet were surrounded by chaperones.

When she whimpered, he pulled back and lifted her chin. "You can always tell me when you're hurting, and I'll hold you and we'll pray through it, okay?"

She nodded. Jet didn't cry anymore as they shared dessert, but she was quiet. They needed some privacy, so he paid the tab, leaving a tip for the chef, then stepped outside of the restaurant where the limousine was waiting.

Inside, she relaxed against his chest after he instructed the driver to take a long scenic route back into the city. He loved the smell of her hair and began to toy with a few strands. "Will you marry me tomorrow?" he teased.

She whipped her head around. "Of course not!"

"Babe, I can't do the whole year planning thing. I've been wanting to marry you since the day you were baptized and God presented my bride to me."

"Well, in that case, I'd better call Layla. She'll be my maid of honor. Of course, Dori will be our flower girl... Do you think Levi and Karyn will mind Little Levi being our ring bearer?"

"Nope." He grinned. "So how long does your fiancé have to wait for our honeymoon?"

She twisted her lips. "Six-month minimum. I just started a new job."

"I was going to negotiate two months until you mentioned the job."

Arriving back at her place, Rossi escorted her to the door. He watched as Jet turned around and squinted in the direction of the park where the musicians had set the mood for a memorable night.

"Every time I open my door I will always remember this day—always." She smiled.

He took a series of deep breaths when she stared into his eyes. The moonlight captured the seduction that she probably didn't know she possessed. Rossi stepped back. "Call me, not only tonight, but whenever you're sad, hurting, or want someone to listen to a corny joke."

She lightly tapped his shoulder. "Hey, I have a good sense of humor." She paused. "Thank you for understanding how much I loved Diane. It doesn't take away from how much I love you." She wrapped her arms around his waist, and he trapped her in an embrace. When she looked up, he refused to indulge in a kiss, so he pulled back. "Four months. I'll buy a couple of franchises if I have to bribe your boss."

Chapter 28

Jet woke the next morning, stretched, and wiggled her fingers, admiring her engagement ring. *Fairytales do come true.* She smiled as last night's events flooded her mind. Yes, she guessed she would always mourn her loss, Diane especially, but through Jesus, she had gained a good godly man. The Holy Ghost fell on her Spirit, she slid to her knees, and began to speak in an unknown language.

He'll take care of you, God spoke as she whispered her Amen.

In her pajamas, she raced downstairs to the front door and opened it. It was early, and only a few joggers and dog walkers were out, but through that reality, her mind replayed the most romantic scene that took place practically in front of her doorstep.

She went back to her bedroom and called Layla. Her friend sounded zoned out, but that didn't stop Jet from screaming, "I'm engaged."

"'Bout time. Took you long enough. Congratulations. Now I'm going back to sleep to find my prince in my dreams."

"Fairytales do come true," she sang, then added, "with God all things are possible." Jet said her goodbyes, then returned upstairs to shower and dress. She couldn't sleep another minute. She was too hyped.

Rossi called not even an hour later while she was cooking omelets. Jet not only knew better, but had a better understanding of why inviting him wasn't a good idea. After last night, their hormones were too heightened for temptation.

"How's my beautiful fiancée this morning?" His husky voice seemed even sexier.

Staring at her engagement ring, she exhaled. "Incredibly happy, but hungry. I was about to eat, then call you afterward."

"I'm a happy man this morning too. I love you so much."

Her heart warmed, hearing him adding the "so much" part. "I love you too."

"I know you want to get started planning for our wedding in three months—"

She gasped and laughed. "We agreed on four months. Keep it up, Minister Rossi, and I'll make you wait three years."

"Jesetta Hutchens, stop teasing." He paused. "There's somewhere I want you to go with me today."

"Okay." She paused to say grace, then took a bite. "Where?"

"You'll see. Pick you up in thirty minutes." He disconnected, then seconds later, texted her:

Forgot to say I love you.

She texted back, No you didn't. You've been saying it for years. It's only now I'm hearing it.

The man was prompt. Jet had to give Rossi that when he rang her doorbell exactly a half hour later.

"Where are we going?" she asked once she snapped her seatbelt. Rossi frowned and twisted his lips, but said nothing. That made her worry. "Is everything okay?"

He turned and winked. "Absolutely."

Where was he taking her? Wedding shopping already? But there were no shops, malls, or bakeries in the direction he was traveling on Lucas and Hunt Road. Then it dawned on her that they were headed toward St. Peter's Cemetery.

She had avoided this area of town to resist temptations to stop and have some tranquil moments recalling memories with Diane. Her heart pounded in her throat when Rossi turned into the entrance and down the narrow road that would take them to Section 25, Block D, Lot 4 and Plot 6 to Diane Hutchens Tolliver's resting place—correction—her remains. Didn't he know this had been her hangout and she was trying to wean herself?

"What–what are we doing here?" she asked when he parked.

He shut the engine off and faced her. She couldn't read his expression. Without a word, he got out and came around to open her door.

"Baby." He reached for her hand, and in almost a trance, she took it and stepped out.

She swallowed as Rossi wrapped his strong arm around her waist. They stopped in front of the tombstone. Jet resisted the urge to kneel and sweep off the dried leaves that rested on the grave. She looked at Rossi for answers, but he only stared at Diane's headstone.

"Lord Jesus, up in heaven, Hallelujah be Your name. We stand here today, talking to You for we know Diane's soul rests with You. I have a message." He squeezed Jet's hand and smiled. "Tell Diane, I'll take care of her sister. Tell her thank you for sending Jet my way…"

Jet began to bawl, and Rossi held her in his arms. His embrace was comforting and secure. She had picked the right man to fall in love with.

***

Wednesday morning, Rossi strolled into the office humming the song he'd heard on the radio. He passed Levi in the hall, and they exchanged a fist bump as a greeting. Since they had come to an understanding, the Lord had blessed their company with a new contract worth $1.7 million. They would hire local skilled workers and train others in an apprenticeship at a lower pay scale. That also meant more commerce for local businesses.

"My cousin's engaged?" Levi chuckled. "I still can't believe you asked Jet and she said yes. That's a match made in heaven I never saw coming."

Rossi laughed too and leaned against the door frame outside Levi's office. "Me either when we first met, but God planted a Jesetta Hutchens seed in my heart, and when it was time to sprout, it did." He grinned. "I'm happy."

He continued down the hall to his own office. Minutes later, he got a phone call that made him unhappy. Halo's application for the APA franchise was rejected. Rossi's heart dropped as he tried to lift his friend's spirits.

"I got the thanks, but no thanks letter today." Halo paused. "Buttercup and I had so many plans. Just like a black man will always wonder if they don't get a job, promotion, or loans because of the color of our skin, I always wonder if my felony background will always close doors of opportunity for me."

"We'll figure it out. Halo's House is a done deal. Let me give Jet a call and tell her."

"I'm sure she already knows," Halo said dryly before ending the call.

Rossi paused. Did she know and didn't tell him? Nope, the seed the devil was teasing Halo with, Rossi refused to buy. He called his fiancée. "I just got off the phone with Halo. His franchise application got denied."

Jet gasped. "Oh no! I'm so sorry to hear that. How is he?"

"Devastated." *Lord, please turn his tears of sorrow into tears of joy.*

"I hope he doesn't think I had something to do with it. I don't process those applications. APA is real strict on their franchises. They're all about protecting their brand and work very closely with league operators to keep a clean image. Maybe he didn't get past his background check. What can we do to help him?"

"Pray, babe."

"I can do that. Please let him know I had nothing to do with their decision, and I want to see him blessed."

"Amen," he said. "I will. See you when I pick you up for church."

Walking out of his office, he found Levi and gave him the bad news. Once his cousin got over the shock, they began to brainstorm about other options to bless Halo and Buttercup. "That would have been a good investment. Other franchises probably had the same requirements. Let's pray and see what God's game plan is."

"Agreed." So for the remainder of the day, he prayed, and before leaving work, he called Halo to check up on him and deliver Jet's message. "She really is sorry."

"Thanks."

That evening while waiting for Jet to get home from work, he reviewed his notes for the youth Bible lesson he was teaching. Luke 10:25–37. As he was about to check the time, his phone vibrated from a text.

Just getting home. Give me 15 mins.

Rossi exhaled, glad that he and Jet wouldn't be late. He grinned. I'll see you in 17.

While en route to church, they discussed Halo's situation. "Levi and I thought about Chaz. This might be the only thing to keep my brother's interest in the business world. Otherwise, he may be in school forever."

Jet laughed. "He did seem pretty fascinated that I worked for the association, and plays like a pro."

They arrived at church with less than five minutes to spare. They veered right to the chapel where the youth were waiting for their service to begin.

They entered, and all eyes were on them. It felt good that he could now call Jet his fiancée. Once she chose where she wanted to sit, he joined her on his knees for them to say a prayer of thanks before he took his post on the front row or in the pulpit.

After a few songs and prayer requests, he asked the young crowd of about thirty to open their Bibles, tablets, or smartphones.

"Anybody who calls themselves a Christian wants to go to heaven. True?" He paused and waited for their response, then continued. "As I studied Luke, chapter ten, God increased my understanding about the Good Samaritan. Number one, the man who approached Jesus already had the answer. In verse twenty-seven, he told Jesus, *Thou shall love the Lord thy God with all thy heart, and with all thy soul, and with all thy strength, and with all thy mind; and thy neighbor as thyself.* He quoted five points of the law." Rossi shook his head.

"Sometimes I believe we think we're smarter than God. *Hmph.* Imagine that." He made eye contact with several students in the audience. "We, as saints, already have the answer to what we must do to enter into heaven. Can you imagine the relationship we would have with God if we surrendered our hearts and souls totally to Him? That alone will give us a spiritual strength to serve Him. If we want to live for Jesus, this is what we must focus on." As he gave them examples, he thought about the beggar who approached him and Jet in the park one evening.

Jet didn't know it at the time, but Rossi would have rather given the man money than give up his favorite meal. But to give the man money when he was hungry wouldn't have pleased the Lord.

Rossi listened to their questions and how to apply the scriptures to everyday situations at school, home, and for those who had jobs. Glancing at Jet, he watched her make notes on her tablet. She looked up and caught his stare. She smiled and he did his best not to respond with a wink. He closed out the teen class with an announcement. They had to get a pool franchise going. That would give the young people a safe environment to have fun and compete for money and prizes toward scholarships.

"I know we didn't have any activities planned this Friday, so I thought it would be nice to have a game night at Cue Cushion on Woodson Road in Overland to shoot pool or play darts."

While many cheered, they had no idea they would be his and Jet's chaperones. Rossi couldn't wait to get married.

Chapter 29

Three months later...

"Here comes the bride," a small voice echoed from the sanctuary when her flower girl Dori, her maid of honor Layla, and her bridesmaid Octavia slipped out the door to take their positions, leaving her alone with her thoughts.

Jet frowned from inside her dressing room. Was that Little Levi's voice she heard? She frowned. As the ring bearer, he wasn't on the program to say anything. When she echoes of chuckles, she relaxed. Whatever antics a child did at weddings were always amusing, so that was good.

As long as there weren't any delays to become Mrs. Rossi Tolliver, she didn't care. She scrutinized her reflection once more, waiting for her cue. Jet smiled, thinking about what Dori had said.

"You look like one of my princess dolls."

Scrutinizing her reflection, Jet agreed.

Surprisingly, she and Buttercup had brokered a sister-in-Christ friendship. The woman had created a masterpiece out of Jet's hair for her wedding day. That was her olive branch after things worked out for Halo's Hall, Buttercup's husband's business venture. Chaz Tolliver had become an APA franchise operator.

Lifting her dress, Jet peeped down at her toes, pedicured compliments of Karyn. It was her slippers that gave her pause. Before she slipped her feet into them, Layla had discovered etchings on the soles of her wedding shoes.

With every step we take was written with neat penmanship on her left shoe, and *Jesus will be beside us* was penned on her right. She and Layla had both fanned themselves until her friend stated, "Whew. Girl, I'm going to find me a Tolliver man." Layla beamed as if it was a done deal.

If there was ever any doubt in her mind that Rossi wasn't handpicked for her, it was dismissed. "Stand still. He'll find you."

Now as she waited for her cue, Jet replayed the words she told Layla. Rossi had found her heart. The knock on the door startled her. Her heart pounded as she patted her chest. Opening the door, Karyn was on the other side.

"It's show time." Her eyes twinkled.

Jet nodded and stepped out. It was bittersweet that her walk to the altar would be without an escort, but she knew once she saw Rossi, the sadness would be gone. "With each step we take," she repeated as she made her way to the sanctuary. She'd voiced her concern to Rossi that she didn't have anyone to give her away, and he had responded, "Jesus gave you to me."

Now as she neared the double doors, her hearted pounded even harder with nervousness. She was actually getting married. The doors opened, and Jet blinked. From the entrance to the altar there were at least a dozen Tolliver men posted on each side forming a Soul Train line. But their stance was more of a military salute. What was going on?

Rossi stood at the altar, breathtaking in his black tux to match the men in the aisle. He lifted his arm as if beckoning her to him. On wobbly legs, she responded to his summons. Levi stepped out from the formation, smiled, and bent his arm to escort her.

She choked with emotions as she looped her arm through his. As they glided down the aisle, the Tolliver men saluted her before they walked behind her to the altar as if they were part of the procession. Who planned this, Layla? When? And how could they pull off something this coordinated behind her back? Jet would find the culprit later…to thank them for making sure she didn't feel alone walking down the aisle.

Pastor Brown asked, "Who gives this woman away?"

Jet's heart dropped. Again, this wasn't part of the program, because she had no one.

"Me!" Dori said proudly. "She's my auntie."

The crowd chuckled, and Jet blinked.

"I do," Levi said, then lowered his voice. "Diane would have it no other way. We love you." He kissed her cheek, then faced Rossi. "She's all yours."

The rest of the ceremony was a blur as Jet watched Rossi's loving expression from his vows to his lips on hers once they were pronounced husband and wife. "There's a lifetime of romance coming up," he whispered.

Book Club Discussion

1. Levi wasn't totally sold on Jet's salvation. How do you respond when the most unlikely person to get saved turns his or her life around?
2. Discuss Rossi's timing to propose to Jet right after the shooting.
3. Discuss whether you incorporate fasting when you're praying for someone or a difficult situation.
4. How did Karyn washing Jet's feet and praying impact their relationship? If applicable, discuss your experience from participating in a feet washing consecration service.
5. How would you describe Nalani's reaction to the news Rossi had chosen Jet as his wife?
6. Compare the moment in your life when you let go of a burden to when Jet released her burden of Diane's death.
7. Rossi was the perfect man of God—until it involved Jet. What are some of your buttons the devil pushes to act contrary to showing love to a sister or brother in Christ?

Author's Note:

I hope you enjoyed Jesetta and Rossi's story. They were first introduced in *Crowning Glory*. Nalani had a fan club who wanted her to be Rossi's love interest in the sequel, but it was as if Rossi was saying, "Hold up, Jesetta has my heart." I guess that is the way love is, your heart knows for sure. If you haven't read the other stories in Restore My Soul series, make sure you pick up your copy of *Crowning Glory* and *JET The Back Story*.

Octavia and Landon also have their own story in Redeeming Heart.

And finally, Rossi is a family namesake. We have four generations of Rossi's in my family: grandfather, father, brother, and nephew.

Thanks so much for spending your down time with me, and I hope you were blessed. Please post an honest review on Amazon, Goodreads, or on your blog, then visit www.patsimmons.net and sign up for my monthly newsletter. You'll receive a free eBook as my way of saying thanks.

Until next time, read, relax, and read some more!

About the Author

Pat is the multi-published author of more than thirty Christian titles, and is a three-time recipient of the Emma Rodgers Award for Best Inspirational Romance. She has been a featured speaker and workshop presenter at various venues across the country.

As a self-proclaimed genealogy sleuth, Pat is passionate about researching her ancestors and then casting them in starring roles in her novels. She describes the evidence of the gift of the Holy Ghost as an amazing, unforgettable, life-altering experience. God is the Author who advances the stories she writes.

Pat currently oversees the media publicity for the annual RT Booklovers Conventions. She has a B.S. in mass communications from Emerson College in Boston, Massachusetts.

Pat converted her sofa-strapped, sports fanatic husband into an amateur travel agent, untrained bodyguard, GPS-guided chauffeur, and administrative assistant who is constantly on probation. They have a son and a daughter.

Read more about Pat and her books by visiting www.patsimmons.net or on social media.

Other Christian titles include:

The Guilty series
Book I: *Guilty of Love*
Book II: *Not Guilty of Love*
Book III: *Still Guilty*
Book IV: *The Acquittal*

The Jamieson Legacy
Book I: *Guilty by Association*
Book II: *The Guilt Trip*
Book III: *Free from Guilt*
Book IV: *The Confession*

The Carmen Sisters
Book I: *No Easy Catch*
Book II: *In Defense of Love*
Book III: *Driven to Be Loved*
Book IV: *Redeeming Heart*

Love at the Crossroads
Book I: *Stopping Traffic*
Book II: *A Baby for Christmas*
Book III: *The Keepsake*
Book IV: *What God Has for Me*
Book V: *Every Woman Needs A Praying Man*

Making Love Work Anthology
Book I: *Love at Work*
Book II: *Words of Love*
Book III: *A Mother's Love*

Restore My Soul series
Crowning Glory
Jet: The Back Story
Love Led by the Spirit

Single titles
Talk to Me
Her Dress (novella)
Christmas Greetings
Couple by Christmas

Anderson Brothers
Book I: Love for the Holidays
(Three novellas): *A Christian Christmas, A Christian Easter, and A Christian Father's Day*
Book II: *A Woman After David's Heart (Valentine's Day)*
Book III: *A Noelle for Nathan*
(Book 3 of the Andersen Brothers)

223

Restore My Soul series

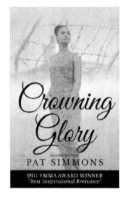

Crowning Glory, Book 1. Cinderella had a prince; Karyn Wallace has a King. While Karyn served four years in prison for an unthinkable crime, she embraced salvation through Crowns for Christ outreach ministry. After her release, Karyn stays strong and confident, despite the stigma society places on ex-offenders. Since Christ strengthens the underdog, Karyn refuses to sway away from the scripture, "He who the Son has set free is free indeed." Levi Tolliver, for the most part, is a practicing Christian. One contradiction is he doesn't believe in turning the other cheek. He's steadfast there is a price to pay for every sin committed, especially after the untimely death of his wife during a robbery. Then Karyn enters Levi's life. He is enthralled not only with her beauty, but her sweet spirit until he learns about her incarceration. If Levi can accept that Christ paid Karyn's debt in full, then a treasure awaits him. This is a powerful tale and reminds readers of the permanency of redemption.

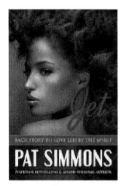

Jet: The Back Story to Love Led By the Spirit, Book 2. To say Jesetta "Jet" Hutchens has issues is an understatement. In *Crowning Glory,* Book 1 of the Restoring My Soul series, she releases a firestorm of anger with an unforgiving heart. But every hurting soul has a history. In *Jet: The Back Story to Love Led by the Spirit,* Jet doesn't know how to cope with the loss of her younger sister, Diane.

But God sets her on the road to a spiritual recovery. To make sure she doesn't get lost, Jesus sends the handsome and single Minister Rossi Tolliver to be her guide.

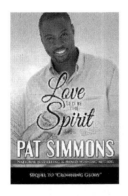

Psalm 147:3 says Jesus can heal the brokenhearted and bind up their wounds. That sets the stage for *Love Led by the Spirit.*

Love Led By the Spirit, Book 3. Minister Rossi Tolliver is ready to settle down. Besides the outwardly attraction, he desires a woman who is sweet, humble, and loves church folks. Sounds simple enough on paper, but when he gets off his knees, praying for that special someone to come into his life, God opens his eyes to the woman who has been there all along. There is only a slight problem. Love is the farthest thing from Jesetta "Jet" Hutchens' mind. But Rossi, the man and the minister, is hard to resist. Is Jet ready to allow the Holy Spirit to lead her to love?

LOVE AT THE CROSSROADS SERIES

Stopping Traffic, Book 1. Candace Clark has a phobia about crossing the street, and for good reason. As fate would have it, her daughter's principal assigns her to crossing guard duties as part of the school's Parent Participation program. With no choice in the matter, Candace begrudgingly accepts her stop sign and safety vest, then reports to her designated crosswalk. Once Candace is determined to overcome her fears, God opens the door for a blessing, and Royce Kavanaugh enters into her life, a firefighter built to rescue any damsel in distress. When a spark of attraction ignites, Candace and Royce soon discover there's more than one way to stop traffic.

A Baby For Christmas, Book 2. Yes, diamonds are a girl's best friend, but in Solae Wyatt-Palmer's case, she desires something more valuable. Captain Hershel Kavanaugh is a divorcee and the father of two adorable little boys. Solae has never been married and longs to be a mother. Although Hershel showers her with expensive gifts, his hesitation about proposing causes Solae to walk and never look back. As the holidays approach, Hershel must convince Solae that she has everything he could ever want for Christmas.

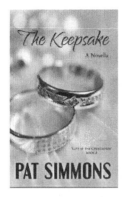

The Keepsake, Book 3. Until death us do part…or until Desiree walks away. Desiree "Desi" Bishop is devastated when she finds evidence of her husband's affair. God knew she didn't get married only to one day have to stand before a judge and file for a divorce. But Desi wants out no matter how much her heart says to forgive Michael. That isn't easier said than done. She sees God's one acceptable reason for a divorce as the only opt-out clause in her marriage. Michael Bishop is a repenting man who loves his wife of three years. If only…he had paid attention to the red flags God sent to keep him from falling into the devil's snares. But Michael didn't and he had fallen. Although God had forgiven him instantly when he repented, Desi's forgiveness is moving as a snail's pace. In the end, after all the tears have been shed and forgiveness granted and received, the couple learns that some marriages are worth keeping

What God Has For Me, Book 4. Halcyon Holland is leaving her live-in boyfriend, taking their daughter and the baby in her belly with her. She's tired of waiting for the ring, so she buys herself one. When her ex doesn't reconcile their relationship, Halcyon begins to second-guess whether or not she compromised her chance for a happily ever after. After all, what man in his right mind would want to deal with the community stigma of 'baby mama drama?' But Zachary Bishop has had his eye on Halcyon since the first time he saw her. Without a ring on her finger, Zachary prays that she will come to her senses and not only leave Scott, but come back to God. What one man doesn't cherish, Zach is ready to treasure. Not deterred by Halcyon's broken spirit, Zachary is on a mission to offer her a second chance at love that she can't refuse. And as far as her adorable children are concerned, Zachary's love is unconditional for a ready-made family. Halcyon will soon learn that her past circumstances won't hinder the Lord's blessings, because what God has for her, is for her…and him…and the children.

Every Woman Needs A Praying Man, Book 5. First impressions can make or break a business deal and they definitely could be a relationship buster, but an ill-timed panic attack draws two strangers together. Unlike firefighters who run into danger, instincts tell businessman Tyson Graham to head the other way as fast as he can when he meets a certain damsel in distress. Days later, the same woman struts through his door for a job interview. Monica Wyatt might possess the outwardly beauty and the brains on paper, but Tyson doesn't trust her to work for his firm, or maybe he doesn't trust his heart around her.

A Christian Christmas. Christian's Christmas will never be the same for Joy Knight if Christian Andersen has his way. Not to be confused with a secret Santa, Christian and his family are busier than Santa's elves making sure the Lord's blessings are distributed to those less fortunate by Christmas day. Joy is playing the hand that life dealt her, rearing four children in a home that is on the brink of foreclosure. She's not looking for a handout, but when Christian rescues her in the checkout line; her niece thinks Christian is an angel. Joy thinks he's just another man who will eventually leave, disappointing her and the children. Although Christian is a servant of the Lord, he is a flesh and blood man and all he wants for Christmas is Joy Knight. Can time spent with Christian turn Joy's attention from her financial woes to the real meaning of Christmas—and true love?

A Christian Easter., How to celebrate Easter becomes a balancing act for Christian and Joy Andersen and their four children. Chocolate bunnies, colorful stuffed baskets and flashy fashion shows are their competition. Despite the enticements, Christian refuses to succumb without a fight. And it becomes a tug of war when his recently adopted ten year-old daughter, Bethani, wants to participate in her friend's Easter tradition.

Christian hopes he has instilled Proverbs 22:6, into the children's heart in the short time of being their dad.

A Christian Father's Day. Three fathers, one Father's Day and four children. Will the real dad, please stand up. It's never too late to be a father—or is it? Christian Andersen was looking forward to spending his first Father's day with his adopted children---all four of them. But Father's day becomes more complicated than Christian or Joy ever imagined. Christian finds himself faced with living up to his name when things don't go his way to enjoy an idyllic once a year celebration. But he depends on God to guide him through the journey.

(All three of Christian's individual stories are in the Love for the Holidays anthology (Book 1 of the Andersen Brothers series)

A Woman After David's Heart, Book 2, David Andersen doesn't have a problem indulging in Valentine's Day, per se, but not on a first date. Considering it was the love fest of the year, he didn't want a woman to get any ideas that a wedding ring was forthcoming before he got a chance to know her. So he has no choice but to wait until the whole Valentine's Day hoopla was over, then he would make his move on a sister in his church he can't take his eyes off of. For the past two years and counting, Valerie Hart hasn't been the recipient of a romantic Valentine's Day dinner invitation. To fill the void, Valerie keeps herself busy with God's business, hoping the Lord will send her perfect mate soon. Unfortunately, with no prospects in sight, it looks like that won't happen again this year. A Woman After David's Heart is a Valentine romance novella that can be enjoyed with or without a box of chocolates.

A Noelle For Nathan, Book 3, is a story of kindness, selflessness, and falling in love during the Christmas season. Andersen Investors & Consultants, LLC, CFO Nathan Andersen (A Christian Christmas) isn't looking for attention when he buys a homeless man a meal, but grade school teacher Noelle Foster is watching his every move with admiration. His generosity makes him a man after her own heart. While donors give more to children and families in need around the holiday season, Noelle Foster believes in giving year-round after seeing many of her students struggle with hunger and finding a warm bed at night. At a second-chance meeting, sparks fly when Noelle and Nathan share a kindred spirit with their passion to help those less fortunate. Whether they're doing charity work or attending Christmas parties, the couple becomes inseparable. Although Noelle and Nathan exchange gifts, the biggest present is the one from Christ.

A Mother's Love. To Jillian Carter, it's bad when her own daughter beats her to the altar. She became a teenage mother when she confused love for lust one summer. Despite the sins of her past, Jesus forgave her and blessed her to be the best Christian example for Shana. Jillian is not looking forward to becoming an empty-nester at thirty-nine. The old adage, she's not losing a daughter, but gaining a son-in-law is not comforting as she braces for a lonely life ahead. What she doesn't expect is for two men to vie for her affections: Shana's biological father who breezes back into their lives as a redeemed man and practicing Christian. Not only is Alex still goof looking, but he's willing to right the wrong he's done in the past. Not if Dr. Dexter Harris has anything to say about it. The widower father of the groom has set his sights on Jillian and he's willing to pull out all the stops to woo her. Now the choice is hers. Who will be the next mother's love?

Love At Work. How do two people go undercover to hide an office romance in a busy television newsroom? In plain sight, of course. Desiree King is an assignment editor at KDPX-TV in St. Louis, MO. She dispatches a team to wherever breaking news happens. Her focus is to stay ahead of the competition. Overall, she's easy-going, respectable, and compassionate. But when it comes to dating a fellow coworker, she refuses to cross that professional line. Award-winning investigative reporter Bryan Mitchell makes life challenging for Desiree with his thoughtful gestures, sweet notes, and support. He tries to convince Desiree that as Christians, they could show coworkers how to blend their personal and private lives without compromising their morals.

Words Of Love. Call it old fashion, but Simone French was smitten with a love letter. Not a text, email, or Facebook post, but a love letter sent through snail mail. The prose wasn't the corny roses-are-red-and-violets-are-blue stuff. The first letter contained short accolades for a job well done. Soon after, the missives were filled with passionate words from a man who confessed the hidden secrets of his soul. He revealed his unspoken weaknesses, listed his uncompromising desires, and unapologetically noted his subtle strengths. Yes, Rice Taylor was ready to surrender to love. *Whew.* Closing her eyes, Simone inhaled the faint lingering smell of roses on the beige plain stationery. She had a testimony. If anyone would listen, she would proclaim that love was truly blind.

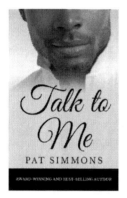

Talk To Me. Despite being deaf as a result of a fireworks explosion, CEO of a St. Louis non-profit company, Noel Richardson, expertly navigates the hearing world. What some view as a disability, Noel views as a challenge—his lack of hearing has never held him back. It also helps that he has great looks, numerous university degrees, and full bank accounts. But those assets don't define him as a man who longs for the right woman in his life. Deciding to visit a church service, Noel is blind-sided by the most beautiful and graceful Deaf interpreter he's ever seen. Mackenzie Norton challenges him on every level through words and signing, but as their love grows, their faith is tested. When their church holds a yearly revival, they witness the healing power of God in others. Mackenzie has faith to believe that Noel can also get in on the blessing. Since faith comes by hearing, whose voice does Noel hear in his heart, Mackenzie or God's?

TESTIMONY: *If I Should Die Before I Wake.* It is of the Lord's mercies that we are not consumed, because His compassions fail not. They are new every morning, great is Thy faithfulness. Lamentations 3:22-23, God's mercies are sure; His promises are fulfilled; but a dawn of a new morning is God' grace. If you need a testimony about God's grace, then If I Should Die Before I Wake will encourage your soul. Nothing happens in our lives by chance. If you need a miracle, God's got that too. Trust Him. Has it been a while since you've had a testimony? Increase your prayer life, build your faith and walk in victory because without a test, there is no testimony. (eBook only)

Her Dress. Sometimes a woman just wants to splurge on something new, especially when she's about to attend an event with movers and shakers. Find out what happens when Pepper Trudeau is all dressed up and goes to the ball, but another woman is modeling the same attire.

At first, Pepper is embarrassed, then the night gets interesting when she meets Drake Logan. *Her Dress* is a romantic novella about the all too common occurrence—two women shopping at the same place. Maybe having the same taste isn't all bad. Sometimes a good dress is all you need to meet the man of your dreams. (eBook only)

Saige Carter loves everything about Christmas: the shopping, the food, the lights, and of course, Christmas wouldn't be complete without family and friends to share in the traditions they've created together. Plus, Saige is extra excited about her line of Christmas greeting cards hitting store shelves, but when she gets devastating news around the holidays, she wonders if she'll ever look at Christmas the same again.

Daniel Washington is no Scrooge, but he'd rather skip the holidays altogether than spend them with his estranged family. After one too many arguments around the dinner table one year, Daniel had enough and walked away from the drama. As one year has turned into many, no one seems willing to take the first step toward reconciliation. When Daniel reads one of Saige's greeting cards, he's unsure if the words inside are enough to erase the pain and bring about forgiveness. Once God reveals to them His purpose for their lives, they will have a reason to rejoice.

Holidays haven't been the same for Derek Washington since his divorce. He and his ex-wife, Robyn, go out the way to avoid each other. This Christmas may be different when he decides to gives his son, Tyler, the family he once had before the split.

Derek's going to need the Lord's intervention to soften his ex-wife's heart to agree. God's help doesn't come in the way he expected, but it's all good, because everything falls in place for them to be a couple by Christmas.

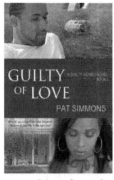

Guilty of Love. When do you know the most important decision of your life is the right one?

Reaping the seeds from what she's sown; Cheney Reynolds moves into a historic neighborhood in Ferguson, Missouri, and becomes a reclusive. Her first neighbor, the incomparable Mrs. Beatrice Tilley Beacon aka Grandma BB, is an opinionated childless widow. Grandma BB is a self-proclaimed expert on topics Cheney isn't seeking advice—everything from landscaping to hip-hop dancing to romance. Then there is Parke Kokumuo Jamison VI, a direct descendant of a royal African tribe. He learned his family ancestry, African history, and lineage preservation before he could count. Unwittingly, they are drawn to each other, but it takes Christ to weave their lives into a spiritual bliss while He exonerates their past indiscretions.

Not Guilty. One man, one woman, one God and one big problem. Malcolm Jamieson wasn't the man who got away, but the man God instructed Hallison Dinkins to set free. Instead of their explosive love affair leading them to the wedding altar, God diverted Hallison to the prayer altar during her first visit back to church in years.

Malcolm was convinced that his woman had loss her mind to break off their engagement. Didn't Hallison know that Malcolm, a tenth generation descendant of a royal African tribe, couldn't be replaced? Once Malcolm concedes that their relationship can't be savaged, he issues Hallison his own edict, "If we're meant to be with each other, we'll find our way back. If not, that means that there's a love stronger than what we had." His words begin to haunt Hallison until she begins to regret their break up, and that's where their story begins. Someone has to retreat, and God never loses a battle.

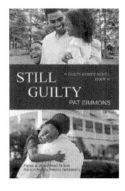

Still Guilty. Cheney Reynolds Jamieson made a choice years ago that is now shaping her future and the future of the men she loves. A botched abortion left her unable to carry a baby to term, and her husband, Parke K. Jamison VI, is expected to produce heirs. With a wife who cannot give him a child, Parke vows to find and get custody of his illegitimate son by any means necessary. Meanwhile, Cheney's twin brother, Rainey, struggles with his anger over his ex-girlfriend's actions that haunt him, and their father, Dr. Roland Reynolds, fights to keep an old secret in the past.

Follow the paths of this family as they try to determine what God wants for them and how they can follow His guidance. Still Guilty by Pat Simmons is the third installment of the popular Guilty series. Read the other books in the series: Guilty of Love and Not Guilty of Love, and learn more about the Jamieson legacy in Guilty by Association, The Guilt Trip, and Free from Guilt. The Acquittal starts off the Guilty Parties series.

The Acquittal. Two worlds apart, but their hearts dance to the same African drum beat. On a professional level, Dr. Rainey Reynolds is a competent, highly sought-after orthodontist. Inwardly, he needs to be set free from the chaos of revelations that make him question if happiness is obtainable. To get away from the drama, Rainey is willing to leave the country under the guise of a mission trip with Dentist Without Borders. Will changing his surroundings really change him? If one woman can heal his wounds, then he will believe that there is really peace after the storm.

Ghanaian beauty Josephine Abena Yaa Amoah returns to Africa after completing her studies as an exchange student in St. Louis, Missouri. Although her heart bleeds for his peace, she knows she must step back and pray for Rainey's surrender to Christ in order for God to acquit him of his self-inflicted mental torture. In the Motherland of Ghana, Africa, Rainey not only visits the places of his ancestors, will he embrace the liberty that Christ's Blood really does set every man free.

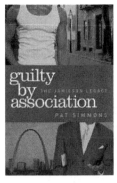

Guilty By Association. How important is a name? To the St. Louis Jamiesons who are tenth generation descendants of a royal African tribe—everything. To the Boston Jamiesons whose father never married their mother—there is no loyalty or legacy. Kidd Jamieson suffers from the "angry" male syndrome because his father was an absent in the home, but insisted his two sons carry his last name. It takes an old woman who mingles genealogy truths and Bible verses together for Kidd to realize his worth as a strong black man. He learns it's not his association with the name that identifies him, but the man he becomes that defines him.

The Guilt Trip. Aaron "Ace" Jamieson is living a carefree life. He's good-looking, respectable when he's in the mood, but his weakness is women. If a woman tries to ambush him with a pregnancy, he takes off in the other direction. It's a lesson learned from his absentee father that responsibility is optional. Talise Rogers has a bright future ahead of her. She's pretty and has no problem catching a man's eye, which is exactly what she does with Ace. Trapping Ace Jamieson is the furthest thing from Taleigh's mind when she learns she pregnant and Ace rejects her. "I want nothing from you Ace, not even your name." And Talise meant it.

Free From Guilt. It's salvation round-up time and Cameron Jamieson's name is on God's hit list. Although his brothers and cousins embraced God—thanks to the women in their lives—the two-degreed MIT graduate isn't going to let any woman take him down that path without a fight. He's satisfied with his career, social calendar, and good genes. But God uses a beautiful messenger, Gabrielle Dupree, to show him that he's in a spiritual deficit. Cameron learns the hard way that man's wisdom is like foolishness to God. For every philosophical argument he throws her way, Gabrielle exposes him to scriptures that makes him question his worldly knowledge.

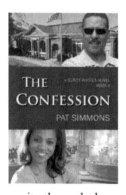

The Confession. Sandra Nicholson had made good and bad choices throughout the years, but the best one was to give her life to Christ when her sons were small and to rear them up in the best Christian way she knew how. That was thirty something years ago and Sandra has evolved from a young single mother of two rambunctious boys, Kidd and Ace Jamieson, to a godly woman seasoned with wisdom. Despite the challenges and trials of rearing two strong-willed personalities, Sandra maintained her sanity through the grace of God, which kept gray strands at bay.

Now, Sandra Nicholson is on the threshold of happiness, but Kidd believes no man is good enough for his mother, especially if her love interest could be a man just like his absentee father.

No Easy Catch. Shae Carmen hasn't lost her faith in God, only the men she's come across. Shae's recent heartbreak was discovering that her boyfriend was not only married, but on the verge of reconciling with his estranged wife. Humiliated, Shae begins to second guess herself as why she didn't see the signs that he was nothing more than a devil's decoy masquerading as a devout Christian man. St. Louis Outfielder Rahn Maxwell finds himself a victim of an attempted carjacking. The Lord guides him out of harms' way by opening the gunmen's eyes to Rahn's identity. The crook instead becomes infatuated fan and asks for Rahn's autograph, and as a good will gesture, directs Rahn out of the ambush! When the news media gets wind of what happened with the baseball player, Shae's television station lands an exclusive interview. Shae and Rahn's chance meeting sets in motion a relationship where Rahn not only surrenders to Christ, but pursues Shae with a purpose to prove that good men are still out there. After letting her guard down, Shae is faced with another scandal that rocks her world. This time the stakes are higher. Not only is her heart on the line, so is her professional credibility. She and Rahn are at odds as how to handle it and friction erupts between them. Will she strike out at love again? The Lord shows Rahn that nothing happens by chance, and everything is done for Him to get the glory.

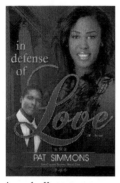

In Defense of Love. Lately, nothing in Garrett Nash's life has made sense. When two people close to the U.S. Marshal wrong him deeply, Garrett expects God to remove them from his life. Instead, the Lord relocates Garrett to another city to start over, as if he were the offender instead of the victim.

Criminal attorney Shari Carmen is comfortable in her own skin—most of the time. Being a "dark and lovely" African-American sister has its challenges, especially when it comes to relationships. Although she's a fireball in the courtroom, she knows how to fade into the background and keep the proverbial spotlight off her personal life. But literal spotlights are a different matter altogether.

While playing tenor saxophone at an anniversary party, she grabs the attention of Garrett Nash. And as God draws them closer together, He makes another request of Garrett, one to which it will prove far more difficult to say "Yes, Lord."

Redeeming Heart. Landon Thomas (*In Defense of Love*) brings a new definition to the word "prodigal," as in prodigal son, brother or anything else imaginable. It's a good thing that God's love covers a multitude of sins, but He isn't letting Landon off easy. His journey from riches to rags proves to be humbling and a lesson well learned.

Real Estate Agent Octavia Winston is a woman on a mission, whether it's God's or hers professionally. One thing is for certain, she's not about to compromise when it comes to a Christian mate, so why did God send a homeless man to steal her heart?

Minister Rossi Tolliver (*Crowning Glory*) knows how to minister to God's lost sheep and through God's redemption, the game changes for Landon and Octavia.

Driven to Be Loved. On the surface, Brecee Carmen has nothing in common with Adrian Cole. She is a pediatrician certified in trauma care; he is a transportation problem solver for a luxury car dealership (a.k.a., a car salesman). Despite their slow but steady attraction to each other, neither one of them are sure that they're compatible. To complicate matters, Brecee is the sole unattached Carmen when it seems as though everyone else around her—family and friends—are finding love, except her.

Through a series of discoveries, Adrian and Brecee learn that things don't happen by coincidence. Generational forces are at work, keeping promises, protecting family members, and perhaps even drawing Adrian back to the church. For Brecee and Adrian, God has been hard at work, playing matchmaker all along the way for their paths cross at the right time and the right place.

Check out my fellow Christian fiction authors writing about faith, family and love. You won't be disappointed!

www.blackchristianreads.com

62345954R00139

Made in the USA
Lexington, KY
04 April 2017